The
Greatest
Softball
Game

The Greatest Softball Game

The Greatest Games Series with Jake & Matti, Volume 1

K G Wauthier

Published by K G Wauthier, 2022.

THE GREATEST SOFTBALL GAME

First edition. July 15, 2022.

Copyright © 2022 K G Wauthier.

ISBN: 978-1955699051

Written by K G Wauthier.

Table of Contents

K G WAUTHIER

———— ⟨∾⟩ ————

ISBN: 978-1-955699-05-1

———— ⟨∾⟩ ————

I want to give special thanks to my editors,
Greg Younger
Paula Braley
and
The men and women of the
Withlacoochee Area Writers Association

Chapter 1
The Wedding Announcement

J ake was on the phone with his mother, nearing the end of their weekly conversation. He opted to call a little earlier than usual due to his plans that evening in Montana. He missed his dad, who was still out on his kayak, fishing in northwest Florida.

"By the way, Mom, would you be offended if Matti and I wanted to get married on your anniversary with Dad? The date's worked out well for you guys. This one coming up is number fifty-two, is it not? If it's okay with the two of you, we'd like to."

"Offended? We'd be honored!" She knew her husband, Greg, would be, too. They were very much in love and proud they had weathered the *storm of marriage* for over five decades. They would quickly tell anyone there were times it would have been easier to throw in the proverbial towel. Together, they had experienced periods of ultimate euphoria and happiness. But there were also times of utter anguish, too. Yet, through it all, they held on to one another and were happier now than ever.

Linda was excited about Jake marrying Matti. She and Greg loved Matti when she was an employee at their farm twenty years earlier. She was great with the horses, and the clients loved her as well. Matti would do her chores, feeding horses, mucking stalls, fixing fences, and the like, often with her baby daughter, Shoshoni, strapped to her back like a papoose.

Matti was a tall, blonde, beautiful young lady. She was well-spoken and an excellent horsewoman. Linda and Greg were deeply saddened when Matti didn't show up for work one day and never returned. She, and her husband at the time, moved out of state. Greg and Linda never knew why—for eighteen years.

Jake served in the Army in Iraq, Operation Desert Storm, and Germany. A decorated soldier, a veteran of six years, he finally decided it was time to pursue other goals.

When Jake re-entered civilian life, he had connections through an Army friend who landed him a management position with a manufacturer in the southeast. It was a good job, but it required him to be indoors all day and, too often, six or seven days a week.

He ultimately went to work for his parents on their horse farm when a position as the breeding manager-in-training became available. The pay wasn't as good, but it met all the other criteria Jake was looking for: Outside, no necktie, and freedom. It was perfect.

Jake's original plan wasn't to work with his parents on the farm, but his stint in the military gave him a new appreciation for the value of family. He was proud to join the operation, especially considering both his mom and dad asked him to quit his job to fill a position due to the planned expansion of their business.

During his first year, he rode, two days each week, with the large animal vet they had on retainer. Jake served as his assistant, or what the vet called his "vet tech." Working with cattle, horses, llamas, goats, whatever the vet was called to treat, Jake was there. The experience was invaluable.

As time went on, Jake served as the liaison with the vet whenever he was at the farm. With upwards of a hundred-fifty horses routinely on the property, the vet was there a lot.

Jake's job was to keep the records and ensure the vet's time there was as limited as possible. The correct horses needed to be up and prepped. Staff needed to be available to move horses, and paperwork had to be readied and in order.

On the days the vet was to be there, it was customary to try to schedule several horses, often ten or more, during breeding season. Efficiency was key.

Jake learned quickly, lessening the need for the vet's involvement on the farm. His acumen was quickly becoming evident to everyone. By minimizing the vet's time on the farm, Jake could keep operational costs down. Greg and Linda appreciated that.

Jake had things running smoothly. However, if a member of his staff were to quit or be let go for cause, a replacement would be needed. It would be Linda's role to put out feelers—Standard Operating Procedure.

Chapter 2
The Interview

When Matti Crenshaw came down the lane, she was married with a child, a baby only a few months old. She had read about the place in a feature article in the newspaper and realized it was within a stone's throw of where she was living.

After turning between the two brick pillars at the property's entrance, Matti navigated the long road between pastures populated with beautiful horses. She was unsure where she was going since no buildings were visible from the road off which she turned at the main entrance to the ranch, but it had to be the right place. The name, logo, and address were proudly emblazoned in bronze plaques embedded in the brick pillars at the entrance.

It was obvious to her the facility was well-maintained, and the animals living there were content. She had seen a classified ad indicating they were looking for help. Matti loved animals, particularly horses, and was glad she'd called about the job.

In 1999, hiring decisions started with Linda. She was the one who posted ads when a position became available, and it was she who answered any calls received in response. If she liked what she heard on the phone, an in-person meeting was scheduled.

If she felt the individual might be suitable, she would pass them on to Jake for a final interview. If they didn't pass muster with Linda, they never got the chance to meet Jake.

When Linda got the call from Matti, she was reluctant to offer an interview because they had tried females in that position before, and none had ever stayed long. Jake fired one after the second day because she wasn't strong enough to meet the job's demands. The most recent quit after about a month because she refused to accept how hard Jake pushed her.

When Linda asked Jake about the incident, he informed her that a woman working in the barn was a *disruption.*

"The other staff members find it difficult, and the normal flow of things too often get screwed up. The guys have to watch what they say. Or, they're constantly making remarks that can have sexual connotations, and then I have to deal with that.

"And, you know, much of what we do here at a *breeding farm* is all about sex, so it's hard to avoid. It's just a problem I'd rather not have to deal with. That's all, Mom."

Despite Linda's reluctance, Matti managed to get her to agree to meet in person. Once they met, Linda was so impressed with Matti she couldn't help but believe Jake would forgive her for granting an interview with him, too.

She had everything he was looking for. She was tall and fit. She had horse experience. She lived right down the road, within walking distance, so a flat tire wouldn't be an excuse for not coming to work. She was beautiful and carried herself with grace. *Those traits go a long way when you're selling beautiful horses.*

Linda ended the interview by telling Matti she would get back with her. Then, she would try to set up a second interview, "...this time with Jake, the breeding manager.

"Probably tomorrow, if that's okay? Can I call you later to set up a time?" Linda asked. She didn't want to have that conversation in front of Matti. She didn't want her to overhear the argument she knew would ensue.

Later that afternoon, Matti received the call informing her to return to the farm the next day at one o'clock to meet with Jake.

Linda convinced him to at least talk to Matti about the position. He agreed but made no bones about his opposition to the idea.

During her interview with Linda, Matti concluded Jake wasn't keen on hiring a female for the position. She rightly figured that Jake wouldn't be influenced by fancy clothes and pretty make-up—at least not unduly so.

She arrived wearing neat, clean blue jeans—ironed and creased but not starched. Clean, but not polished, lace-up riding boots, and a well-fitted, red t-shirt emblazoned with the words "Roll-Tide" stretched perfectly across her ample breasts.

Her long, blonde hair was pulled back in a ponytail that poked through the hole in the back of an orange University of Tennessee baseball cap. She chose to forego make-up, just a bit of mascara to make her eyes pop. She was pretty enough without it anyway.

It was the way she carried herself that mattered. Her tall, upright frame and "Roll-Tide" made quite an entrance.

Upon Matti's arrival, Linda made the introduction. Jake looked at Matti and asked, "How *the hell* does that work?"

Linda, shocked and amazed, said, "Jake! What are you doing?"

Matti immediately chimed in, "It's okay. He's talking about the UT hat and the Alabama shirt." She quickly looked to Jake with a raised eyebrow and finished with, "Right?"

"Precisely! How does that happen?"

"Well, it's complicated. My dad gave me this shirt. He *loves* Alabama. I like how it looks, and I love my dad. I wear it mostly to make him happy, but I told him I'd only do so if I could wear something bearing my favorite school, Tennessee, at the same time. So, there you have it."

Of course, she wasn't telling the whole truth. Matti couldn't give two hoots in Hades about her dad, and she hated Alabama, but she had heard Jake was a big fan. She had worn the shirt for effect. She couldn't bring herself to wear the shirt without showing her true colors at the same time. So far, her plan seemed to be working—maybe.

"So, you're really a UT fan?"

Matti nodded.

"We don't allow Tennessee fans to work here. I guess the interview's over."

Linda interrupted, "Jake! Stop it. You're scaring Matti to death."

In reality, Linda breathed a sigh of relief as she saw Jake's willingness to banter about college athletics as a sign Matti had a chance to prove herself in the interview. *Heck, it looks like Jake might be trying to hold back a smile.*

Matti was showing off her grit. She wanted to show Jake that she was up to the job. Matti was savvy about many things, including college football, and willing to stand her ground. She did her homework to find out Jake was an Alabama fan but wasn't going to pretend to be one to get the job.

Matti loved what she had seen of the facility so far. It was good-sized but clean and well-kept. From the feature article she had read to what she had observed during the drive in, she could see the owners loved the horses. She could tell they cared about how they were treated, which Matti especially liked.

As soon as Linda saw that Jake wouldn't bite Matti's head off, she excused herself from the meeting so the interview could continue without her interference, as was customary.

It didn't take long for Jake to test Matti's knowledge of horses and her experience around a barn. He soon learned why Linda was so impressed. Matti's answers were quick, sure, and sharp. She was intelligent, confident, and witty.

Jake began to realize he had lost his ability to resist. From the moment Jake laid eyes on her, he knew he wanted her. He admired the way she carried herself. Her innate beauty captivated him. She wasn't *perfect*, but her flaws made him feel she might be attainable since, after all, he wasn't perfect either.

But it wasn't just that. There was something different, a feeling Jake couldn't quite understand.

"If I were to hire you, when could you start?"

"I could start now if you want. Or tomorrow could work, too. Whatever works best for you. What time should I report for duty?"

"8 AM should be fine," Jake assured her.

As Matti was about to leave his office, Jake stood to escort her to the door. For the first time, she realized he towered above her. Matti's initial thought was, "Wow! Finally, a man I could date wearing high heels."

Being nearly six feet tall was a challenge for Matti, and she often found herself forced to compromise in her choices. Jake, at 6' 4", would eliminate that problem. Not only was he tall, but his chest and shoulders were broad, and his arms were strong and muscular. He looked like he could hunt bears with a stick.

"Go find Linda. I'm sure she's got some paperwork you'll need to fill out, okay? I'll see you tomorrow."

When Matti found Linda to fill out the forms, Linda was quite pleased.

Jake, of course, played it as though he was doing it to appease his mother as if it was at her insistence. "If this doesn't work out, it's on you, Mother. I've told you before, hiring females in this role is a bad idea."

"I know, Jake. You're right. It probably won't work, but I think Matti has a real shot at being the right person this time. Let's hope your dad doesn't blow a gasket."

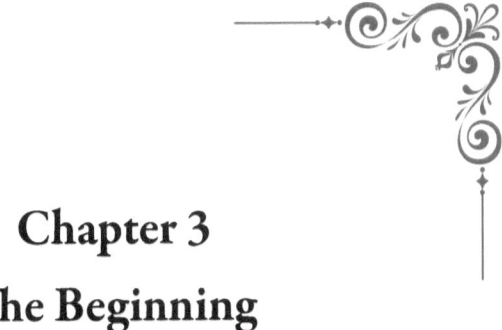

Chapter 3
The Beginning

During the interview, Matti shared that she had a daughter, "...she's only four months old. My husband works the night and early morning shift for a local trucking company, so he can take care of little Shoshoni during the day while I'm here at the farm."

Truth be told, Matti had two daughters. Greg, Linda, and Jake only knew about the baby, but she had another. Matti conceived her first daughter at her sixteenth birthday party, something that certainly wasn't planned and for which she clearly wasn't prepared. Some speculate she wasn't a willing participant in the copulation.

Matti gave birth and named her daughter Cayuga. Shortly after, Matti's rights as a mother were usurped by the child's maternal grandmother.

Not long after coming home from the hospital with Cayuga, it was made clear, since Matti didn't have the means to provide for this new baby, she shouldn't expect to have much say in her upbringing. Matti should, she was told, "... focus on finishing high school."

Matti was born in the beautiful Blue Ridge Mountains in southwestern North Carolina, near the Nantahala National Forest. She loved it there, and her whole family lived in the area, but she found living with her mother and stepdad—with Cayuga, under those conditions—untenable.

She and her biological father didn't get along either, so living with him and his new wife was out of the question, too.

She loved her paternal grandmother, though. They both shared similar feelings for Matti's father. They discussed the possibility of living together until Matti graduated. "That's a splendid idea, my dear. You know I would love your company. You're welcome in my home anytime, for as long as you'd like. But what to do about Cayuga?" her grandmother asked.

Matti had already come to grips with reality. Moving out of her mother's house meant leaving her first child behind, at least for a while.

When she worked at the farm, Matti was married to Bryce, but he was not the father of either of her daughters. He married her after she had become pregnant with Shoshoni, knowing the baby wasn't his. Matti was grateful, the only emotion she felt toward him.

Vanilla was the only way to describe Matti's husband. He was neither handsome nor ugly, tall nor short, strong nor weak. He was just Bryce. He came into her life at a pivotal time, and he was *there*. Matti's gratitude faded when Jake entered the picture.

Matti was frustrated. She'd been with several men. Two daughters proved that. But a *truly meaningful* relationship with a man escaped her. Sex was *fun,* but she craved the intimacy of a loving man to *love*, and be loved back—something she'd never experienced.

When Matti came to work for the farm, she already possessed considerable horse experience. That trait, along with the beauty and grace with which she carried herself, landed her the job. When Matti walked, she seemed to flow. When she ran, she appeared to glide. She never seemed to be in a hurry but covered a lot of ground... fast.

"When you're in the business of selling beautiful horses, style and grace have *everything* to do with it," Linda had said to Greg when defending her decision to hire Matti initially.

Jake was aware Matti was married and had a daughter. He also knew she was a beautiful woman but was, as far as he was concerned, another member of the staff.

He wouldn't conduct himself differently, at least any less gruff, around her because she was a woman. To do so would be sexist, after all. And he already had a rub against hiring *another woman* in the first place.

Jake had his reputation with the rest of the staff to consider. He was a taskmaster. He couldn't be seen as *soft* on Matti.

For weeks, Jake was tough on her. Matti accepted it, but as time passed, she began to think he had something against her. That's what he intended. He tried his best not to *like* her despite his strong feelings. He wasn't sure it was safe for her to be there. He *was* sexist in that he didn't feel women were, by and large, as strong, or courageous as men.

One morning, Jake noticed Matti had arrived at work wearing something wrapped around her torso, almost like a backpack, but different. He looked closer to see it was her baby. She was carrying her like a papoose, as if she were an Indian squaw. Jake was having none of that. He motioned to her, "In my office, please," and they headed in that direction.

Once inside, he said, "What the *hell* do you think you're doing? This is no place for a baby. That wasn't part of the deal."

"Look, Jake. With what you're paying me, I can't afford a babysitter. These horses are used to me. They love me. They wouldn't hurt me for anything. I've been bringing Shoshoni to see them after work for weeks now. The horses love her, too. And she loves them back. It'll be okay.

"Besides, it's not like it'll be every day. It's just that Bryce is out of town on a three-day run. He's home most days and can watch Shoshoni, so it'll only be when he's out of town. Please. Give it a chance. It won't be a problem. She won't slow me down. I promise. Please?"

Jake's blood was about to boil. His face was turning red when he said, "Oh, this *really* pisses me off. I wouldn't let any of my male employees bring their kids to work. Why should I let you bring a baby? Oh my God! You're not still breastfeeding, are you?"

"No. She's on a bottle and baby food now." She quickly adopted an ornery look, tilted her head, and asked, "Would it help if I was?" giggling coyly.

"No!" Jake said, almost screaming... unable to hide his smile. "This is SOOOO against my better judgment. And I'm still pissed. If she gets hurt, it's on you. And she'd better not slow you down, or I'll dock your pay. Get back to work."

"Thanks," then playfully, "Love you, Jake," as she bounced out of his office.

As Matti walked out the door, Jake yelled, "Riiight!" Then, under his breath, "What could *possibly* go wrong?"

Jake knew he had to make concessions for Matti when she had Shoshoni in tow. He would assign her simpler tasks like feeding pasture horses, cleaning empty stalls, and fixing fences—things that were unlikely to put her or the baby in harm's way.

While this was somewhat troubling to him, her overall value was worth it. She could be counted on to be there. Her prowess with equine showed. It was clear to everyone. The horses loved her, and that meant a lot.

Whether he was willing to admit it or not, Jake was smitten. He had sent his live-in girlfriend—everyone called her his "play-pretty"—packing a month previously. Everybody noticed.

When her baby was not in tow, Jake put Matti in more challenging situations to see what she could handle. No matter the task, she never flinched. She was up to it. Matti proved to have the strength and determination equal to almost any other staff member.

One day, a few weeks later, Matti showed her mettle when she stood her ground in front of an out-of-control two-year-old colt. He had managed to get loose. As he was trying to make his escape, he started toward Matti. She threw both arms in the air and screamed, blocking his path.

Of course, the colt outweighed her by a factor of ten and could have run her over without the slightest effort. She could have been killed, but her actions caused the young steed to hesitate and alter his course. Unfortunately, his shoulder hit her and knocked her against the wall, from which she bounced to the barn floor.

She suffered some nasty scrapes and bruises as a result. However, her actions and the resulting commotion, enabled Jake to gain control of the youngster and prevent what could have been a bigger disaster.

Jake quickly put the colt in a nearby stall and went to Matti, who was still on the barn floor. "Are you okay?" Jake asked as he reached down to help her, seizing the opportunity to wrap her in his arms. He could have just as easily offered a hand, but he couldn't resist the temptation.

"That was impressive. I've seen big men back away in situations like that. Hell, if it had been any of my other staff, they probably would have. You may be a girl, but you got balls!"

Matti replied, "Thank you... I think. That was supposed to be a compliment, wasn't it? You were speaking metaphorically, right?" Then, with a wry smile, she added, "Because I can assure you, I don't."

Jake was the master of the double entendre, and making sexual innuendos was his specialty. Matti's remark caught him off guard. All he could think of to say was, "Well, that's good to know," as he gently brushed some sawdust from just above her eyebrow, trying his best to avoid looking directly into her baby blues.

Chapter 4
The Breeding Manager

Jake's primary role at the farm was *breeding manager*. His job was to ensure the intended mares got pregnant by the appropriate stallions every year.

With artificial insemination being standard operating procedure at their farm, Jake's job included collecting the semen, inseminating the mares, scheduling the vet for ultrasounds, and keeping all records necessary to facilitate a satisfactory outcome. For a good portion of the year, there was a lot of sex taking place on the farm.

Jake didn't like breeding a mare unless someone else in the barn was close enough to lend a hand if something went wrong. When dealing with animals that weigh well over a thousand pounds in a confined space while performing *any* procedure, anything can go wrong at any moment—and often does. It is essential to have another person present.

When Jake was ready to breed on this day, he realized Matti was the only staff member available to help him. She had come to work without her daughter. "Would you help me breed *Miss Maggie Mae*?"

"Uh, I don't think so. What do you think I am, some kinda pervert? Why would you need my help anyway? And how did you get her away from Rod Stewart? Wasn't she his lover?" She giggled.

Jake found her cleverness cute but tried his best not to show it. "The mare, you idiot."

She smiled. "Ohhh."

Matti had never assisted in this procedure before, so Jake made sure he explained every step—carefully. He figured it to be an excellent teaching opportunity—on, perhaps, more than one level.

After Jake had Maggie adequately secured in the stocks, a custom-built enclosure made from three-and-one-half-inch diameter iron pipe to minimize the chance of injury should a horse panic, he wrapped her tail and tied it up and off to the side to keep it out of the way so the hair wouldn't interfere with the breeding process.

The stocks was equipped with a door at the front about chest high and another at the back, the top of which came to about nine inches above an average horse's hocks, but low enough her backside was accessible for breeding.

A hook was welded to the outside on the front upright where the horse's lead could be secured and another at the rear where the horse's tail could be tied for palpation.

Once Jake felt Maggie was comfortable, he began explaining to Matti how important it was to keep talking to the subject of their work as it was "... impolite to assume mares were different somehow than humans."

He continued, "It's okay to talk among ourselves as long as our tone is always soft and level, as though we're talking to her. We must always include *her* in our conversation. After all, she's the reason we're here. Does that make sense?"

Matti agreed. She found this side of him new, soft, caring.

"The first thing we're going to do is wash her. Usually, the spray of water startles them, so I need you to go up to her head to calm her while I start. She may jump forward a little, so be prepared for that."

With a nod of his head toward the front of the mare, Jake asked, "Would you do that for me?"

Matti promptly obliged. She left Jake's side, rubbed Maggie's nose, and began talking softly.

When Jake began spraying the mare's hind end with water, the mare jumped and danced but quickly settled down. When she calmed, Jake signaled for Matti to return to the business end, where she could watch what he was about to do.

Jake began applying a mild liquid soap, and, using the back of his hand, he gently cleaned the mare's vulva and surrounding area. After it appeared to be thoroughly clean, at least to Matti, Jake rinsed the area and carefully wiped it with a clean, folded paper towel. He showed the towel to Matti, revealing numerous particles of soil and debris. After discarding the towel, he repeated the washing and rinsing steps until the paper towels showed no contamination, which took four washings.

"Okay. Now we're ready." Jake looked at Matti and asked, "Hand me that glove, please?"

Matti pointed inquisitively at the folded vinyl sleeve in the package marked "sterile" on the table, and Jake said, "Yeah, that's it. Thanks."

Jake carefully tore open the sealed wrapper and let it unfold, touching only the corners of the glove's sleeve, avoiding contamination. He gently blew into the end to fill it with air so he could slide it over his left arm more easily.

Matti said, "That thing goes all the way up to your shoulder. Is that really necessary?"

Jake looked at her, smiled, and said, "Have you seen the size of a stallion's erect penis? Up close and personal, I mean?"

Matti's face immediately flushed red. She tried to look away from Jake's eyes but couldn't. "Oh, my God."

Jake returned the smile she was trying to hide and said, "Hand me that lube, please."

Thoroughly enjoying the moment as she pointed to it, he nodded. Jake took from her the tube in his ungloved hand and said, "How am I supposed to use this?" Matti looked at him, puzzled until she realized she needed to remove the lid.

"Oh. So sorry."

Jake held the tube firmly as Matti unscrewed the cap. Once it was off, he squeezed the first little bit into the trash can sitting nearby and then a liberal amount onto the back of his gloved hand, which he would ultimately use to smear around Maggie's private parts.

Matti asked, "Why did you squirt the first bit into the trash?"

"It may have been contaminated from previous use or by exposure to the air. We don't want to carry anything into the mare that could cause an infection. It's a good habit to get into. I do it even with brand new tubes we've just opened."

Jake then picked up the twenty-four-inch-long sterile pipette they'd set aside using his right hand, the ungloved one, and used his teeth to tear off the end of the wrapper near the attachment port. He spat out the wrapper end and pushed the pipette down against his leg to expose the end from the sleeve to handle it with the gloved fingers without contamination.

He then asked Matti for the syringe of semen from the incubator, which he attached to the pipette. Once connected, Jake used the plunger on the syringe to force semen up to within an inch of its end.

When Matti asked, "Why did you do that?"

Jake replied, "To minimize the introduction of air into Maggie's uterus. It could cause unnecessary pain, and who knows what contaminants could be in that air bubble?"

"Wow. Never thought of that," Matti said.

"Okay, remember, we need to keep talking to the mare. Hey baby. We're going to do some lovin' now. Is that okay? Is that good for you? Are you a little horny? Do you feel sexy right now? I

THE GREATEST SOFTBALL GAME

suppose not. But it's okay. It's something we've gotta do. Doc says it's your time."

It was all Matti could do not to laugh, but she did her best to maintain her composure.

Jake smiled at his assistant, then continued, "Okay, Honey, here we go."

The lube may have been cold when it touched the mare's vulva because she got a little jumpy, making Matti step back.

Standing shoulder to shoulder next to Jake at the business end of a mare can be dangerous, especially when she's got two powerful weapons like those back hooves at her disposal.

The mare was in the stocks, but there had been occasions when horses had gotten out of control despite being so constrained. Jake himself had a mare jump, lift both hind hooves above the back door of the stocks, hit him square in the chest, and place both back down right from where they started.

Jake said her back feet returned to their original position before he hit the opposite wall of the barn aisle. He gained a lot of respect for the power of a mare's hind hooves, "...even when she's in the stocks."

Jake instructed Matti, "...go up to the front. Talk to her to calm her down for a moment. Just whisper sweet nothings in her ear and pet her nose. It works wonders. Trust me."

"I suppose you're gonna tell me that works with women too, ain't ya, Jake?"

He looked up at Matti, smiled, winked, and said, "Try it on her, see if it works. If it does, maybe I'll try it on you someday." Then, after a pause, "Remember, talk softly."

Matti smiled and started talking to Miss Maggie Mae.

After a minute or two of Matti's soothing comfort, Jake gently touched the mare's vulva again, and she settled down. He continued rubbing her, and it didn't take long before he knew Matti could return to his shoulder.

Jake started softly speaking to Maggie and, in mid-sentence, in the same tone, said to Matti, "I think you can, slowly, come back here beside me, and we can move forward. She'll be okay now."

He then went back to his conversation with the mare as though it was part of the same paragraph, massaging Maggie's vulva with the back of his gloved hand and distributing the lube.

When Matti arrived, she stood close to Jake but was careful not to touch him. She watched as he continued his conversation. "We don't want to be in any hurry. No female of any species wants it to be a 'Wham-bam-thank you-Ma'am' kind of thing. You have to take it slow."

He gently parted the lips of her labia with two fingers, and he continued there, massaging a bit more and talking to the mare until Jake said, "It's okay, baby. It's okay."

Jake cut his cobalt eyes toward Matti and said, "We don't want to penetrate too quickly. That would be rude." His gaze caught her by surprise, but Jake saw the slight curl of a smile, and she swallowed uncomfortably.

Jake continued, "She'll let me know when she's ready."

Almost on cue, the mare exhaled and made a gesture of relaxation that was evident even to Matti.

"There. Did you see that?" Jake, still looking at Matti, saw her nod and smile.

"Yeah. I think she just gave you the okay. Right?"

"Exactly. She relaxed. She told me she was ready to be penetrated. Her way of saying 'Yes.'"

To get all the mileage out of this experience he could, Jake shaped his hand like a spear to facilitate penetration as gently as possible, explaining every step graphically. "I want to make sure this is not painful for her, so I'll make my hand as small as I can, forming it like this. And there needs to be plenty of lube. Lube is good!"

He took his time as he gently inserted his hand, holding the pipette between his first two fingers, and glided the assembly into her vagina. He described everything about Maggie's vaginal vault and how it felt inside—all the folds, soft and smooth, warm and wet. He lingered there and explained, "Here I must let my fingers be my eyes in the search for the opening of her cervix...which can sometimes take, who knows how long? You have to *feel* your way around until you find it."

Before it was over, Jake's arm was fully up past his elbow when he said, "Ah, there it is. I've reached the holy grail." Looking directly into Matti's eyes, he continued, "It is here through which I will pass my finger... and along it, the pipette. Let's do this."

Matti's eyes were as big as saucers. She had seen a stallion's erect penis before, but only from a distance. Never had she thought about how much of it would penetrate a mare's vagina during the mating process. This was graphic and brought a whole new perspective to things.

As Jake passed his index finger through the mare's cervix, he said, "Oh, darlin', your cervix is wide open. You're ready, aren't you? When the vet said you needed to be bred today, he wasn't kidding.

"Matti, you can tell how close a woman, I mean a mare, sorry, is to ovulation by how *open* her cervix is. If she's close, it will be wide open to let the sperm cells in. If not, that sphincter will be closed to keep them out, for there is no point in letting them in to contaminate the uterus."

Jake continued, "A stallion's penis isn't designed to penetrate the cervix. Its head, when close to ejaculation, becomes enlarged and flat. It's designed, if he's a good breeder, to press up against the cervix. If she's ready, and about to ovulate, it will be open, and the stallion's semen, or at least a good portion of it, can shoot right into the uterus when ejaculation occurs. That's the way God designed it to work.

"With this pipette, I can ensure that all this semen is deposited directly in there. I can ensure it happens on the right day without harming the mare and prevent disease, too. By using artificial insemination, we can also protect the mares and stallions from getting hurt. Live cover mating between horses is a brutal, vicious, and often bloody affair. I know of several horses who have been severely injured in the process and one stallion whose breeding career was ended by an errant kick.

"Now that I've deposited the semen, I'm going to withdraw the pipette." Again, Jake looked directly into Matti's eyes and smiled, "But, as I withdraw, I'm going to massage the sphincter of her cervix to make sure it closes adequately to keep all that precious stuff inside where it can do its job. Then, I can slowly come out of her, gently, politely, and with a great big thank you, conclude this session."

Jake kept his eyes locked on Matti's as he finished his dialogue and removed his arm from Maggie. He stepped back, pulled off the glove, along with the pipette and syringe, and tossed them into the trash can beside the breeding station.

He rinsed the mare's backside, took down and unwrapped her tail, grabbed a paper towel to dry off his hands, and walked around to the mare's head. There, he began petting her nose and forehead, whispering sweet nothings in her ear—his way of expressing his gratitude all over again.

Jake looked at Matti and asked if she would take Miss Maggie Mae and put her in a stall for a couple of hours before turning her out to pasture. Before handing the lead to Matti, Jake asked, "Did you enjoy the session?"

Matti replied, "I did! I learned a lot." Then, with her ornery smile, "But there for a second, while you were rubbing her nose, I thought you were gonna offer her a cigarette."

Jake laughed, and as Matti was about to take the lead from his hand, he asked her, "Did I get you wet?"

Matti's head snapped to meet his eyes, trying her best to look offended.

"When I sprayed her off after we were done... What? Surely you don't think I meant anything else, do you?" Jake protested in jest.

"I know exactly what you meant." After a pause, as she walked away with the mare, Matti said, "But you'll never really know, will you?"

After a few steps, she heard him say in a low voice, "I already do."

Matti knew that Jake knew she had become aroused during his poetic description of the procedure. After all, that was his intention. It was foreplay—and it worked. Thinking about it and realizing Jake knew made her smile as she kissed Maggie on the nose before removing her halter and walking out of the stall to close the door.

Chapter 5
The Collection

It was early May. The weather in north Georgia was becoming quite warm. No visitors were expected, but a stallion needed to be collected for a couple of mares who were about to ovulate.

There was also a pasture that had been unused during the winter. Jake referred to it as the *back forty*, even though it wasn't that big. It was south of the big barn, separated by a large, wooded area at the back of the property—secluded. It was a perfect place for older horses or an occasional stallion to be left alone to run off some steam.

It needed some attention. Mowed, fencing mended, and a general tidying up. It was a one-person task Jake expected to take a good portion of a day to complete. The night before, he had assigned Matti to the job.

With a firm grasp on what her day would entail, and Shoshoni with Bryce at home, Matti figured it would be an opportunity to get some sun. She would be alone in a pasture in a secluded part of the farm where no one would see her. She showed up for work wearing very short, cut-off jeans, boots, and a halter top. Her long blonde hair was pulled back in a ponytail, which covered a good portion of her otherwise exposed back.

As luck would have it—good luck for Jake—the staff member he had planned to help him with the collection, called in sick that morning. Jake suspected the *brown-bottle flu*, an infraction for which, if true, he would pay dearly. Nonetheless, he wasn't there.

Jake needed a replacement. Matti had already demonstrated her ability to handle horses, including the stallions, and Jake thought this might be a good opportunity for her to broaden her skills. He was confident she was capable.

The procedure would require three personnel. One to position, and potentially escape with, a pre-selected mare, in heat, into a wooden *teasing box*. Another to maneuver the stallion through the process. Jake would handle the AV, the artificial vagina.

Jake had a staffer who was experienced with controlling a mare during a collection, but stallions are so valuable, and unpredictable, only a handful of individuals were allowed to even enter their stalls, let alone handle them.

Matti was one of the few, but semen collection would be a new challenge for her.

He hadn't expected her to arrive to work wearing shorts and braless in a halter top. She was wearing her usual boots, and he noticed her gloves stuffed into her back pockets.

In the break room, where the staff gathered each morning to clock in and slurp down a cup of coffee before starting their day, Jake found Matti. He motioned for her to follow him to where he could get her off by herself. Once away from everyone, Jake said, "What made you decide to come to work dressed like that?"

"You assigned me to the back forty today. Remember? You said it would probably take all day. There's never anybody back there. I figured I could get some sun."

"Oh, yeah. I forgot. Well, things have changed, maybe. Can I ask a personal question? A very personal question?"

"That depends. What would you like to know?"

"You're not on your menstrual cycle, are you?"

Jake could see the anger building in Matti's face as her lips contorted to form the words, "What the hell kind of question is that? And, what the hell business is it of yours?" Matti's reply, with her furrowed brow and raging eyes, left no doubt she was offended.

Jake was quick to respond, "Wait! I need some help collecting a stallion. I'd like you to do it, but if you're on your period, you're out! I didn't mean to offend. I'm sorry."

Matti had seen from personal experience how stallions react when a woman on her cycle gets too close. She immediately realized why Jake had to ask her. "If you think I can handle it, I'd love to. It sounds exciting, and I could learn a lot. I'm sorry I snapped at you."

Jake smiled, doing his best to stifle the remark that immediately jumped into his mind, opting instead to ask her to stick around until he had everything ready so he could go over what everybody needed to do. "It's okay. Meet me at the breeding lab in fifteen minutes."

As she turned to begin walking away, Jake couldn't resist any longer, saying, "So, I take it that's a 'no' then?"

Matti didn't even turn around. She just looked down, trying to stifle her laughter, shook her head, and kept walking. It was as if somehow she knew it was coming. Then Matti reached back for her gloves, placed them in her right hand, slapped them loudly into her left, and hollered, "Fifteen minutes. At the breeding lab. Don't keep me waiting."

Jake used the time to prepare everything, all the elements needed to complete the task. He checked the incubator setting, 101 degrees Fahrenheit, the natural body temperature of a horse. He had placed a bottle of *extender* therein the night before.

Record-keeping was essential. The required forms were assembled, laid out, and readied for when Jake would analyze the semen post-collection.

Jake also prepared several other materials he would need: sterile cotton, 60ml syringes, shipping containers for the off-premises mares whose owners had placed orders, and the AV.

By the time Jake was finishing up, Matti and Tony, the mare handler for the day's operation, arrived at the breeding lab.

"Ah, just in time," Jake quipped as he led them outside near the breeding dummy, securely mounted on two steel posts buried in concrete, deep in the ground. "I'd like to walk through what's about to happen. Tony, you'll be handling Angels Envy today."

Tony nodded his understanding.

"You've done this before, so it should be almost routine for you. Right?"

Without waiting for any acknowledgment from Tony, Jake continued, "But this time, we're collecting Shahman. He can be a handful. Be ready. If I give the word, open that door and get Angel the hell out of here fast. Got it?"

"Got it, boss," Tony responded, shaking his head exuberantly for added emphasis.

Jake turned his attention to Matti and pointed. "As you can see, the teasing box is approximately the height of the mare's legs, with a door at each end. It leaves most of her body exposed. The procedure requires her handler to lead the mare into the box and remain, with lead in hand, in case anything should go wrong.

"Whenever there's a stallion, who's always eager to breed, a mare in heat, confined, then you throw three human beings in the mix, to try to *control* things, *Murphy's Law* often comes into play.

"The *box* is intended to prevent the stallion from kicking the mare's legs, and the mare from doing the same to her suitor. One errant kick from a mare can end a stallion's breeding career forever. It's happened before.

"It'll be your responsibility, Matti, as the stallion handler to prevent him from becoming too aggressive and harming or mounting the mare during the teasing process. The idea is for the stallion to mount the breeding dummy, which, as you can see..." as Jake, standing next to it, patted it with his hand, "is a mere yard and a half away. The breeding dummy. Not the mare, not me, and certainly not you. Got it?" and they all chuckled.

"Yeah, that's the plan. Right?" Matti joked.

"Correct. Glad to see you catch on fast. But all these stallions have been through this drill dozens of times. Everything's going to be okay. They know what they're supposed to do. You just need to guide them.

"Them? I thought we were collecting *a* stallion?" Matti quipped.

"We are. But once you're *experienced*, you may become my *go-to* person for collections. Who knows? Today, you'll be handling the *big guy*. I know you've handled him before, but never in this capacity. This time, I want him in a different headstall. That one," and Jake pointed to the one hanging on the wall next to the breeding-lab door.

"You'll notice it's equipped with a chain attached to the lead. I want the chain run through Shahman's mouth, above his tongue. Understood?"

Matti nodded in the affirmative, but her eyebrow was slightly raised, even though she may not have noticed it. It was the most aggressive she'd ever known Jake to be toward a horse.

Jake saw it and said, "You'll understand why when we get into it. Just follow my instructions without question throughout the process, and everything will be fine. Okay?"

"Okay," she replied.

"Good. The first thing you'll do is bring him up to meet Angels Envy. Once you put that halter on him, he'll know he's heading for the breeding shed, so he'll start behaving all excited right from the git-go. All pumped up, blowin' and snortin' for all his buddies—showin' off somethin' awful, so be ready."

Matti was confident. "I'm ready," she said.

"Good. Make sure you're wearin' your gloves before you even go into his stall. Once you're in there, it's too late.

"By the time he sees Angel, he'll get really amped. Lead him up to her. He'll scream. She'll scream back and act like she's gonna kick the shit out of him. It's just foreplay. Just don't let him get too aggressive. Don't let him try to mount her. He'll try. As soon as he starts up, jerk him down, and damn sure, don't let him bite her. Trust me. He'll want to." With a big grin, he continued, "She's so pretty, he won't be able to contain himself."

Matti couldn't help but laugh.

"He'll start building an erection quickly. I'll watch for that. You just pay attention to what he's doing with regard to Angel. When he's ready, I'll have you pull him away," and Jake walked them over to an area on the other side of the breeding dummy. "Over here to where I will wash his erect penis. This is where the *fun* begins. He won't be in the mood for me to do what I've gotta do, but Matti, you need to hold on to him and try to get him to stand still."

At nearly a scream, laughing but trying to be serious simultaneously, Matti asked, "How am I supposed to do that?"

Only half joking, Jake replied, "Hey, you're the horsewoman. I thought you could get a horse to do anything. Did I say it was going to be easy?

"He'll dance around a lot, blow and snort, and prob'ly stomp his hooves, but keep him under control as best you can. It'll be fun. You'll see." Jake never lost his wide grin.

An apprehensive Matti replied, "I'll bet."

"Once we finish that step, you'll take him back to Angel, where he'll get super excited—quickly. I'll watch his erection, and when he's ready, I'll yell something like, *It's time, To the dummy*, or something like that. It'll be your cue to do whatever you need to pull him away and put him in front of the *pretend mare*.

"Maybe we should name her. What do you think? What would be a good name? How about Mildred? Do you like Mildred?"

Matti laughed, "Mildred? Where did you come up with that? Did you have an aunt you hated with that name?"

Tony couldn't control himself. "That's my mother's name," he said.

They all laughed hysterically until Jake finally said, "Well, I suppose Mildred's out then."

"No. I think Mildred fits perfectly," Tony replied. "I can't wait to share with my mom that we named a horse after her," and the uproar began again.

"Okay. 'Mildred' it is, then. I hope she makes your mother proud, Tony.

"Now, back to the matter at hand. Matti, once you pull Shahman away from Angel, he'll be ready to breed anything. That's where you've got to be careful that you don't get between him and *Mildred*. That may sound funny, but I'm not kidding. You've got to be fast. He will be up on two legs looking for that dummy. Don't let him come down on you.

"Once he lands on *Mildred*, I'll take care of the rest."

Jake looked at his charges and said, "Okay. Everybody understands their role and knows what we're gonna do, right?"

They nodded in agreement, and Jake continued. "All right then. Tony, you bring up Angel and put her in the teasing box. While you're doing that, I'll prepare the AV and fill the bucket for washing the big guy.

"Matti, grab the headstall and mosey on over to the stallion barn, but don't go near Shahman's stall. I'll holler when it's time to hook him up. Okay?"

"Got it," she replied.

"Okay. Let's do this. Remember, Matti, don't go near the stallion's stall until I holler. And have your gloves on when you go in."

"I remember. I'm not a child."

"Yeah. I saw that right off," Jake replied as he watched her walk away in those cut-off jeans.

Matti heard him, looked back, smiled, and continued on her way, but not before adding a little extra sway in each step.

Jake's eyes feasted on the sight before he returned to the lab to fill the AV bladder with the necessary amount of water at precisely 104 degrees Fahrenheit. Next, he inserted the collection sleeve and bottle. Once affixed, he applied copious amounts of lubricant to the sleeve's interior inside the AV using a palpation glove.

A trick Jake had learned was to use the glove as a seal. He'd remove his arm, leaving the glove inside, and fold the cuff over the opening to prevent contamination from getting to the interior of the AV. He then prepared a bucket two-thirds full of warm water and numerous chunks of sterile cotton he'd use to clean Shahman's organ.

As he walked out of the lab and strategically placed the bucket, Jake saw Tony approaching with Angel, so he signaled Matti. "Time to hook up the *Big Guy*."

Matti took a deep breath and headed for his stall.

When the stallion saw Matti, he approached the door like always. He had a fondness for Matti. The feeling was mutual. She scratched his nose through the bars of the stall door before opening it. She stepped in and quickly closed it behind her. When he saw the headstall she was carrying, Shahman got excited, as Jake had predicted.

Matti hated putting the big and seemingly bulky headgear on such a beautiful face, but the idea of running the chain through his mouth and over his tongue made her skin crawl. *Why on earth is such a thing necessary? I'm sure Jake has his reasons.*

It wouldn't take long for her to discover why. As soon as she slid the leather of the headstall past his ears, the stallion's demeanor changed dramatically. It was as if he had transformed from Dr. Jekyll to Mr. Hyde.

Suddenly, Matti was glad Jake had told her to don the gloves before entering his stall. Her eyes became as big as silver dollars, and she could feel her heart pounding.

He started prancing in place, eager for the door to open so he could meet his chosen mate for the evening, afternoon, or morning. He didn't care what time of day it was. He was ready!

Now Matti was somewhat hesitant to slide the door open. She'd never seen the Big Guy in this kind of state before. Self-doubt crept in. *Holy shit! Am I going to be able to handle him like this?*

Look at him. Amped up this way. He is incredible, isn't he? C'mon! Cowgirl up! Jake's got faith in you. You can do this.

"Hell yeah! Let's do this." She pushed the door open. Shahman nearly knocked her over, rushing past her as if she didn't exist. She jerked hard on the lead to slow him down so she could catch up and regain some semblance of control. It was then she discovered the value of the chain. It wasn't that it leveled the playing field, but it gave Matti a chance to gain his respect.

The Big Guy continued to prance down the barn aisle, making his way toward the breeding shed, letting his rival stallions know today was *his* day.

As they approached the corner of the breeding shed, Jake motioned Matti to proceed with the stallion, taking him up to the mare's nose to get familiar with her. Shahman didn't need much coaxing. He knew the drill.

After a short period of romance and foreplay, the Big Guy became aggressive. The way most stallions demonstrate their masculinity in the presence of a mare in heat, realizing they might get lucky.

Once Shahman was becoming aroused and starting to *drop*, as they say in the horse breeding vernacular, Jake instructed Matti to drag him away from the mare, which, she learned, was no small task.

Matti found the enamored steed unwilling to leave the target of his desires. She knew the farm had a policy about handling the horses gently and respectfully, so she was reluctant to use anything that might be considered excessive force. However, it was apparent the stallion was ignoring her.

Finally, she took charge, stepped back, and put her whole body into it. She jerked his head so hard he had no choice but to pay attention. It took all she could do to pry him away, but her efforts made an impact, and she prevailed.

She led Shahman over a few feet away from Angel to Jake, where, with his bucket filled with warm water and individual chunks of surgical cotton, he began washing the stallion's extended organ to remove any dirt and debris.

Jake explained the importance of cleanliness to Matti. He went into great detail as he held Shahman's massive phallus in one hand and washed it with a drenched mass of soft cotton.

The stallion danced. It was difficult to tell if it was out of anger or if the Big Guy was enjoying it. As Jake washed him, he was careful to emphasize why what he was doing was essential. "Contamination can kill semen, infect a uterus, compromise a pregnancy, or all of the above," he explained.

Every time one chunk of cotton would become soiled, he would toss it on the ground and grab another out of the bucket until the appendage was finally clean, to Jake's satisfaction. "Cleanliness is next to Godliness," he exclaimed.

After cleaning, more teasing was needed to ensure the stallion returned to an exceedingly aroused state. It didn't take long. Almost instantly, Shahman started arching his neck. His tail was standing straight up, and his ears were pricked forward. He was kicking the teasing box and doing everything he could to let her know he would have her! Finally, his member was engorged and throbbing, and Jake yelled, "Okay, he's ready."

Matti squealed, "I'd say so!" as she, with all her might, dragged the stallion away from Angel and led him over to *Mildred*, just a meter and a half away from the teasing box.

With the AV in his left hand, Jake watched as the eager stag pawed and pivoted up in the air. Before landing perfectly in position, he used his right hand to remove and toss aside the glove, sealing the AV's opening. He then guided Shahman's throbbing phallus into the freshly exposed lube of the AV. It all seemed to happen in one swift motion, a product of Jake's experience, much to the stallion's delight.

With a bit of expert stimulation on Jake's part, Shahman's tail began to flag, and he deposited nearly 300 ml of semen into the collection bottle. Mission accomplished.

As soon as the Big Guy ejaculated, Jake opened the valve on the AV to release much of the warm water in the bladder, thus relieving the pressure, enabling its comfortable removal from the satisfied steed's member, now gradually becoming flaccid, without discomfort.

Upon ejaculation, Shahman virtually collapsed his weight upon *Mildred* as though he had exhausted every bit of energy he had saved up over the last week. Nevertheless, the whole episode was carnal, exciting, and humorous.

"It looks like that took a lot out of him. Do you suppose *he'd* like a cigarette?" Matti asked.

Jake laughed and told Matti to wait until the once-proud steed was "... regaining some sense of dignity, and a desire to dismount." Only then was she to lead him back to his stall.

After assessing the situation, Jake said, "Tony, I think it's safe to go ahead and turn Angel back out to pasture and resume your regular duties. Matti, once you feel comfortable putting Shahman back, come to the breeding lab for further instructions. Okay?"

By the time Matti had returned to the breeding lab, Jake was well on his way to finishing up much of what he needed to do. He had a drop of semen on a slide under the microscope from where he had evaluated its forward motility. When she entered, Matti said, "That was awesome! What's next?"

I'm glad you enjoyed it. You did great. I thought you might like learning more about what we do on the breeding side here. Wanna see what we just did?"

"Sure."

"Okay. First of all, a little critique. You did great. Overall, you handled Shahman well. You do, however, need to be a little quicker. When I say, 'Pull him away!' You need to do it NOW! Jerk his head off if you need to, but pull him away. You can't let him get the upper hand.

"To do that, you need to position yourself to have leverage at all times. You don't necessarily need to use it, but you must always be prepared to, if need be.

"There was that one point, just before I cleaned him when you were slow, but you recovered and learned from it. You did well.

"That was the *only* thing that I can say that needs work. The *only* thing, and that very fact, *amazed* me. Congratulations."

"Wow. Thank you. I've never been *criticized* so beautifully, so nicely, in my life. Thank you. I was a little *flat-footed* there for a moment, wasn't I?"

"You were, but you recovered well. You looked like you got mad and threw your whole upper body into it." Flashing a big smile, "In that halter top, *it was impressive*! I enjoyed it immensely."

Matti was looking straight into Jake's eyes when those words came out of his mouth. Her face immediately flushed bright red.

She had nice breasts and looked good in the halter top. She wasn't wearing a bra, and the top *was* quite revealing.

Matti hadn't planned on working with Jake that day. She wondered just how much of her Jake had actually seen. *I wouldn't have worn that top if I'd known I'd be working with him. I am kinda glad it worked out the way it did. Why am I not angry?*

"Well, I guess I'm glad I was able to *impress* you, at least," Matti said teasingly as she flashed a wicked smile back at him.

Jake responded, "Was there anything about the process you found surprising or have questions about?"

"Yeah. The amount of time you spent cleaning his penis after he dropped. That surprised me."

This provided Jake the perfect segue to share with Matti the basic construction of the artificial vagina, how it's assembled, and how the semen collection occurs. He figured once she understood the AV and how it works, it would be obvious how debris from a dirty penis could contaminate the semen.

With a clear understanding of the AV, Jake decided it was an excellent time to continue Matti's education. "Come over here and take a look at what clean, uncontaminated semen looks like under a microscope."

As they walked across the room and neared the microscope, Jake said, "This is what we just collected." He reached over to guide Matti into place. In so doing, he touched her gently on the small of her bare back. His touch sent a shock wave through Matti, as powerful as a bolt of electricity. She didn't know if Jake knew how it affected her or not. She must have flinched. But did she?

Every tiny hair on her body stood on end. Suddenly, she wanted to rip her clothes off and have her way with Jake right there in the lab. She could envision the image clearly in her mind.

She composed herself, as best she could, and looked into the microscope. After what seemed like several minutes of instructions on adjusting the aperture, the focus, and every other thing, Matti couldn't see what Jake was describing.

Frustrated, Jake finally looked into the scope. "Shit! They're all dead. We've been talking way too long. The heat from the lamp below has killed all the sperm cells. No wonder you couldn't see them."

Jake and Matti both began laughing hysterically. Precisely what Matti needed to regain her composure since she was so close to being completely out of control. It gave her a convenient excuse for being so red-faced and emotionally charged.

Jake rescued the moment. "No problem. We'll toss that slide, get a new one, put a drop of this *extended* semen on it...." Jake let the sentence trail off as he placed a thin glass cover slip on top of the droplet before sliding the new one onto the platform and into the field of view.

"Voila!" Jake exclaimed. That's more like it. "When I checked it before, it was 95% forwardly motile. You can imagine how deflated I was to see it all dead when you looked at it. Here, look again to see what good semen looks like."

Matti bent down again to gaze into the microscope. Again, Jake couldn't resist placing his hand on her bare back. Again, Matti experienced the same flush of excitement.

This time, instead of resisting the feeling, she went with it and didn't attempt to hide anything. No. She lifted her head from the microscope to look into Jake's eyes, smiled for a long second, and then looked back at the semen on the slide. Jake's hand remained comfortably on Matti's bare back—and Matti was good with that.

While studying what she was observing, Matti said, "These little guys look like they're wigglin' around goin' crazy. What does that mean?"

"They're just swimming 'around goin' crazy' because they're in a little drop with nowhere to go. That's semen with which I've already mixed an extender—a combination food source and antibiotic that extends its life expectancy and enables us to keep it, or even ship it, via overnight delivery anywhere in the country for use up to five days after it's collected.

That way, we can service multiple mares with a single ejaculate. It also enables us to breed mares on consecutive days, if necessary, without overusing our stallions."

Jake continued, "If you look closely, there are most likely some dead sperm cells. Do you see any?"

After a moment of intense peering through the aperture, Matti finally said, "Oh, yes. A few, but not very many."

Jake had taken a seat next to Matti to fill out some remaining paperwork before saying, "That's good. That means the extender is doing its job. Now, if you look hard enough, you should see that most are capable of moving forward, but some can't. They wiggle but go nowhere. Do you see any of those? Can you tell the difference?"

"Yes! I see some of those, and I *can* tell the difference." Matti was proud of herself for being able to identify them so quickly. "I'm pretty sure I see more of those than dead ones."

"Very good. Typically, that's the case."

Matti jumped in again. "Boy, some of these guys are just swimming like gangbusters. They're going at it like there's no tomorrow." She couldn't help but giggle as she finished the statement.

Jake chuckled back and said, "Those are, more than likely, the male cells."

Matti looked up, sure he was joking. They both had a good laugh before Jake continued. "Actually, it's true. The stallion controls the sex of the offspring. He produces male and female sperm cells."

She chimed in. "It's that x and y chromosome thing, right?"

"Precisely. The males are typically stronger and swim faster—"

Matti protested, "Uh, huh."

"But there's a trade-off. They use up their energy in a hurry and die off quicker. The females take their time getting to their destination and live longer.

A theory suggests that if a mare ovulates within eight hours of being inseminated, she will, more often than not, produce a colt. After eight hours, most male sperm cells have died off, so the odds are a filly will be the result."

Jake was on a roll, "The cells on that slide are limited in where they can go, so they just look like they are swimming *helter-skelter*. Without additional fluid, they can go no further. They will exhaust themselves and die."

He slowed his words and continued softly, "In the warm environment of the mare's vagina, they get all giddy. When that precious egg makes its way down that fallopian tube into the uterus, that's like manna from heaven. Those little guys go bonkers. Unlike on this slide, those cells will have a destination. Their mission will be clear when that happens.

"Once they reach the egg, it becomes a contest. Who will it be that can penetrate that membrane, fertilize it, and create the next masterpiece? The competition will be fierce. But the egg must be willing. That's always the question. Is the precious *egg* willing? Will she say *yes* or reject her suitor?"

Matti knew that remark was directed squarely at her. It confirmed what she already knew. They were going to have sex. It was just a matter of time.

Jake finished up by saying, "About the only thing left to do here is drawing the semen up in 60 ml doses and preparing them for shipment or storage. Do you want to help with that?"

"I do. I want to see this thing through."

Jake instructed Matti, and together, they drew up the syringes and packaged two for shipment and the others for storage. During the process, Matti asked, "How long will this extended semen last?"

"Great question. From our stallions, typically five to seven days, unless something goes wrong, either in shipment or how it's stored after it gets to its destination."

"Really? I noticed you said, 'From *our* stallions.' Do some stallions' semen not fare so well?"

"Some don't ship well at all. Some of it is because of how it's collected and handled, but sometimes it's just the stallion. It's crazy, I know."

"How do you extend it? Do you just dump a bottle of the extender in on top of the stallion's stuff?"

"Ha. Not exactly," Jake replied. "First, I have to measure the semen's concentration in this here machine," and he took a step to reach the small vial still stored therein. "It's called a *densimeter*. It reads how many cells per milliliter. Once I have that number, and knowing the volume he produced, I can calculate how much extender to add, based on the forward motility percentage, to provide five hundred million forwardly motile sperm cells per 60 ml dose."

"How did you know how much Shahman produced? Did you measure it?"

"Well, kinda." Jake held up the bottle and pointed to the lines and numbers on the side. "The collection bottle gave me that information, and I wrote it down before you came in.

"Once I have that data, I can take the extender out of the incubator and mix the correct amount gently with the semen before drawing the mixture up into the syringes. Last night, I put the extender in the incubator to bring it up to temp. Any temperature differential can kill sperm cells."

"Holy crap. There's a lot to this, huh?"

Jake smiled, "It took me a while to learn it. I can't lie."

"I've got some more paperwork and other chores to do. So why don't you spend the rest of the day doing what you originally had on your schedule?"

"Working out in the *back forty*?"

"Yeah. I think that's what it was. Right?"

"Should I take the tractor and bush hog?"

"No. I don't think you'll have time to mow. Just work on the fence and try to pile some of the downed tree limbs, ones you can handle, around the paddock so we can come by and haul them away with the trailer later. Throw whatever tools you think you'll need in that five-gallon bucket hangin' off the back of the 4-wheeler.

"Some of those limbs will take a chainsaw to cut into smaller pieces. I'll be out in a little while with the saw to help. Okay?"

"Okay. See you later."

Chapter 6
The First Kiss

I t was a lovely day a little after two o'clock, exceptionally warm and sunny, with scattered clouds. The *back forty* was a beautiful part of the farm. Separated from the main barn by a couple hundred yards of forest and surrounded by trees. Perfect.

Matti had been out there for more than three hours—by herself. Jake decided he should take her something cold to drink. Some water, yes, but maybe a cold beer or two would be a nice touch.

He grabbed a blanket and a couple of towels out of the bunkhouse. He tossed them, along with a cooler containing some ice, a bottle of water, four beers, potato chips, and two halves of a pastrami sandwich he had made, into the vintage Army jeep he often used around the farm.

He was ready to leave to find Matti when he remembered, *Oh, shit. I need to grab that chainsaw.* So he set it, along with fuel and chain lubricant, into the back.

When Jake pulled up, he found Matti hard at work—dripping with sweat. "I figured you might need a break and a nice cold drink of water."

"How sweet are you?" Matti exclaimed.

Jake motioned to the passenger seat and said, "Hop in. I know a nice shady spot where we can relax for a few minutes."

Realizing shade was within easy walking distance, Matti jumped in anyway. Jake handed her the bottle of water as he took off toward an area through the woods next to a small creek nearby. Matti had never seen this place before. She was taken by its beauty.

"I'm not sure anybody else knows about this, but it's one of my favorite havens on the farm. I come here occasionally, and I'd just as soon keep it a secret if you know what I mean."

He removed the blanket and cooler from the jeep, headed to a grassy area a few steps from the creek bank, sat the cooler down, and asked Matti to help him spread the blanket.

"Wow. This is nice." Matti's words were a mix of surprise, gratitude, and suspicion.

As they sat, Jake opened the cooler, pulled out a bottle of beer, twisted off the cap, and offered it to Matti. "I thought a nice cold beer might taste good after being in the sun for so long. What do you think?"

Perfect. "That sounds delicious." Matti eagerly took the beer and downed a big swallow.

Jake pulled another from the ice, and they toasted the occasion by clinking their bottles together. Then, after taking a swig of his, he dug into the cooler again, retrieving the sandwich he had made, neatly packaged in a plastic bag. He held it up to Matti and said, "I also thought you might be hungry. I was and figured you had to be.

"Working that hard, you had to have worked up an appetite, and nothing goes with a pastrami sandwich like a nice cold beer. What do you say? Will you share it with me? Please? It's a picnic on a beautiful, sunny day. You can't turn me down, can you?"

Looking at the sandwich, Matti could see how massive it was and that it was already cut in two. She was hungry. *I really have no choice, right? Jake's the boss' son, so I'm kinda under orders.*

"That sounds wonderful. Thank you, Jake," Matti replied. "Before I eat a sandwich with these filthy hands, I think I'll wash them in the creek."

As she walked the few feet over to the water's edge, Jake joined her to wash his as well and said in a low voice, "I sometimes come down here on a hot day, strip off naked, and wash my whole body." Then he pointed to his left and continued, "Just downstream a few yards, it gets about waist-deep with a pebbly bottom. It's pretty nice. Just sayin.'"

Matti looked up at him and smiled. "I was only planning on eating half a sandwich. Washing my hands should be enough. Thanks for the information, though."

The comment brought a chuckle, and they headed back to the blanket.

Jake handed Matti one of the towels so they could dry their hands. He loosened the wrapping, handed her a paper napkin, and held the sandwich out, saying, "Madam."

Matti removed the half closest to her, placed it on her napkin, and smiled, "Thank you, kind sir."

Once he had done the same for himself, they were about to take a bite when Jake said, "Oh, I almost forgot. I brought some chips, too."

He reached into the cooler, grabbed the bag, and set it on the blanket between them. It would go unopened.

They started talking. First, it was about what Matti had been doing since she had arrived there in the *back forty*—the fence work she'd done, challenges she'd faced, limbs that still needed to be cut. Then, the conversation moved back to the collection.

Soon, they realized they hadn't taken a bite of the sandwich. So Jake said, "Hey, let's eat! We can talk and eat, too, you know. I'm mean, I know it's not polite to talk with our mouths full, but...."

Matti admired the pastrami sandwich that Jake had made especially for her. The meat was piled high and topped off with Jake's unique touches. She bit into it and said ... with her mouth full, "Holy crap! That's the best sandwich I've ever put in my mouth! What is it?"

Jake burst out laughing. "Ha! I just said, 'It's not polite to talk with your mouth full.'"

Jake took a quick bite of his, and they laughed hysterically together.

After they semi-composed themselves and swallowed, Jake responded, "That's my pastrami special. I made it just for you. I'm glad you like it. It's like a Reuben, except I use pastrami. I pile it high, add a little sauerkraut, pepper jack cheese, and my secret, special sauce."

Matti would come to learn he was a master in the kitchen.

They laughed some more and continued their conversation, sandwich, and beer. When the food items were gone, they continued to talk for a while. Finally, Jake looked into Matti's eyes and said, "You know, I'm enjoying this so much, I don't want it to end."

Matti replied, "Me, too."

He reached into the cooler. "Luckily, I brought one more beer each. May I open this one for you?"

"I would appreciate it if you would."

As Jake leaned over to hand the opened bottle to her, he watched her drink from it. As she swallowed, he said, "I envy the mouth of that bottle."

"Oh. Why is that?"

"I would much rather it were my lips pressing against yours than that stupid bottle."

Matti smiled wryly. "Why would you want to do that?"

"Because I've wanted to kiss you all day. For weeks, actually."

"What's stopping you?"

Jake leaned close and softly touched his lips to hers. Almost instantly, Matti's mouth opened slightly. An invitation of which Jake took full advantage. Their embrace became more intense. Matti fumbled to find a place to set her beer off the blanket. When she released it, it fell over and spilled half its contents. Neither cared, as Jake's hand had found Matti's breast.

Jake pulled her closer. Their breathing quickened. Suddenly, Matti pulled away, stiffened her posture, and took a long sip of what remained of her beer. She reached down, pulled off her left boot and sock, then the right, stood up, and started toward the creek.

"Where are you going?"

About halfway to the water's edge, Matti stopped, said nothing, reached around, and began untying the knot in the back of her halter top. Once accomplished, with her back fully exposed to Jake, she undid the knot behind her neck and allowed the top to fall to her waist, holding it in her hand.

She turned to face Jake, giving him a full view of her bare breasts. She looked into his eyes, retraced the few steps in his direction, and dropped her top onto the blanket. With her eyes fixed on his, Matti unbuckled her belt, unbuttoned, and slowly unzipped her cutoff jeans.

Without shifting her gaze, she let them fall to her ankles, stepped out with one leg, and used the other to lift them onto the blanket with her toes, the nails of which were painted to match her fingernails. She paused briefly before seductively removing her sexy panties.

Matti stood there, naked, looking squarely into Jake's eyes, and she said, "I thought it might be a good time for that *cool bath*." She motioned with both hands, coyly pointing to her neatly trimmed, but not shaved, bush, and said, "Did you notice? No balls."

Jake sat there staring for a moment, in stunned disbelief, taking in the sight of her. She was even more beautiful than he'd expected. Then, after a few seconds, grinning like the proverbial cat that ate the canary, he said, "Yeah. I *definitely* noticed that. Yes, I did!"

Matti smiled as she reached up to remove her UT hat, pulled her ponytail through the hole in the back, and laid it on top of her pile of clothes. She shook her head, ran her fingers through the hair in front, looked down at him again, and said, "Are you coming?"

Without waiting for an answer, Matti turned and headed for the creek.

"I think a quick bath is an excellent idea," Jake said as he jumped up and began ripping off his clothes to join the beautiful, bare-naked woman stepping into the creek.

In little more than an instant, they were completely submerged in the cool water with the pebbly bottom, wrapped in each other's embrace. Their kisses were deep and urgent. Matti wrapped her legs around Jake, eagerly welcoming him inside. As he penetrated her, she moaned softly.

When he was fully deep inside, she whispered in his ear, "See. I told you the other day. If I had 'balls,' they'd just be in the way."

Chapter 7
The Affair

Jake and Matti seemed perfect for each other. Jake was divorced from his first wife, and the relationship with his *play-pretty* had been over for a while. There was just one problem. Matti was married to somebody else.

Nonetheless, their affair was blossoming. They laughed, and they loved. They slipped off every chance they got to their secret place. Trouble was, those opportunities were few and far between. They both agreed they had to keep their affair secret.

Matti was married and had a baby daughter, for heaven's sake. "If Bryce finds out, it'll kill him. There's no tellin' what he'll do, and I can't make it on my own without him.

"And, with the circles your folks travel in, your mom and dad will never be okay with you *hookin' up* with the *barn help*. That'll never fly. We've got to keep this under the radar. I have to admit, I want you all the time."

And so, it went—for months. They worked together, and from all outward appearances, few could tell there was anything more between them but a professional friendship.

From the very beginning, Jake treated Matti like every other staff member. That she was female made no difference to him. He told the same jokes in front of her as he would a male coworker, so his sexual innuendos didn't surprise anyone. They were no big deal, and Matti wasn't shy about responding in kind from day one. Everybody got a kick out of it, and nothing ever changed.

Even if a coworker did suspect something, Jake didn't care. He knew no coworker would have the guts to tell his parents or the wherewithal to figure out who Matti's husband was. He didn't figure they were bright enough to dig into it or cared enough to give a shit.

They would live out their love affair whenever they got the opportunity—a good thing for Jake. Matti couldn't get enough of him. Whenever no one was around, and he came by, she'd pull him around the corner, wrap her arms around his neck, and kiss him deeply. She knew she would instantly get a rise in his groin. She'd then pull away and head off with a "...gotta go. I love you."

After several of those episodes, Jake said, "You're killing me! Why do you ambush me like that?"

Matti replied, in a whisper, "Because I want you to know how I feel. How bad I want you. I ache for you all the time, Jake, but I hafta go."

"My God. You are amazing. Where are you going?"

Matti giggled as she trotted away. "My boss is a son-of-a-bitch. He works me like a dog. I wish I had more time. I love you. Bye."

Jake lived in a house on the property, but it was right on the *beaten path*, as they say, so having sex there, at least during the day, was out of the question. They had to find other venues for their daytime lovemaking—and they did.

The sex between them was great. Matti was on birth control, so there was no worry about an unwanted pregnancy. When an opportunity presented itself, they would seize it—behind a barn, in the woods, anywhere they thought no one might catch them.

One evening, after everyone else had left the farm, Matti had just finished sanitizing a stall in preparation for a world-famous stallion scheduled to arrive for a public presentation the next day.

She had laid in fresh, sweet straw, waist-deep, soft, and fluffy. She called Jake on his cell phone to ask him to inspect her work to ensure it was acceptable since she had never prepared a stall for such a situation before.

When Jake came down to inspect, it was near dusk. Matti hadn't turned the lights on in the barn, so the interior was getting dark with lots of shadows. Jake immediately saw the open stall door, but no Matti.

When he approached the stall and peered inside, he found his lover lying seductively in the straw pile. With her shirt unbuttoned down to past her bra, exposing much of her chest, she sported a shaft of wheat, with the seedhead still attached, clenched between her teeth.

Jake couldn't resist the temptation.

After they straightened their clothes, Jake said, "I think you did a fine job preparing that stall, Matti. A fine job, indeed."

Matti smiled, kissed him, and said, "I love you, Jake."

As they started out of the stall together, Jake looked back and said, "Uh-oh. I think we smooshed the straw down a bit. Maybe we should add a little more. What do you think?"

Matti looked in, nodded, and said, "If we don't, we'll be discovered for sure. Everybody'll know what we've done."

Matti headed over to grab two more bales of straw, and Jake walked back in to start fluffing what was already there. When she returned, Jake pulled out his knife to cut the twine. They finished the task in little more than a minute.

When they got to the end of the barn aisle, Jake turned Matti toward him, kissed her deeply, looked her in the eye, and said, "I love you. Now, go home. I'll pots around here for a while. Even though I don't think there's anyone around, we can't risk being seen leaving together. It won't look good for you."

"Okay." Matti turned to head home.

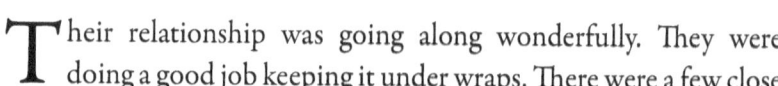

Their relationship was going along wonderfully. They were doing a good job keeping it under wraps. There were a few close calls, but they eluded discovery for several months.

Their visits to their favorite spot by the creek were few. It was challenging to carve out enough time to slip away without causing suspicion, so they couldn't get there as often as they would have liked.

Bryce's job required him to be on the road, sometimes for two or more nights at a time. On those occasions, Matti would sometimes spend the night with Jake and bring Shoshoni with her.

Jake would wait until all staff members, including Matti, left the farm to ensure nobody knew what was happening. Then, once he was comfortable all was safe, he would pick up Matti and Shoshoni for the sleepover. Then, before daylight, he would deliver them back home to get ready to come to work just like any other day.

Jake used Matti's hunger for him to his advantage. His words, the way he delivered them, could arouse her and get her juices flowing. Jake could make love to her in ways she had never imagined. He could bring her to orgasm without penetration. He had explored and tasted every crevice of her body. When they made love, it was not unusual for her to experience orgasm three or more times and be entirely spent before Jake would finally finish. They were great together.

Jake loved everything about Matti. He loved how she looked, loved, and moved—so graceful in everything she did. Jake also loved her scent. Even when she was working hard, dirty, and sweaty, the lady produced an aroma he found intoxicating. For him, Matti was perfect. She was intense, daring, and playful.

They had come to the realization that what they had together was real. They were meant for each other and had fallen in love. This wasn't superficial love. Not just lust. This was the real thing. But what to do?

M ost of the staff was afraid of Jake. He was big, strong, and short-tempered, a taskmaster. He had a reputation for firing staff members, often because they made a stupid mistake or just made him angry, usually over something foolish.

With Matti, it was different. He loved her and knew her intimately. There was nothing he wouldn't do for her, but he also recognized the situation in which they found themselves.

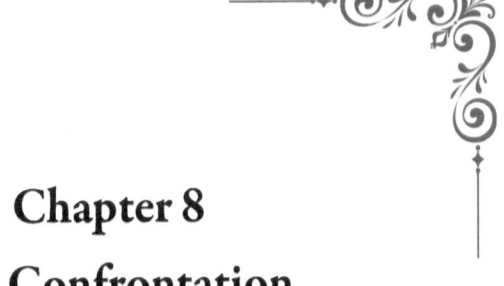

Chapter 8
The Confrontation

As the months passed and Matti's affair with Jake grew, Bryce began to realize he was losing his wife. One evening, over dinner, Bryce informed Matti he'd found a job opportunity she'd find irresistible.

"We've been offered the position in New York State, in wine country, managing a ranch up there. Obviously, I can't do it without you. It includes housing and a good salary. They've got horses, cattle, hay, and timber. Check out the website on your computer. It looks like an incredible facility. The owners don't live on the property. Not even in the same state."

"Where *do* they live then?"

"Connecticut, I think," Bryce replied. "Is that important? It's what's called a 'gentleman's farm' kind of thing. Mainly a tax write-off, I suspect."

Matti, shaken, replied, "I guess not. I didn't know we were looking for a new job. This is all kinda sudden, don't you think?"

"Well, maybe, but you've been dreaming about this kind of opportunity ever since I've known you. I understand you've always wanted to move west, but this could be the next best thing. What do you say?"

Matti opened her computer, and Bryce guided her to the website. "I can't deny it is a beautiful place."

"Good. I already told the owners we'd take it."

Shocked, Matti screeched, "What? You told them we'd take it? Before you talked to me?"

Bryce assertively responded, "Yeah. I knew you'd love it after you saw the website. It's your dream job. It's all you've ever talked about."

Pointing to the computer screen, he continued, "What's not to like about this place? You can't turn it down, right? It's not Montana, but it might be a stepping-stone to getting there."

"When would we have to leave?"

"Tomorrow is your day off, right?"

Matti confirmed it was.

"We could start packing tonight, finish up tomorrow, and head north before dark."

Devastated, Matti shot back, "You're telling me you want me to leave my job, one that I *love*, in the middle of the night, without notice, to run off with you to New York to something you *say* is going to be wonderful?"

Bryce paused, looked her square in the eye, and said, "*One* you love or a *job* you love, Matti?"

That question froze her. She couldn't move—couldn't speak. The tears welling up told everything. Her face was bright red.

"I know, Matti. I've known for a while. But I love you. I don't care. I want you—and Shoshoni. I want to provide for you, and this is my chance. But, unfortunately, staying here, under these circumstances, will never be an opportunity for you, even if I'm out of the picture.

"Jake's parents aren't going to let you marry their son. If you had met him under other circumstances, maybe. But you met him as a *barn hand*. That can't work in the circles they operate. You're from the wrong side of the tracks, babe. I'm sorry."

THE GREATEST SOFTBALL GAME

Bryce didn't always make sense, but this time, she knew he was right.

Jake's parents routinely had movie stars, professional athletes, politicians, and even members of royal families visit their farm. Their son needed to marry a member of *society*, after all.

I don't fit the image of what Jake's parents have in mind for their son.

Matti never gave a college education a second thought, given her situation. Being a single mother, twice at such a young age, was pretty clear evidence of her "... poor judgment and lack of self-control." She heard that a lot from her parents.

She was angry with Bryce for forcing her to choose, even though she knew he was right. She was, after all, carrying on an affair, right under his nose, with the son of her employer, with whom she worked every day.

She also knew any long-term relationship with Jake was likely a *pipe dream*. From her perspective, falling in love with the son of a rich and famous cattle rancher and horse breeder, one known worldwide—her just being a hired hand with a young child—was simply beyond comprehension. That could never happen.

But months earlier, Matti had already resigned herself. *It's okay. I can live with that.*

Now that she and Bryce were having this conversation, Matti was starting to wonder whether what she had with Jake was love or simply lust. When she thought about it, she had to admit their time together, while tender and sweet, when time permitted, always ended in passionate lovemaking.

When they were rushed, and only a few minutes were afforded them, quick and hurried, half-clothed sex would suffice, and it was magnificent. They were perfect for each other. Their mutual orgasms were ecstasy. The kind people fantasize over—write books about. They couldn't get enough of each other.

The idea of leaving was more than she could take. But she also knew Jake's mother had almost discovered their affair when she nearly walked in on them once. They had experienced several close calls by other staff members as well. Matti knew they couldn't keep their relationship a secret forever. Sooner or later, someone would discover the truth.

Matti didn't expect it would be Bryce who figured it out. But she realized if she didn't leave with him, he would probably meet with Jake's parents to explain the situation, causing Matti to lose her position with the farm.

Either way, she loses—Jake *and* her job.

Chapter 9
The Departure

Matti, the epitome of an outdoorswoman, had a burning desire to visit the West, particularly Montana and the Bitterroot Valley. She was almost obsessed with how badly our government treated the American Indians, hence the names she chose for her daughters.

By the end of the next day, Matti, Bryce, and Shoshoni were headed north to New York. Not Montana, but maybe a step, even though not in the correct compass direction.

They completed the two-day trip from the horse farm in northwest Georgia to their new destination, and it was beautiful, just as Bryce had described.

Matti's sadness over leaving Jake lingered. Departing without saying goodbye haunted her. She thought about seeing him one last time to tell him what had happened but realized she couldn't. If she went to see him, she knew she'd change her mind and wouldn't leave. She had to make a clean break, so she left without a word to anyone.

Fortunately for Matti, she and Bryce had two vehicles, so they drove separately. At least she'd have the opportunity to cry it out on the way. It would be a long trip.

The image of Jake's face never left Matti's mind's eye. She missed him so much. The sight of her husband made her angry.

Over the next few months, their attempts at intimacy always ended poorly. Their relationship grew more and more platonic. The marriage failed before they had completed a year in New York together.

Knowing he had no expertise in running the operation, Bryce acquiesced to Matti's request for a divorce and moved on. By the time the property owners realized it had occurred, Matti had established herself as *the* ranch manager and continued in that role without so much as a hiccup.

M atti was living in beautiful wine country, raising her little girl as a single mom. They were doing well enough, but life in the middle of nowhere can get lonely. She hadn't been intimate with Bryce during the last six months they were married, nor had there been any other men in her life since. It was taking a toll.

A year after Matti's divorce, she saw on social media that Jake was getting married. She was devastated. She cried inconsolably and was a wreck for days. For weeks, she'd burst into tears for no apparent reason.

After struggling through the emotional pain, she forced herself to accept reality. *The love of my life has moved on.*

Matti's loneliness was quickly reaching a breaking point when she began to notice Karson, a man a few years her senior. He was starting to show an interest in her, and Shoshoni.

He owned an over-the-road semi with which he hauled hay and other goods, often from Montana, occasionally for the farm she managed. She had grown to know him as a trustworthy member of the *team* and appreciated him. She enjoyed talking with him about his trips out west but didn't view him as a love interest.

Karson and Shoshoni had developed an excellent relationship as he liked kids and brought her trinkets he'd pick up while on the road.

Whenever he'd arrive at the farm with his load of hay, he was always friendly, respectful, and supportive of Matti. She appreciated that he would go out of his way to assist whenever she needed help.

One day, after his truck had been unloaded, Karson asked, "Matti, it's getting late, and I've been on the road all day. Would it be alright if I slept here tonight instead of drivin' all the way into town?" He had a sleeper cab, so accommodations weren't an issue.

Matti replied, "Sure, you can. We have a bunkhouse on the property. It has a shower down there and several cots. It ain't a hotel by a long shot, but it's not bad if you'd like to sleep there instead of your truck for a change. Shoshoni just checked on it the other day, so it should be in pretty good shape.

"Why don't you have supper with us tonight? Not sure what we're havin' yet, but you're welcome if you want."

"I'd be honored, once I get these last three days of grime off me. Thank you, Matti."

After a while, Karson's stays in the bunkhouse became routine and sometimes extended. Occasionally, they would last several days before he would leave to collect a load to haul to destinations west of the Mississippi.

It was becoming clear—Karson was interested in a different form of relationship than anything Matti had in mind. He didn't seem her type at all. The man was eight years her senior and wore every day of it. He wasn't tall enough, which meant she could never wear heels again. He wasn't Jake.

Nonetheless, it does get lonely living alone on a big ranch. It was a beautiful place but a long way from civilization. The only men that were ever around were day workers or delivery personnel. When Karson would deliver hay, Matti noticed her mood improved. He would lend a hand with the chores around the farm and fix things she couldn't get to. He was a great help.

Matti realized when Karson was there, she was happier. They would spend hours talking about Montana and share meals at the dining table until one evening, Matti suggested he stop using the bunkhouse and sleep in the extra, unused bedroom instead.

During one of their conversations, Matti discovered Karson was divorced, the father of a son and daughter who were both now young adults. She shared the news about her divorce, too, but didn't mention her continuing love for Jake.

As time passed, their relationship grew. Matti hated to admit it, but when Karson was around, the load of running the place was easier to manage. She could do more of the things she enjoyed instead of putting out fires all day.

Matti decided it was time to give him an enticement to keep him coming back and stay longer.

After dinner, Karson helped her clean up the kitchen. They were about to head into the living area where Shoshoni was watching television when Karson said, "Thank you for dinner. You know I have to hit the road in the morning, so I think I'm gonna shower and call it a night if you don't mind. I've got some bookwork to catch up on and need a good night's sleep."

"Sure. That's fine. What time do you think you'll be leaving?"

"Before sunrise, I suspect."

"I figured. Okay, have a good night, then," and Matti kissed him on the cheek.

A plan flashed in Matti's brain as Karson headed for the hall bathroom. She watched TV with her daughter for a while before retiring to shower in the master bath as usual. Then, figuring Shoshoni would already be in her room, she could slip into Karson's unnoticed. When she quietly tapped on Karson's door, he answered, "Yeah."

Matti whispered, "May I come in?"

"Sure."

Matti opened the door, wearing only her robe. Karson had just finished filling out his log in preparation for leaving the following day and climbed into bed. He propped himself up and said, "Wow! You look beautiful. Is anything wrong?"

"Thank you. Nothing's wrong, except that you're leaving in the morning, and that makes me sad. I decided I want you to have something before you go."

"Oh? What would that be?"

Matti untied the belt of her robe, opened it slowly, and allowed it to fall to the floor. She looked him in the eye and said, "Me."

Karson stared for a long moment, unable to believe his good fortune. Then he tossed back his covers and reached out his hand. Matti smiled and joined him.

Their relationship blossomed over the following months until they eventually wed.

Matti now had a new last name. She and her husband started making a pretty good life for themselves. Karson took on the responsibility of being a *dad*, and Shoshoni loved him for it. He was a good man.

He continued to drive over the road, and Matti managed the ranch in New York State until Karson's connections in Montana eventually opened the door to an opportunity there—one he and Matti could not ignore. They ultimately moved there, fulfilling Matti's lifelong dream. She was ecstatic.

Upon their arrival, they discovered the position they had secured was perfect. It included a lovely log home they would occupy. When they walked up the steps to the porch, they were met by a friendly-looking man.

"Welcome to your new home. I'm Harold, but my friends call me *Hal*. I'm who you'll be replacing. I've been here since my friends purchased the place about seven years ago. I love them, but it's time for me to move on.

"I've purchased a motorhome and intend to spend what years I have left traveling this beautiful country. It's parked around back, but I can move it if you'd like. I thought I'd stay a few days to familiarize you with the surroundings and share some of the idiosyncrasies of your new bosses, if you know what I mean."

Matti blurted out, "Oh, that'd be great! It's good to meet you, Hal. I'm Matti." Gesturing, she continued, "This is my husband, Karson, and my daughter, Shoshoni. I didn't catch your last name."

"Hughes. Harold, *Hal* Hughes."

"Huh. You're not related to Howard, are you?" Karson asked, only half-joking.

"No, but I get asked that all the time. Come on, let me show you around the place.

"First, standing here on the porch, turn around and look out. It's easy to see this home is beautifully positioned, so any visitor can be seen coming at least a mile away.

"You'll also notice we're in a picturesque valley, and you can see it contains a small herd of Hereford cattle."

"... 'a small herd?' It looks like a pretty big herd to me," replied Matti.

"By Western standards, that's a small herd, indeed," Hal laughed. "The cattle belong to our neighbor to the south. The land is ours. Their contact information, a copy of their lease, and other pertinent paperwork are in a file cabinet I'll familiarize you with later. It's their responsibility to maintain those pastures throughout the lease that endures for the next four years. The pastures wrap around about as far as you can see."

"Wow. It is beautiful," Matti replied as she took it all in.

Hal walked them around the porch. "You'll notice this porch extends around all four sides—"

Matti interrupted, joking, "That should make it easy to become disoriented."

Hal laughed, "Perhaps, but only for a short while. Behind the house, the elevation increases quickly. These tall trees are Ponderosa Pines, and they grace the mountainsides around these parts."

From the rear, the view of the mountains was breathtaking. The property Matti and Karson were hired to manage was over a thousand acres, but it backed up to tens of thousands of acres belonging to the Bureau of Land Management (BLM), home to prime elk, deer, and bear hunting property.

"There's a beautiful trout stream just a short walk behind the house through the woods. It flows into the Big Hole River a few miles from here."

Matti replied, "It just keeps getting better, Hal. This is about as close to Heaven as it gets."

"That's what Ted says. Let's go inside." Hal opened the door to the home they'd be occupying, built by the original owner a few decades before. A three thousand square foot log home that looked like it belonged there. To say the new managers were pleased would be an understatement.

Their responsibility in this new position was to manage and maintain the property. Matti and Karson were provided an annual budget with which they were expected to achieve the goal. They could do much of the work themselves or hire subcontractors as needed. It was their job to ensure everything was ready for the owners when they came to enjoy their piece of *Heaven*, which they did two or three times a year.

When the owners came, they stayed in the newer, more grandiose home they had built in a more secluded part of the property. It was their private retreat, where they could escape the spotlight of their regular lives, if only for a little while.

They were obscenely wealthy—and famous. They could afford the extravagance and treasured the privacy.

All they required of Matti and Karson was that they kept the place up to their standards within the budget provided—and discretion. Who visited and what happened there was never to be discussed with anyone. It was private property, and the owners considered it their sanctuary.

Hal had done an excellent job, and the owners were sad to see him leave. His departure was amicable. He stayed around long enough to help Matti and Karson acclimate to the lay of the land, the responsibilities of the position, and the owners' quirks, like showing up unexpectedly.

After a few months, Matti's skills with horses endeared her to the new owners. They loved to ride up into the mountains, so they kept a small group of horses on the property just for that purpose. Her ability to keep them fit and ready to be ridden made the owners quite happy. They learned there was a difference between feeding and turning a horse out occasionally versus *caring* for one.

Matti's love for horses showed. She could *look* at a horse and sense it wasn't feeling well and instinctively know how to resolve most issues.

Like humans, horses need exercise to stay physically fit and mentally well. Matti knew she needed to become intimately familiar with the property. She also needed to familiarize herself with every trail and mountain pass like the back of her hand, and there was no better way than on the back of a horse.

And the best way to exercise horses is to take them on the trails the owners would ride when they came to visit. The plan would pay dividends in multiple ways.

On the owners' next visit, they found the horses fit, happy, and willing on the trails. It was an enjoyable ride.

When they returned to the barn, they found Matti waiting for them to put the horses up for the night. But, of course, Matti wouldn't think of doing that without grooming them, checking for any issues or injuries, and ensuring they ate and drank normally.

As the owners dismounted, a conversation ensued. Both were full of compliments about how much they enjoyed the ride and how well-behaved the horses were. "What did you do, drug them or something?" asked the husband jokingly.

"No. I just treat them well. I love them—listen and learn from them. They talk to me."

His wife asked, "What do you mean, you 'listen and learn from them?'"

Matti replied, "Well, if I ask them to do something and they resist, I try to figure out if they're being stubborn or if there's a problem. I try never to force them if they're shying away. I've learned horses are often aware of things humans are not. Sometimes, they know what I don't. So, I try to learn from them.

"It could be something wrong with them physically, or it could be the environment. I remember when my horse was aware of a snake I didn't see. I wanted to go on, but he wouldn't. No matter how I insisted, he wouldn't move. Then I heard the rattler. We quickly backed out and headed off in another direction. I reached down and hugged his neck."

The wife, again, "Well, whatever you've done, you've got quite a gift."

Her husband, "Indeed. Thank you. Keep up the good work."

"Well, thank you, both. It's my pleasure, believe me," Matti replied, wearing a big smile.

Chapter 10
New Challenge

Later that evening, the property owner, Ted, called Matti to ask if she'd have three horses prepared by 9 AM the following day for another trail ride. He preferred different mounts for his wife and himself and asked if she'd accompany them "... on a different route of your choosing."

Surprised by the request, Matti responded, "That's fine, I think. Are you sure you want me to come along? Is something wrong?"

Ted assured her everything was fine. "Nothing's wrong. We think we could learn a lot from you. That's all. Oh, what about your daughter?"

"That won't be a problem. Karson is here. He can watch Shoshoni. I'll be ready with the horses by nine. See you then."

Matti arrived at the barn at six to feed the horses and clean the stalls. Then, while the steeds were enjoying breakfast, she began the process of deciding which horses would be chosen for the day's ride.

Any lacking a healthy appetite or thirst would be eliminated from consideration, along with the two from the previous day's ride. Then, she inspected each carefully, felt their legs for heat, picked and examined their hooves, brushed them, and listened for feedback. Finally, she decided on two bay geldings and a beautiful palomino mare.

Ted's wife, Janet—his third or fourth, but who's counting—was a beautiful woman with long blonde hair. Matti thought Janet would look amazing atop that gorgeous steed with the nearly white mane and tail.

Matti took great pains brushing the mare so she would shine brilliantly in the sunlight. In the process, she noticed the lovely lady was a little more fidgety than usual. The reason suddenly revealed itself when it came time to comb out her tail. *I hope this doesn't upset the apple cart.*

Then, she selected a fancy, complimentary saddle and polished the silver appointments to make everything perfect.

Ted and Janet showed up at the barn about fifteen minutes early, in time to watch his employee finish tacking up the last horse, the palomino. Ted knew immediately what Matti had planned. The mare's mane and tail matched Janet's hair perfectly. She would look like a queen sitting on such a beautiful animal.

Ted smiled knowingly.

Matti returned the smile, nodded, and continued about her business.

Janet couldn't hide her excitement, but there was something wrong. She didn't seem herself.

When Matti had everything ready, she proudly led the mare to Janet and said, "Madame, this lady's for you. May I give you a leg up?"

"Thank you. If you'll just hold on to her, please, that'll be fine. I'm quite capable of mounting my own horse."

Somewhat taken aback, Matti responded, "Yes, ma'am."

As Janet threw her leg over, her mount became restless and started dancing around. Matti kept hold of the reins, just behind the bit, and gently said, "Eeeaaasy, mare."

Instead of releasing the reins, she walked with the horse, maintaining light pressure, and said to Janet, "Hold on to the horn, ma'am."

As Matti worked to calm the horse, she settled down some, but the situation was not good. The horse was uncooperative, and Janet was becoming agitated.

Matti had spent considerable time with the palomino mare since she'd been there and knew there was a problem. She was worried enough to ask, "Ma'am, would you allow me to walk you and your lady over to the round pen so you can work with her in a confined space before we head off on the trail? I'd feel safer if we did that."

The question seemed to make Janet even more upset, so Matti added, "I sense something is going on here that I might be able to help with. Will you let me do that? Please?"

Janet, rather angrily, said, "Oh, alright. Let's go."

Matti asked, "May I have the reins, please?"

Ted followed, looking concerned, fearing this might lead to an ugly end.

Matti led the mare, with Janet aboard, into the eighty-foot diameter round pen and latched the gate behind them, leaving Ted standing outside.

She led them to the opposite side of the pen before turning to Janet to say, in a very soft voice, with her back to Ted to keep him from hearing, "Ma'am, while tacking up this mare, I noticed she's about to ovulate. That's why she's acting a bit cranky this morning." Then with an ornery smile, Matti concluded by saying, "She's pissed there isn't a stallion around to scratch that itch, if you know what I mean."

Janet laughed before responding. How do you know she's about to ovulate?"

"I used to work on a large horse breeding farm and was heavily involved in the process. I got pretty good at reading them and their physiology by how they behaved."

Matti continued, "Now, I'm going to hand you these reins, but first, promise me to stay out of her mouth. She's very sensitive about that, and if you're rough on her, we're all gonna have an awful day."

"What do you mean 'stay out of her mouth?'"

"Oh. Sorry. Remember, these reins are attached to a bit, and it can inflict pain—more than you might expect. You don't need to be rough. Gentle pressure should be all that's necessary. Please be mindful of that and don't jerk on them, okay?"

Then Matti lowered her voice to a whisper, "I don't mean to offend, but looking at you and your demeanor today, you seem a little off, too—a little agitated. Not yourself. Is there any chance you're about to start your period or just started, maybe? Both of you suffering from PMS may not be a good thing."

With that, Janet broke into a great laugh. "Under normal circumstances, I'd be furious with an employee who spoke to me like that, but for some reason, I'm not. Why is that Matti? Truth is, you're right. I'm supposed to start today or tomorrow. I guess I'm not *myself*. Maybe you both sensed it.

"Okay, what should *we* do?"

Matti suggested they try a few laps around the round pen to see if they could work out their differences, with Janet now aware of the situation. Sure enough, after several laps, and some patience on Janet's part, things started coming together. The ride was able to commence as planned.

Janet finished the ride looking beautiful aboard the gorgeous palomino mare, and her horsemanship skills improved mightily, too.

Matti was confident her value to Ted and Janet increased considerably as well. It was a good day.

Ted and Janet had scheduled to visit early in the fall hunting season. The afternoon they arrived, it was snowing, but it was supposed to clear overnight. Ted had asked Matti if she would lead the couple up into the mountains on a hunt. "Hopefully, a trophy, but short of that, at least some meat for *your* freezer."

"Sure. I'd love to. But to get where I'd like to take you, we should prob'ly head out early, before daybreak. Is that okay with you?"

"Sure. That's fine. What time do you want us at the barn?"

"How about five? That'll give us time to get there and settle in before the herd starts moving. Is that too early?"

"No. That's good. We'll see you then."

"Perfect. I'll leave a light on for ya,'" Matti giggled.

She was pumped. She immediately cleaned and inspected her Winchester 30-30 and 40 mm Glock. Ammunition was also prepared for the day's hunt. She didn't figure she'd be taking any shots. She wasn't going to be *hunting*. These weapons were for self-defense or in case any unforeseen situations arose.

She laid out the clothes she would wear since she'd be getting up in the middle of the night, around three, to be at the barn to prepare the horses for a 5 AM departure.

I t was about twenty degrees when Ted and Janet arrived at the barn. "Mornin' Matti."

"Good morning, Sir." Nodding quickly toward Janet, Matti followed with, "Ma'am. How're y'all this fine, chilly mornin'?"

Janet forced a smile, but her husband jubilantly said, "We're great, aren't we, Sweetheart? And so enthusiastic about being dragged out of bed at this ungodly hour." He chuckled as he looked in his bride's direction.

Janet managed a guttural "Ugh."

Turning back to his guide for the day, he said, "Why four horses, Matti? Is someone else coming with us?"

"Well, I'm sorry to make you get up so early, but we need to get into position before daylight, and it's going to take a while to get to where I'm pretty sure we'll see an elk. I've been watching their patterns lately, and I think I know a great place.

"And, no. No one is coming with us. You never know what might happen up in the mountains, in the winter—with guns. Better to be prepared. And, if the hunt is successful, we'll need a way to get the carcass down the mountain. An extra horse could come in mighty handy—even if we don't have a proper harness for carrying such things. Just sayin'. Hint, hint."

Matti chuckled as she closed that statement, hoping she didn't overstep her bounds but trying to illustrate a point. All four horses were saddled, and in no time, they headed out to a place she had selected on one of her scouting trips earlier in the season.

They arrived where they could safely dismount and hobble the horses. Matti led them on foot about a hundred yards or more to a point that provided a good view of a pass regularly used by one of the elk herds she'd been watching. There was room for all three to stay hidden together since Ted had no interest in taking an animal. "Today is all about Janet," he told Matti.

The hunt turned out to be a success. Before 10 AM, Janet killed her first *trophy*, a nice 4 x 5 bull elk Ted was proud to have mounted to hang prominently in their home on the property, and Matti could keep the meat for their freezer.

The following spring, Ted called his now trusted guide and asked if she'd be interested in attending an upcoming outfitters school that was about to start. It was a rigorous course that would require her to be away from home for days at a time over several weeks, but he had an idea.

"Would that be something you'd be interested in? If so, I'd be willing to pay for the course. You did such a great job with Janet and me. You seem like a natural."

"I'd love to, but why would you want me to do that? What good would it do for you? What's the *why*?"

"Janet and I were thinking, we've got all this land, and we're not sharing it with anyone. That seems like a shame. What if we made it available to a few people each year for hunting? Only people *we* choose, *we* screen, and *we* allow. We could charge a fee that would be enough to cover some of the costs to help pay your salary and some of the upkeep of the property. It sounds like a win-win to me. What do you say?"

"My gut says 'Yes!' But I'd better talk it over with Karson and Shoshoni to get their input. Can I let you know in a day or two? Would that be okay?"

"Sounds good to me. I'll let Janet know we've talked, and we should expect to hear back from you soon. Time is of the essence, though. The course starts a week from Monday."

"Holy crap! That's what, ten, eleven days?"

"Correct. One or the other, I'm not even sure what day today is. I just know we don't have much time."

"Okay, I'll talk to my family tonight over supper. Thanks, Ted. It sounds exciting."

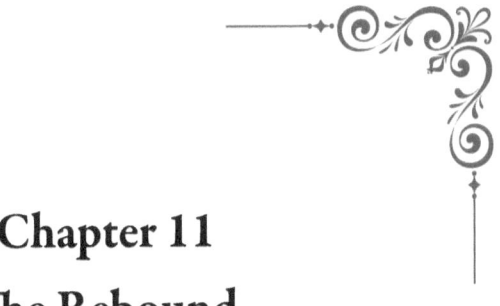

Chapter 11
The Rebound

Jake lived in a house on the farm, but as far as staff were concerned, it was considered off-limits, except in case of emergency. He liked it that way.

It was a modest home, but there was a good-sized pond, stocked with crappie and bass, often visited by ducks and Canadian geese, right out his back door where he could fish. It was comfortable.

His mood had become sullen and dark after Matti left. He would go to work, do his job, and retreat to the house. He didn't socialize with his parents any more than necessary.

On one particular Friday, Linda coaxed him to have lunch with her. During the meal, she said, "I'm worried about you. You haven't had a serious relationship with a woman in what? Three years? Are you okay?

Jake's facial expression betrayed his efforts to be civil. His clenched jaw, reddening face, careful choice of words. "Nothing's wrong, Mother. I'm fine. And it hasn't been that long."

Linda paused before continuing. "Well, I didn't mean to upset you, but it seems like it. You've been in this lousy mood for a while now. Why don't you go out anymore? Have you been out on a date since you kicked out your 'play-pretty?'

"I hear there's a rodeo going on this weekend on the other side of the mountain. You should go. At least it'll get you off the farm for the evening."

"Where did you hear that?"

"Jenny, our housekeeper, said her granddaughter is competing this evening—said she's pretty good. Several of her family will be there to cheer her on. Heck, you might even have a good time. You should go."

He took his mom's advice, and Jenny's granddaughter won her competition. Unfortunately, he didn't see Jenny in the crowd, so he didn't introduce himself to any family members when they gathered around to congratulate the young cowgirl as she collected her belt buckle.

Instead, he watched as a stranger, but he noticed a raven-haired woman in the group whose beauty stood out like a rose in a field of wheat.

The next day, Jake was having lunch with his mother when Jenny entered the room. Linda seized the opportunity to say, "Jenny. My son tells me he went to the rodeo last night and saw your granddaughter win."

Jenny had lived all her seventy-eight years in northwest Georgia and probably only left the state twice. She replied, "What about that? She's sumpin', ain't she? Did ya' have a good time?"

Jake chuckled and replied, "She is, and I did. Jenny, who was that tall, beautiful lady in the group with the long black hair in the cowboy hat?"

"Oh, that musta been my daughter. She's a pistol."

He quickly responded, "So, she's the mother of the young lady who won last night?"

"Uh, huh."

"Was her husband there? I didn't see a man in the group."

"Don't know, but doubt it. They're divorced."

"Oh. That's good to know. What's her name, Jenny?"

"Christy. Would ya' like to meet her? She's got three kids from six to sixteen. She divorced her husband a little more'n a year ago."

It took six months of dating for that to change. Christy was reluctant at first. Being eight years Jake's senior, the thought of being called a *cougar* made her very uncomfortable. But, ultimately, she gave in to his charms, and they tied the knot.

Jake moved into the home Christy had won in the divorce. He commuted to the farm instead of living on the premises, which changed the daily routine considerably—much to his father's chagrin.

It wasn't long before Jake mentioned to his dad, "I think Christy might be interested in working at the farm."

"Oh?"

"Yeah. I think she'd be open to it. She's got lots of *ag* experience—horses, cattle, chickens. She grew up in 4-H and is raisin' her kids in it, too. Her daughter has a barrel horse that she competes with. She's pretty savvy, Pop."

Linda and Greg discussed it and agreed the newlyweds working side by side every day in the same division of the company was a bad idea. Linda suggested, "But if they could maintain separation by dealing with different species in another part of the business, that might work."

Greg objected, "We're not ready for that right now. Maybe sometime soon. We'll see how things go. How's that?"

Linda agreed, "I'm good with that, Honey. Taking on another employee in that kind of position doesn't make sense right now. Besides, the idea of our son trying to blend in with three kids trying to make sense of living through a divorce will be challenging enough."

After nearly a year, Greg and Linda decided it was time to grow the farm's cattle operation. An opportunity became available for someone with Christy's experience. She joined the business to head up the expansion.

Over time, she fit into the family well. She and Greg bonded beautifully. She taught him a lot about cattle he didn't know. After all, he was more of a *horseman* than a *cattleman*. They bought an outstanding bull, leased an additional two hundred acres of land, and began transforming the herd into one that could be certified *Registered Angus*.

During the transition, non-Angus beef calves they were selling were lucky to bring $0.90 per pound at the stockyard, and they were spending a lot on new stock for their change in direction, additional equipment, land, and other expenses Greg hadn't even thought about.

As they say, timing is everything. Unfortunately, they picked the wrong time. The price of beef, even Angus beef, flat-lined. It was going to take a while for their investment to pay off.

At the same time, the horse side of the operation was flourishing. Everything they were breeding was hitting. They were selling foals before they were born. The babies they were producing were selling for prices higher than anyone in the industry.

Horses from their breeding program were winning.

THE GREATEST SOFTBALL GAME

In the waning years of the last century, when Greg was still working in corporate America, and a year after he and Linda first got involved with Arabian horses, the folks from whom they purchased their first filly suggested she be shown to enhance her value. The show they recommended was the largest in the world for their specialized segment of the industry. There would be horses in attendance from all over the world—over six hundred typically on hand to compete.

That was music to their ears, the greatest compliment imaginable. Linda looked up at her husband, teary-eyed, and said, "Our baby must be something special. Maybe we *should* show her off."

Greg interpreted it as *he* should show as an amateur. Of course, that was not at all what the farm had in mind, but they acquiesced, as long as they could also show her in the professional classes as well.

Everyone agreed. Greg diverted homeward-bound business trips to include long layovers in Texas to receive lessons on presenting a horse in a halter class. Four separate sessions were arranged, but he had no practical experience.

At the show, Sharon, the trainer schooling Greg watched with him during a professional class of older geldings and talked him through each step of the presentation. "Now watch as this handler enters. His crew will have the horse all jazzed up back in the warm-up area. When he's ready, he'll enter the arena, and the crowd'll take over from there, cheerin', whistlin', stompin'. The horse will have its tail up over its back, not knowin' what the hell's goin' on.

"It's your job to take advantage of that, cause that's when an Arabian horse looks the most beautiful. Give your filly as much lead as you can, and run like a junkyard dog is chasing you.

"It won't take long for you to tire in this soft footing. When that happens, slow down and try to get her to trot. That's the *Holy Grail*. Keep doing that until the judge turns his back. As long as he's lookin', you keep runnin'. Got it?"

After watching the handler enter the ring and listening to what Sharon described, Greg said, "That's easy for you to say. I'm twice his age."

"Suck it up, Buttercup. You wanna win this thing or not? Now watch. After each horse enters, the ring steward will guide them to a position along the rail where they will wait for the next competitor.

"Once they're all in, each will present individually before the judges, where they'll have time to walk around, up close and personal, to examine the horse's conformation and how well it was prepared. It's your job to present her in her best light, showing off her best physical traits.

"Remember, it's kinda like a bodybuilder competition. You want her to tighten her body, flex her muscles, and get her to show off her beautiful neck.

Before his class, Sharon explained she wanted Greg to enter the arena last so he could watch a few of the other handlers present their horses. "This will give you a feel for your competition and what you need to do," she said.

After the first several had shown, she led him back to his filly so they could go over final instructions.

Greg's gut was twisted in a knot as he entered the arena, while his filly was being scrutinized, and when they trotted off to join the others to await, horses in hand, the judges' decisions. When the tenth-place winner was announced, he stroked his filly's neck and said, "That's good." Ninth place, he did the same, and the pattern continued until the reserve champion's number was called, and it was not his.

He immediately realized the consequence. With two horses left in the ring, one would exit dejected, and the other would be crowned Champion. He thought about heading for the gate, but he patted his filly's neck instead, more to console himself than her. *Well, it was fun while it lasted, baby girl. How could we expect a little yearling, the only one in the class, led by a novice, to beat seasoned mares? What an idiot!*

The music pounding in Greg's ears was interrupted only long enough to allow the ring announcer to inform the audience of the Reserve Champion's owners, handler, pedigree, and previous accomplishments. The ribbon presentation, photos, and victory lap, to the cheers and applauds of the crowd, had to be completed before the Champion could be called.

Once the announcer quit speaking, the music ensued at an even higher decibel level, adding to the novice handler's anxiety. Greg watched the second-place mare exit the ring. He was sure the ultimate winner was about to be called. But the music kept playing. *What the hell is taking so long?*

Finally, the song ended. The arena fell silent—for what seemed like forever ... at least to Greg.

"Ladies and Gentlemen. I am pleased to introduce our Champion, number 254..." crowd noise drowned out the announcer as she mentioned her name so Greg couldn't hear it. Making it worse, he had forgotten his number.

It wasn't until he looked over to his support base in the stands and they pointed toward center-ring and yelled, "You won!" that he realized what had happened. In his first show, one of such magnitude and importance, with his little yearling filly, he won the Amateur Halter Mare Championship!

Greg was thrilled. He couldn't contain his excitement. In center-ring, his filly was draped with the championship ribbon. He was handed a ribbon and then a trophy. Pictures were taken. During the process, he was so emotional he was shaking. He dropped his whip three times.

Never mind, his filly had been well-trained by the farm from whom he had purchased her at four days of age, and she happened to have grown up to be stunningly beautiful. Greg was hooked.

Over time, he learned the methods professional trainers commonly used to get the horses to perform as they did, and he found them unnecessarily harsh. He decided there had to be a better way. In his spare time after work, he began training horses on the farm in *his* way and continued honing those skills in the show ring.

Greg shared his techniques with his son. Because he was a natural athlete, Jake improvised to create his own style and developed the ability to achieve an even more intense presentation, much to his dad's delight.

Things were humming along well. It was late May. Their show string was ready. Their most important show of the year was fast approaching, slated for the first full week in June.

On Sunday of the Memorial Day weekend, Greg was coaxing his bull out of a thicket where he didn't belong. His boot slipped on a tree root and wedged awkwardly. The bull turned and knocked him to the ground before he could free it, and his leg and ankle broke like a twig.

A week before his breed's most important show and a barn full of horses prepared and ready, Greg's accident rendered him unable to present them. Jake was already slated to show a few, but there was no way one person could handle them all. Help was needed.

Greg was released from the hospital on Wednesday, the day after his surgery, which included a titanium rod, plates, pins, and screws. Within hours of his arrival home, he began schooling Christy on the nuances of presenting a horse in hand while he sat on his golf cart with his leg propped up on the seat.

They worked together, virtually non-stop, until they left for the show on Saturday, despite the surgeon's stern warnings against it. "The last place in the world you need to be is at a horse show! I don't want you putting any weight on that leg. Don't even touch your toe on the ground. And for God's sake, don't let the incisions get wet."

They would take eight horses. Christy would show three. Two, because she and Jake would be in the ring in the same class with different horses, and another *special* filly with a very feminine look. Christy fit the picture better. Jake would show the rest.

Overall, the show was a disappointment for Greg. They still won a lot of ribbons, but he felt he had let his clients down. He told Linda privately, "There's no way anyone could have stepped in on such short notice and done a better job than Christy. Some of those horses had never shown before. They trusted me. To throw newbies in the ring with another newbie was awful.

"They both did incredible work. Jake had to show horses he had no experience with, and we got through this with better placements than I expected. The clients were understanding, and no one came home empty-handed. They were all in the ribbons."

Over the next few years, Christy became increasingly involved in showing the horses. Her abilities improved significantly, and her penchant for wearing flamboyant outfits that accentuated her height, long jet-black hair, striking beauty, and flowing stride made her a crowd favorite.

Each had unique gifts that meshed well with certain horses. Collectively, they were good at pairing each other with the right steeds. Once they figured out those personality quirks, it didn't take long until they became a significant force in the show ring.

The glamor of it all was too much for Christy to ignore. She loved being the center of attention and became more involved in the horse side. The cattle division started taking a back seat.

Things were going *so* well that Greg retired from the corporate world to devote his entire focus to the farm. He built a new, state-of-the-art barn that included an indoor riding & training facility, a 4,000-square-foot client center, a kitchen, four bathrooms, two showers, and offices upstairs for staff.

A review of the numbers made it clear, the horse division was far more lucrative than the cattle side of the business. Their client list continued to grow, requiring more pasture space for the growing herd.

Slowly and systematically they reduced the cattle herd to free up space and give Christy more time to work with the horses.

After a few years, Christy damaged her knee and she could no longer run. It required surgery. Too young for a knee replacement, the surgeon suggested an experimental stem-cell procedure to fill in missing cartilage. It did not turn out well.

She suffered through nearly a year of rehab with disappointing results. A second surgery was performed—more stem cells. Then another. Then something else. Finally, a partial replacement knee was installed.

In the end, after four years of *surgery, rehab, disappointment, repeat*, ended with "... you may never be able to run."

That reality, and the years these *experiments* stole from her, turned Christy into a bitter woman who became someone other than the one with whom Jake had fallen in love. Suddenly, he could do nothing right. She seemed to have forgotten about all the time her husband had taken off work to care for her during her recovery from surgery—to help her through rehab.

The farm suffered. Not only did they lose what Christy brought to the table, but they also lost Jake for extended periods.

Greg and Linda encouraged their daughter-in-law to do other things around the farm when she was able. A woman with many talents, they wanted her to be able to remain an active part.

Christy started picking at everyone, Jake, Linda, and even Greg sometimes, though she seemed to respect him more than the others.

She started criticizing her husband for his performance in the show ring, even when he won. But for some reason, she was especially cruel to Linda. It seemed Christy developed a special hatred for her, which may have led to her eventual undoing with her son.

She officially quit the farm, saying she could be of no benefit anymore since she was *compromised*.

It was about the same time the housing bubble burst and the economy tumbled. Bad news was everywhere. The horse business took it hard.

Most of the one hundred and fifty horses on the farm's property were owned by clients who paid monthly board fees. Revenue from boarders went a long way to covering the farm's monthly overhead, employee salaries, grain, utilities, and the like. It's all good if they pay their bills. If one stops paying and moves his horse, it hurts, but it's okay. But what happens when a client stops paying and doesn't move his? What to do then? Do you stop feeding it? It's not the horse's fault. And how do you stop feeding one when he's in a pasture with others?

It started happening. Not just one client, several. Then many. Horses showed up in the pastures near the main road that no one on the farm had ever seen before, and they weren't always Arabians. People had dropped them off because they could no longer care for them. Had they been vaccinated? To whom did they belong? No one knew. Their herd was growing, along with the farm's overhead.

Equine sales had stopped. Income had slowed to a crawl. The horse business all over the country was in trouble. Greg and Linda knew it. Jake knew it. Christy came to realize it.

When Christy's surgeries didn't work, and it was clear she wasn't coming back, Greg decided to sell off the rest of the cattle herd and not renew the lease of the neighboring land. He used the money to help fund the horse side of the operation during the recession.

Christy blamed herself and her injury for everything. She became even more self-loathing—and it metastasized. She grew to hate everything and everyone. Even her children avoided her.

Jake was miserable. He saw the inevitable. The business was running out of money. Greg continued to do what he could to streamline the operation, but nobody wanted to buy a horse in the United States.

Fortunately, Linda had connections abroad, but the combination of shipping costs and a US recession made them wary. Foreign buyers know how to take advantage of a situation.

After a few years of struggle, Jake finally made the decision to leave the farm. He decided the downsizing made his presence there unnecessary. The need for a breeding manager had diminished to near zero, and the farm was actively marketing both of their champion stallions for sale.

His job no longer viable, Jake figured he'd do his dad a favor, leave on his terms, and save him the agony of having to *terminate* his son.

Together, he and Christy had saved some money. They'd be okay for a while.

Jake had plenty of contacts, but his nearly twenty years in the horse business didn't help since the entire industry was in such bad shape. Nobody needed a breeding manager. And trainers were starving to death since horse show attendance had reached an all-time low. He had an offer from a breeder in Italy, and others from South America, but Christy wouldn't dream of uprooting and moving away from her family.

Their relationship was going from bad to worse. They owned a couple of valuable brood mares and a show filly. The sale from their offspring had, over the years, added to their income substantially. Now, they had become a liability.

"I know my knee isn't your fault, Jake, but you've got to find a way to sell our horses to make up for the lost income. We can't afford to keep feeding them."

"Christy, if I could find somebody to buy a damned horse, I'd sell them in a heartbeat. I've been trying. Mom's been trying, but no one is interested. That's the problem. Finding people to buy horses is hard right now."

Jake's exasperation with her was near a tipping point. He'd been very close to asking for a divorce until he heard about a short-term gig they could do together.

It involved traveling for a marketing company. They'd be promoting gear for a nationally renowned outdoor equipment manufacturer at selected sporting goods stores and major events around the northwest. They'd be manning a pair of specialized trailers set up by the marketer, hyping the product line, and handing out promotional goodies.

It would be a great adventure. Accommodations would be provided at various Airbnbs along the route, plus a daily food allowance, not to mention a considerable salary. The only catch was they'd be gone for three months and wouldn't get home until Christmas Eve.

Jake thought it might be an excellent opportunity for him and Christy to rekindle their relationship. They'd see parts of the country neither had visited before. Their schedule provided days off so they'd have free time for themselves. And it would put a considerable chunk of change in their bank account. It sounded almost too good to be true.

Their trip was to start in San Francisco. From there, they would head north. In total, they'd visit seven states with multiple stops in each.

There were two themed trailers designed to create an outdoor camping scene. Where space permitted, they would be parked end-to-end to form a continuous landscape or used individually in smaller venues.

Each was pulled by a new, 4-door crew cab, dually, pick-up truck. The caravan had one additional matching truck for extra carrying capacity and crew. Jake and his wife were two of eight people staffing the two trailers. Christy was the only female.

Other members of the staff were from various states around the country. All were outdoor types, specifically chosen because they fit the merchandise profile. Her presence worked because she was beautiful and a natural cowgirl, although she still couldn't get around well. She hobbled with a brace on her leg. It didn't matter. Jake sold her other qualities and didn't mention she was nearly a cripple. She could still drive if needed and added a touch of eye candy that employers thought would be nice.

Under normal circumstances, Christy might have fit in with this group for an evening or two, but three months would have been a tough pull at best. These guys tried to watch their language, but they were hard-drinkin', pull-no-punches kinda' cowboys.

The fact they were staying in Airbnbs was good because she wasn't forced to spend too much time with this rowdy bunch of men. Christy could slip off to her room and read a book, which she often did. She stuck it out for the first few nights through dinner and brief fellowship before retiring. Jake followed and *attempted* to engage in conversation, or they'd watch TV when one was available.

Christy rebuffed any attempts at becoming amorous, so Jake quit trying. Finally, one evening, after eating dinner together, he decided to turn on the television. When he picked up the remote, Christy said, "I'd like to read my Bible. Why don't you go downstairs and spend time with the guys? I can't imagine you wanting to watch me read. I can't concentrate on what I want to do with the TV on. Would you mind?"

"Not at all," Jake replied, marking a turning point in their relationship from which it would never recover.

He pulled on his boots and did as she suggested. From that evening until the end of their trip, Jake ate dinner with the men. As he headed down the stairs, a thought ran through his mind. *So much for rekindling.*

One of the men in the group, Ben, was from Montana. Jake loved hearing about his home state. He told of elk hunting, the trout streams, the moose, and the bears. Jake thought it sounded like Heaven. Matti came to mind.

From her most recent text message that simply read, *Happy Birthday*, an act Matti repeated every year since she left, he noticed the area code was from Montana. He wondered if Ben could find out where.

As the marketing trek through the northwest was winding down, Christy spent more and more time in her room in the evenings, preferring her husband's absence to his company. Jake realized how miserable he was in his current situation. He doubted there was any way to repair their relationship. *It's over.*

When Jake and Christy arrived home from their adventure throughout the northwest, it was Christmas Eve. Over the next few days, they dutifully celebrated Christmas with Linda and Greg, Christy's mother, the children, and extended family members.

Over the following several days, Jake attended to repairs around the place, fixing things that had been neglected for the three months they'd been gone. While in the barn one afternoon, Jake's phone rang. He was searching for a misplaced tool.

It was Ben. He shared with him the information Jake was dying to know—the town where Matti lived.

Once satisfied he'd addressed the most pressing issues around the house, Jake sat Christy down to explain his intentions. "Ben's asked me to come and meet his dad. He said something about a job opportunity that'd be *right up my alley*. His dad has a ranch and needs somebody to run it for him, but he wants to meet before offering it to me."

Christy looked surprised. "You mean to Montana? We just got back from there! That's a long way to go for a job interview."

"I know, it's Montana. But I don't have any prospects around here. And Ben says I'm a

shoo-in if I want it. His ranch backs up to the mountains, and they've got two sleds up there he and I can use for a couple of days to go snowmobiling. He says it's great this time of year, so even if it doesn't work out and I turn it down, it'll still be worth the trip."

Of course, that was all a lie. Jake had spoken to Ben, but he had no intention of seeing him while he was there. Jake's sole purpose was to find out if there was any flame left in Matti's heart for him. He was dying to see her again.

Christy did not favor Jake making the trip, and they argued over it for the rest of the day. "This may be the dumbest idea you've ever come up with. Is he gonna buy you a plane ticket?"

"No. We just got off a plane, and you know how I hate to fly, those new rules and all, cramped seats, and being stuck for hours with nasty people in a tube at thirty thousand feet. And takin' guns on a plane is such a hassle.

"I'm gonna drive. Besides, we've been with each other twenty-four/seven for the last three months. I figure a few days apart might do us both some good."

"It'll cost a fortune to drive all that way just for a job interview. What will you do if he doesn't like you?"

"Are you kidding? What's not to like?" Jake jokingly replied.

"Yeah, you think your wit will get you through anything. Do you have any idea what this job will pay?"

Jake quickly pulled the details out of his behind. "Not for sure, but Ben said it comes with housing, a budget to run the ranch, a salary, and a bonus if things turn out well. I'm guessing it should be something I can manage in my favor. Everything is a negotiation, and you know I'm the best-damned negotiator around. Right?

In the end, Jake wasn't going to take *no* for an answer. He headed off to Montana two days later.

Chapter 12
The Reunion

During those early days in the northwest, Matti couldn't have been happier. The house, the ranch, the setting, and now the opportunity to attend outfitters school at Ted's expense—it all screamed Montana! Her lifelong dream.

The rest of the family wasn't as exuberant over her being away at the class, but they finally came around.

She breezed through the course like it was her calling. Although she was the only female enrolled, she outworked, outpaced, and outscored over two-thirds of her classmates.

Some of the men taking the course with Matti also served as Wildland Firefighters during the season. They shared stories of what it was like—harrowing experiences, close calls, dangerous situations, trials, and tribulations.

Enthralled, Matti decided that she, too, wanted to learn to fight wildland fires. The men telling the stories agreed she'd be an asset to any team based on what they'd personally witnessed. Then one of them added, "I don't know. Sending someone as *hot* as you to fight a fire makes no sense a'tall. Am I right, or am I right?"

Everyone had a good laugh. Matti blushed but loved the compliment. *It's been a while since I've heard anything like that at home.*

Upon her return to the ranch, she would apply, train, and accept assignments fighting fires every summer thereafter. She enjoyed the work. It was exhilarating—an adrenalin rush. It made her feel good, like she was doing something worthwhile. The money she earned was a pleasant bonus.

Matti's performance in Outfitters School gave Ted all the encouragement he needed. In August, he called. "Matti, I've invited three close friends to join me for a week-long hunting trip into the high country this fall. I'd like you to make that happen for us. Would you be willing to do that?"

"I'd be happy to, but I need a little clarification, please. How much gear can I purchase? We'll need tents, more stock, and a lot of equipment."

"Yes. I know. I'm counting on you to acquire what we'll need. I want this to be a first-class trip. Money is no object. Pay for everything out of the farm budget, and I'll reimburse the account for whatever you spend toward this trip. Just keep track of it all. Okay?"

"Yes, Sir. Do you want to stay on your property or venture onto BLM (Bureau of Land Management)?"

"Since we'd like to schedule the trip for the first week of the season, I'd like to stay on our land unless you think that's a bad idea."

"No. I think that's smart, actually. It'll be a lot safer that way, I suspect. I'll start putting the plan in motion this afternoon. Thanks, Ted."

"My pleasure. I'm looking forward to it."

Matti had weeks to prepare, but she had a lot to do. She had decided they could forego the purchase of additional stock since Ted had allowed her and Karson to board their personal horses in the barn along with Ted's seven.

She felt confident. *Surely, with a livery of nine and only four hunters, we'll have enough ponies for the trip.* Nonetheless, she still had much to acquire. For extended stays like this, they'd need a large wall tent, pack harnesses, outdoor cooking equipment, cots, sleeping bags, a wood-burning stove, and other items too numerous to mention. In addition, she'd need to spend a lot of time in the high country selecting the perfect spot for the hunters.

On her scouting trips, Matti noticed their travel patterns were changing. She found an area, almost like a highway for elk, that a sizable herd used daily and picked out four spots, each with a different view or angle.

Once she identified where the hunters would be stationed, she selected a central campsite in a convenient location about three hundred yards away.

Matti asked Karson to fabricate a sled to haul the stove up the mountain behind one of the horses. "Piece a cake. There's some leftover corner posts behind the barn I can use. A couple boards across the top should do the trick. I'll angle the front of the runners so they'll glide up and over the snow if we get some between now and when we're ready."

"Sounds perfect."

Over the next few days, she solicited Karson's help again. They erected the wall tent, installed the stove, and cut firewood. She had the campsite readied two weeks before the opening of hunting season. Her scouting trips during that time would always include a quiet inspection to ensure there had been no unwelcome visitors and things were as they should be in anticipation of her guests.

By the time the hunters arrived, everything would be prepared. All Matti had to do was escort them to their destination without one or more falling off his horse. The plan was to get to the camp the day before opening season. "Ted, if it's okay with you, I'd like to get there in time to take y'all around to the four spots I've picked out. That way, everybody'll know where each other is, nobody'll shoot in the other's direction, and nobody'll get lost.

"Y'all can decide who gets which position. But remember, you don't have to stay in the same spot every day. You pick. It's up to y'all."

Ted asked, "So, what time do we need to leave the barn?"

Matti had already asked Ted to arrive as early as possible. He told her his jet, with friends aboard, should arrive around 11 AM in Missoula. "So, by the time you have lunch and get to the ranch, can we head outta here by two, then, maybe?"

Ted replied, "We'll do our best."

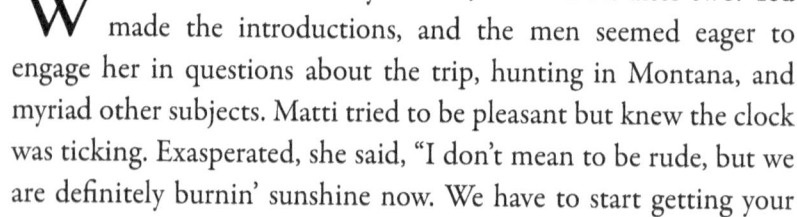

When the hunters finally arrived, it was a bit after two. Ted made the introductions, and the men seemed eager to engage her in questions about the trip, hunting in Montana, and myriad other subjects. Matti tried to be pleasant but knew the clock was ticking. Exasperated, she said, "I don't mean to be rude, but we are definitely burnin' sunshine now. We have to start getting your gear stowed onto these pack horses. We need to be heading to the campsite, or I'm not gonna have time to show you where you'll need to set up to hunt. We'll have plenty of time for all these questions over the next few days. Right now, we've got work to do."

"Yes, ma'am. How can we help?" one of them replied—the cutest one.

Ted responded, "I told you she was a taskmaster."

Matti barely looked up but smiled, saying, "Just bring your stuff over to the barn. This ain't gonna be no picnic, ya' know." She grinned to take the sting out of her words.

As they walked, Matti said, "Y'all *can* ride, can't ya'? Good on a horse, right?"

The cute one, Cliff, responded quickly, "I'm good anywhere. And I can ride, too."

Matti glanced over her shoulder at him, "Uh, huh."

At the barn, the hunters watched Matti strap the first of the bags to a pack horse. Cliff decided to help and hung his to the other side of the same horse. "Is it okay if I hang mine here?"

Matti smiled and said, "Sure. Let's see how well you paid attention." She stepped around the horse and watched him attempt to secure the load.

When he finished and stood back, Matti said, "Not too bad. It *might* still be there when we get to where we're goin'." Turning her attention to the others, she continued. "Y'all want me to load yours, or would you rather try it yourselves? Your rifles'll fit in the scabbards on the saddle horses."

"**O**kay, I think we're ready. There are full canteens on the saddled horses. Take your pick, except that one." She pointed in the direction of the dun on the end. "That's my horse, the one over there. All but one of us will be pulling a pack horse. Who would like to be the odd man out?

Al, another handsome but possibly the least masculine of the three guests, said, "I may be a less accomplished rider than the others, so maybe that should be me."

"Okay, Al, then you take that bay gelding over there. He doesn't like having a pack horse dragged along behind him, so that'll work out well. You bring up the rear. Okay?"

George, another hunter, announced, "Matti, I brought two rifles."

"I'd suggest you lash the other one to the gear on your pack horse, but let's hurry. We've got a long ride ahead of us."

Waiting for a lull in the questioning, Cliff asked, "I know you said the canteens were full, but what about other drinks after we get there? Is there anything at the campsite waiting for us, possibly a little tastier than water?"

Matti mounted before responding, shifted her position in the saddle, and adopted an authoritarian but ornery smile, "Why did I know it would be you who asked that question? There's a large cooler up there that should quench even *your* thirst, Cliff. I think you'll find it to your liking." She chuckled.

The men were in awe during the ride up the mountain. The scenery was breathtaking. The new-fallen snow, hanging in the trees and covering the ground was less than three inches deep. Their path showed only an occasional track left by a passing animal. It was magical.

By and large, the horses behaved themselves despite having greenhorn riders aboard. Matti was peppered with questions during the ride, and she tried to answer some but admonished them to keep their voices down as much as possible. "We are on a hunt, remember."

When they arrived at camp, Matti led her charges into a rope corral she had prepared for the horses a few yards behind the large wall tent they would use for sleeping. "If you fellas'll help me unload this gear and take it inside, I'll water and hay these guys.

"Just carry your stuff into the tent, pick out a cot, and familiarize yourself with the campsite. I'll be done here in a jiffy."

The hunters found everything set up and waiting for them. They entered the tent and found it had a wood-burning stove in place, surrounded by four cots. It was big enough to fit a few more and still afford adequate walkaround space. Cliff opened the door on the stove and found it full of wood with kindling in the bottom. "Looks like Matti has this thing ready to go. About all it needs is a match."

Ted looked at him, pointed to the cup near the stove, and said, "Looks like she's provided them, too."

Seeing the cup, Cliff replied, "Damned if she didn't." He selected one from the container, lifted his right leg to pull the material tight, and slid the head of the match hard against the length of his thigh. "Ignition. Just like in the movies."

While Cliff worked at fire building, the others unpacked their gear. About the time they were finishing up, Matti entered the tent. "How's it coming along?"

Cliff responded, "The fire, I presume?"

"Yeah. I saw the smoke."

"Figures. Pretty well, I think."

"Mind if I take a look?"

"Sure. Go ahead. I don't suppose I could stop you if I wanted to anyway."

"Probably not." Matti giggled as she opened the door a tiny bit. "Oh, that's good. You did a nice job. How many matches did it take ya'?"

"Only one."

"Wow. I'm impressed. There may be hope for you yet. Well done.

"Y'all wanna go on a quick tour?"

They all agreed and followed her outside.

"Okay. Out here, a safe distance in front of the tent is our fire pit. This circle of rocks keeps the fire from spreading out of control. In the center, as you can see, is a neatly stacked pile of hardwood. There's a forged tripod with a grill rack for cooking, and I hope you'll be comfortable in the chairs we brought up."

She walked with them a short distance to a tree with a long rope tied around its trunk and coiled at its base. The other end extended up and over one of the high branches, attached to a waterproof container. "Your food is at the end of that rope. Let me demonstrate how to operate this contraption."

One of the hunters remarked, "Please do."

Matti began the process, untying the knot and gently lowering the food. "Do not ever untie the rope from the container. Remove whatever you want for that meal, then close and seal the bag. Then, *immediately,* re-hang it in the tree. Don't wait until your meal is over. You may never have a chance to hang it back up there if you don't do it right away. Trust me on that point. Do it right then. It might save your life. Don't be *stupid*. Did I make my point?"

She waited for an answer but got only nods, so she said, "I ask again. Did I make my point?"

In unison, they answered, "Yes."

"Good. There are grizzlies in these woods. I hope you noticed I used the plural form of that noun. Now, let me demonstrate how to open and re-seal the container."

When she finished, she said, "Cliff, would you like to hoist the food back to its safe spot, tie it off, and stow the rope?"

"Sure. I can do that. Since we didn't untie the rope from the bag, it's ready to be lifted back in place. Right?"

Matti nodded. "Precisely."

"Okay." Cliff pulled the rope, lifting the container high into the tree. When it got near the branch, he looked at Matti and said, "Close enough?"

Matti looked at the group and asked, "Is it high enough a grizzly can't reach it?"

They all agreed it was.

"Okay then. Tie it off."

By the time Cliff finished tying the knot. Matti said, "Nicely done." Addressing the group, she continued, "When you finish eating, put your scraps, anything that won't burn completely, back into one of the plastic bags from which it came, lower the food container..." she pointed in its direction "...and stow it back in there.

You don't want to attract bears by leaving food where they can smell it."

"You probably noticed those big coolers in the tent. One has water and soft drinks in it. The other has beer and liquor. Since it's been near or below freezing, neither has ice in them. If you like your liquor at room temp, good luck with that. Sorry.

"Now, before it gets too dark, we should head out on foot to the spots I've picked out. I think they'll provide the best chances for success."

George asked, "Should we bring our rifles?"

"Uh, that's a hard *no*, George. I've got my handgun on me in case we need it for protection, but the season doesn't start until sunrise tomorrow. Remember that. Sunrise. C'mon. Let's get to it. We don't have much time."

Ted asked, "Just out of curiosity, how did you get enough water up here to supply us and the horses?"

"Y'all carried a few two-gallon bladders today. I used those to fill the buckets they're drinkin' from right now. Every trip I'd make for the last several weeks, I'd carry at least two full bladders and dump them into those five, five-gallon cans outside until I had 'em all full.

"It's been above freezing during the day until today. So, if you bring those cans, which may now be frozen, into the tent and place them near the stove to thaw, the horses should have enough to drink. I'll keep bringing more on my every trip.

"I'll be leavin' to head back on my pony, and take two others with me, so y'all won't have so many to care for while I'm gone. That'll help some."

"Oh, makes sense. Thanks, Matti.

"No problem. Just make sure they always have plenty of water, and it isn't frozen. Check their buckets for ice on top often. And give them fresh hay twice a day.

"Now, let me get the fire going before I leave. This overnight snow may make it a little more challenging than the stove. It's supposed to get kinda chilly tonight, and you'll need a good, hearty meal.

"Remember, this food has to last you a week. It should be plenty. If it looks like you might run out, just let me know. I'll be back and forth a couple times while you're up here."

Ted responded, "Ah, you are an angel. Thank you, Matti, but you'd better hurry, or you'll be riding home in the dark."

"No problem. I've done that many times before. My horse knows the way. I just give him his head, and he takes me there. That's why there's no way to put a value on him."

All three of Ted's friends filled their tags. Ted had a shot, but chose not to take it.

Matti had gone back twice during the hunt, and since they never killed more than one elk a day, it was easier for her to quarter and haul the carcasses down the mountain than it could have been.

While loading the pack horses with their gear to leave, Matti smiled as she listened to the banter about Ted being the only one with an unfilled tag.

Satisfied the job was complete, she motioned for her boss to follow, away from the others, where she looked at him and said, "I'm sure you saw plenty of elk. Right?"

"I did. They were right where you said they'd be."

"So, you didn't take the shot, huh?"

"Naw. Something wasn't right."

"The one you had in your scope was bigger than any of theirs?"

Ted smiled and turned to walk away.

Matti nodded. "You're a good man, Ted."

Without facing her and continuing on his way, Ted replied, "Thank you, Matti."

As they approached the horses, Matti bellowed, "Everybody got their shit together? Let's mount up. We've got a long ride ahead of us."

She would lead Ted and friends on similar trips during her tenure with the ranch and occasionally accepted opportunities with other outfitters in surrounding states when they arose. She found herself in high demand but had to be selective due to her other obligations.

Karson still owned that long-haul rig and had always found it quite lucrative to haul hay from Montana back east. This arrangement worked well for years since the ranch management didn't require them to be physically on the property simultaneously.

When Karson was home, life was simpler. Matti appreciated having someone there when Shoshoni got home from school. If Karson was on the road, Matti often took care of farm chores during the day and conducted scouting trips after the school bus dropped her daughter off.

One afternoon, as Shoshoni was arriving home, she saw her mother walking up the steps carrying two canteens.

"Hey, Momma."

"You ready?"

"Soon as I go pee."

"Y're burnin' daylight."

"I love you, too, Momma."

"Love you back. See ya' in the barn. Yer horse is already saddled."

"I know. Be right there," Shoshoni giggled as she walked through the open door.

Matti smiled as she went to the kitchen to fill the canteens.

The education her daughter received on these trips was unlike anything taught in public schools. It wasn't long before Shoshoni was an accomplished asset on outfitting trips. She could ride better than most, and her knowledge of the forest was impressive. Matti taught her to shoot at an early age, saying, "You never know when you're going to need to protect yourself."

As the years rolled along, the time Matti and her daughter spent together, working the ranch or in the mountains, drew them closer—until the hormones started kicking in. As she grew more interested in boys, Shoshoni became rebellious.

During fall and early winter, Matti started accepting more outfitting opportunities on the ranch or in different states, each lasting a week, sometimes two, expecting Karson and Shoshoni to take care of the ranch in her absence.

Karson was becoming agitated running the ranch by himself. Too often, he'd have to hire subcontractors to get things done, and that cut into the budget they'd been given. Matti's pay for her outfitting services often failed to make up the difference.

Arguments ensued. Matti protested, "Why on earth did you have to bring in outside labor to get that done?"

"Somebody had to do it. Our daughter is still in school, you know. I was taking care of horses, cleaning stalls, and fixing things around this farm, not to mention stacking the last bales of hay for the winter. Remember, up there where you said they wouldn't fit—those last hundred, some odd bales?"

"That damn sure didn't take you two weeks. Whaddya do the resta the time, sit on your fat ass?"

Karson's face glowed bright red. His fist hit the table. "No! I've been bustin' my *fat ass* on this farm for the last two weeks. It's time I haul some hay back east. It'll give me a chance to cool off."

Over time, he became a workaholic. Too often on the road. Too seldom at home.

The added money was a wash, and the separation made things *more* difficult. When Matti discovered tasks Karson had either forgotten or hadn't addressed, she'd be furious. It compounded their issues.

Increasingly, it seemed, the married couple was always apart. If Karson wasn't on the road, Matti was fighting fires or outfitting in the mountains. Then, one evening, in a state of deep depression, Matti realized she and Karson hadn't been on a *date* in years. She couldn't remember the last time she'd worn a dress, and heels were out of the question.

She walked into the bedroom and slipped on a simple, tight, black evening dress she'd owned for decades. It had spaghetti straps, and it accentuated her curves. She pulled out a pair of red, satin heels. *Look at the dust on these. Where did you come from? What's happened to my life?* She burst into tears.

After removing the soot with a cloth, she slipped her feet into the shoes. Standing tall, she walked toward the master bathroom door and closed it to reveal the full-length mirror on its back. She wiped the tears from her face, and other than her red eyes, hair, and makeup a bit lacking, she was pleased with the reflection peering back at her. The dress fit like a glove and clung to her fit body.

Standing there, she became aware of how lonely she was—how deserted she felt. Even though she'd never had the opportunity to dress up for him, she missed Jake. *Where is he when I need him?*

Shoshoni had become a teenager eager to spend more time with people her age, making the situation even more difficult. When Karson would come home from a long trip, he was dog-tired. All he wanted to do was sleep. Matti could see him aging, fast, right before her eyes. And they weren't having fun anymore.

Driving a truck was killing him—but he wouldn't stop. Matti begged him to quit. His truck was getting old, too. It was only a matter of time before repair costs would become a problem. "Karson, I don't feel like we're married anymore. It's more like we've been living a long-term separation for the last two years. Sell that old truck and stay home with me. Please."

He chose to go into debt to buy a new truck instead.

Matti filed for divorce the following week. It was a difficult decision for her, but she was tired of the way things were. She would have to make some drastic changes.

Karson didn't object, but it would still be nearly a year before the divorce was finalized, ending their nine-year marriage.

When Ted learned of the divorce, he approached Matti. "Is it true?"

"If you mean the divorce, yes. It's still in process, but it's true."

"How can you possibly run this place without help?"

"I can do it. Karson's not here most of the time anyway, that damned truck of his. You know that," Matti insisted.

"Yes, I know, but you seemed to be able to work that out when I needed *you* for the things that made the two of you special to me. Now you won't be available for those things. It's too much on you, all by yourself."

"I've got my daughter."

"I'm sorry, Matti, I can't leave this ranch in the care of an irresponsible high-school girl in your absence. And the bus doesn't drop her off until what, almost four? I'm going to have to make other arrangements. I'll be happy to give you a *great* letter of recommendation. It should help you get about any job you want.

Matti was furious with Karson for placing her in this situation, but she couldn't abide him plunging the family so deeply into debt with the new truck, and now it's cost her the job of her dreams.

She left the rough and tumble life she had lived for so long and landed a job as a Sheriff's deputy. She found more suitable housing for herself and Shoshoni in a small town nearby, where they began their new lives together.

Another year passed after her divorce from Karson, and the relationship between mother and daughter only worsened. Shoshoni, now a senior in high school, was a wild and rebellious young lady.

One morning, Matti was about to take her first sip of coffee at the kitchen table when her daughter, wearing a slinky, see-through nightshirt and the skimpiest of panties, walked in. Matti said, "Good morning."

"What's good about it?" Shoshoni replied as she poured a cup of her own.

"Why do you have to be so foul? Do you not feel well?"

Holding her cup with both hands and looking over the top, her daughter replied, "I don't know why you're so surprised I act like I do, Mother. It's all your fault. You're the one who ruined my life.

"You're the one who separated me from my *dad*. We had a great life when we were with him. Now look at us, living in this dump, and I have to live with the shame of you as a *Deputy Sheriff*. *Mother of God*, what am I supposed to do with that?"

"Karson is not your *dad*. He's your stepfather. And I have a right to be happy, too, damn it!"

"Well, you don't seem very *happy* to me right about now."

"That's beside the point, and my *happiness* has a lot to do with you and your behavior. What the hell has gotten into you? You're out of control. Why don't you put some clothes on? Look at you.

111

You're always running around half-naked. And the clothes you wear to school aren't much better."

"I like my body. I think it's pretty, and I like to show it off. But I'm not out of *control*. I'm in *complete* control. You have no idea, *Mother*. I have men chasing me like I was a dog in heat."

Then, lifting her top and pointing to her skimpy panties, which covered hardly anything, she said, "I control who gets into these. Me and me alone."

"So, you are having sex then."

"Oh, heavens, yes. And I *LOVE* it."

Seeing her mother cringe, Shoshoni shifted her weight, placed a hand on her hip, and said, "I wouldn't *criticize* if I were you, *Mom*. I'm confident I waited longer than you did."

"Well, I hope you don't end up in the same situation *I did*. Please protect yourself."

"I will. As I said, '*I'm in control*.'"

"Mm mm. I heard you. I hope you're right. Do you have a steady boyfriend, or are you playing the field at the moment?"

"Actually, I'm currently dating two guys, both of whom I like a lot. We'll see which one wins out."

"That's *risky business*. What are they like?"

"Well, they're both dark and handsome. One is real tall, while the other is about my height."

"Any other attributes?"

"None I'm willing to share with you."

"Are either of them working? Are they local? Do they have names? How old are they? Anything?"

"They both have jobs, they're older than me, live within a fifty-mile radius, have names, and they both make me—"

"Never mind. That's enough."

"Happy. *Happy* was what I was about to say. Were you thinking I was gonna say something crude, *Momma*?" Shoshoni said with a smirk.

"As much as I'm enjoying this conversation, I have a date this evening, and I must get ready. I'm pretty sure it will be a fantastic night, Mother. I'll do my best to live up to the standards you've set for me." Shoshoni pivoted, coffee cup in hand, and headed for her bedroom.

When Matti and Jake began to click at the horse farm, she remembered how thrilled she was to meet someone with whom she could dress up, wear high heels, and still not be taller than her date. At six-foot-four with broad shoulders, Jake was the perfect man for her.

Ever since she left without saying goodbye, there was hardly a day without Jake's image popping into Matti's mind. She never cared that he didn't respond to her birthday texts. She wanted him to know she hadn't forgotten.

Initially, the sender was evident because it appeared as "Matti" on Jake's caller ID. But when she moved to Montana and changed her phone number, those text messages started arriving with only an incoming number.

Confused at first by an anonymous birthday wish, Jake put it together when he realized the absence of one from Matti. He then set about to search the area code of the text. *So she achieved her dream. Good for her.*

Matti had just returned from work one afternoon and changed clothes when her phone rang. When she looked at the screen, she couldn't believe it. "Jake."

No! That can't be. Cautiously, she answered, "Hello ...."

"Matti?" Jake asked, with a lump in his throat.

Matti's heart felt like it was trying to jump out of her chest. *Did he butt-dialed me or something?*

He had been on her mind every day, from when she first laid eyes on him until that moment he called to ask if they could meet for a cup of coffee.

Matti, in response, asked, "Uh..., we live kinda far apart for us to meet for coffee, don't you think?"

"We do, but I happen to be sitting at a little table in Blu's Bar in Missoula. If my information is correct, it's not that far from you. Is it?"

"Are you serious?"

"Serious as a heart attack."

Matti smiled, remembering that as one of Jake's often-used lines. "I'll be there in twenty minutes!"

Matti ran to her car as she spoke those words, fumbling for her keys on the way. As she drove, tears were streaming down her face. She wasn't sure if they were happy tears or out of fear. Maybe the anticipation of seeing him again. She didn't know what to expect. *I wonder what he looks like after all these years. Why is he here? What's this all about? What should I do? Should I run in and do what I want, wrap my arms around his neck, and kiss him passionately?*

She thought about it and decided she'd better measure her entrance. Maybe he was in Missoula for other reasons and was mad because she kept texting him. Perhaps this wasn't a good visit after all. *Be careful, Matti.*

When she arrived and parked the car, she realized her heart was racing. She held two fingers to her carotid. *My God, it must be at least 200 beats per second!*

No matter what she tried, she couldn't make it slow down. Deep breathing didn't help. Nothing worked. Finally, she adjusted the rear-view mirror, checked her makeup, and touched up her lipstick.

Standing at the big, heavy wooden door, she took another deep breath, pulled it open, entered, pulled off her sunglasses, and waited for her eyes to adjust from the bright sunshine she just left.

Inside the dimly lit bar, a window illuminated the table where Jake was seated. When the door opened, all Jake could see was her silhouette as the door slowly closed behind her. He knew in an instant it was Matti, and his heart leapt. He jumped to his feet, broke into a huge grin, and threw his arms open wide.

He watched the love of his life standing at the door. She saw Jake in the corner. She smiled but strolled toward him as planned, trying to control her emotions. As their eyes locked, neither could look away.

Perhaps without realizing it, Matti walked a little taller. With each step, she added a little strut. Overcome with emotion, she fell into his outstretched arms, displaying a big smile as they swayed back and forth in a lingering embrace that brought back fond memories of the man she still loved.

Standing there, Jake whispered in her ear, "Hi, Matti. It's sooooo good to see you."

Matti held him, squeezing hard, trying her best not to say *I love you* out loud, said instead, "It's good to see you, too, Jake. How have you been? And why are you in Montana? You're a long way from home, aren't you?"

Chapter 13
The Eviction

At Blu's Bar, Jake and Matti talked over coffee, cup after cup. Jake listened as Matti told of her divorce from Bryce not long after leaving the farm.

"I'm not surprised. Did he put two and two together and figure out that we were engaged in ... well, you know ..."

"In what, Jake?"

"I'm guessing *he* called it an affair, but that's not what it was for me. I was devastated when you left. My world fell apart. For years I barely left the farm unless I absolutely had to. Never even looked at another woman."

"Really, Jake? I'm sorry I hurt you so badly. My hatred for Bryce, after he gave me that ultimatum, drove us apart. It only lasted a few more months.

"I took over the reins of that farm in upstate New York and stayed single for a couple of years, but I got mighty lonely, especially after I saw you had gotten married."

"Yeah. I kept hoping you'd divorce him and come back to me, but I finally gave up and moved on. I regret that now."

"Well, Karson kept showing up. He hauled hay from Montana. After a while, he started taking an interest in me. One thing led to another, and it just happened. We got married.

"He kept hauling hay, and one day, he heard about this position managing a gentleman's farm out here through one of his contacts. It worked out perfect for us ... for a long time."

They shared sordid details for hours, back and forth, and reminisced until Matti got to the part about her divorce from Karson and that she and Shoshoni, now nineteen, were living together in a small place in town.

With a laugh, Matti said, "I'm now a deputy sheriff, so watch yourself while you're in my county, mister."

Having occupied the table for so long, the waitress approached the couple carrying the coffee pot and wearing obvious displeasure on her face. "More coffee?"

She and Jake had become acquainted while he awaited Matti's arrival. Jake had bantered with her, consistent with his typical nature in such settings, and he couldn't help but notice her name, *Julie*, printed on the badge pinned above her ample breast. In response to her question, he looked into Matti's eyes and said, "Julie, let me ask my friend if she has time to join me in a beer. We've had enough coffee, I think. Matti ...?"

His date looked up at Julie and said, "Okay, but just one. I have to drive home."

Julie looked to be at least sixty years old and a bit overweight, but it was easy to tell she was a firecracker in her day. She looked at Matti and replied, "Okay, honey. What would you like?"

Noticing a handwritten sign on the wall, Matti replied, "Is that *Blonde Bombshell* you have on tap as good as it sounds?"

Julie replied, "Everybody seems to love it. It's our biggest seller."

"Okay, then. That's what I'll have."

Julie looked at Jake.

He laughed before saying, "With a name like *Blonde Bombshell*, do you have to wonder what I'm having, Julie?"

It wasn't long before two beers appeared in front of them.

They talked for another hour, during which they discussed Jake's plans to leave Christy. As Matti prepared to leave, she said, "Jake, if you'd like to stay at my place, you're welcome. There's room in *my* bed."

"Matti, there's nothing I'd like more. You have no idea how much I yearn for you. I recognized you the second you opened the door. When we hugged, and I breathed you in, it was like old times, but going home with you and doing what I want, can't happen. Not yet.

"I have to do this the right way. I've been married to *her* for fifteen years. I just don't love her anymore—if I ever did. I've always loved you.

"Matti, if you'll have me, I'll be back soon. Three months or so should be enough. Is that acceptable? I've gotta tell her first. I owe her that much."

"That's awfully noble of you. And, of course, I'll *have* you. I've *wanted* you back ever since I was forced to leave all those years ago. If I hafta wait another three months, I suppose I can endure it. I've waited nearly two decades already. But know this: if you *do* come back to me, I'm never letting you go."

Matti grabbed her handbag and fumbled for her keys. Tears welled as she said, "It's probably a good thing you don't come home with me tonight. I've gotta work tomorrow, and if you did, I wouldn't get a wink of sleep. But hell, who am I kidding? I probably won't sleep anyway just thinking about you. There wasn't a day went by you weren't on my mind."

She paused, looked him in the eye, and concluded, "I never stopped loving you, Jake."

"Stop. You're killing me already. You gotta go before this gets outta hand. I was gonna suggest we go someplace for dinner, but we'd better say goodbye now before we get in too deep."

Blinking away the tears, Matti kissed her first two fingers, pressed them tight against Jake's lips, silently mouthed 'I love you,' turned, and headed toward the door.

When she got to her car, she found her phone and texted his. *Hurry back.*

J ake sat at the table, thinking how he would break the news to Christy.

Julie walked up behind, put her hand on his shoulder, and said, "You okay?"

Jake didn't look up, afraid he couldn't hold back his emotions, and said, "Julie, would you bring me one more, please?"

Without answering, the waitress turned to fetch the beverage. As Julie set the beer down in front of her customer, she saw the pain reflected in his face. "Tough to let her walk out the door, huh?"

Jake's voice cracked as he spoke, "Oh, you have no idea. Life tore us apart nearly twenty years ago, but that's about to change, God willing."

Julie touched his shoulder again, saying, "Good luck to you both. I sure hope it works out for y'all. This one's on the house." She winked at him as she walked back toward the bar.

"Thanks, Julie."

While Jake was finishing his beer, various scenarios ran through his mind about how he'd tell Christy and his folks. *I'll give her whatever she wants. Help her liquidate assets so we can divide them accordingly—anything for an amicable split.*

Jake knew Christy wasn't happy in her relationship with him either. *She can't be. Right? Her behavior proves she's miserable. There's nothing left between us.*

W hen Jake called Christy to let her know he was about to cross the Tennessee state line into Georgia and on his way home, she responded, "You're just now calling? Did you have a good trip?"

"I did. I'll tell you all about it when I get there. See you in about a half hour. I'm in some pretty heavy traffic, so I gotta go. Bye." He ended the call.

When he pulled into the driveway, Jake gathered some of his things to carry them into the house. With his arms full, he anticipated Christy might meet him at the door and open it. She did not. She was out in the barn, tending to the horses.

Jake fumbled for the doorknob, dropping some of his gear. "Damn it," he said, as he managed to gain entry and stumble toward the bedroom, where he tossed clothes, a laptop, and other paraphernalia onto the bed.

He then returned to the truck, picking up what he had dropped on the porch along the way for load number two.

He was still in the bedroom, putting things away and sorting dirty clothes, when Christy came into the house and said, "Oh. You're home. I didn't see you drive in."

"Yeah. Just a couple minutes ago."

"So, how *was* your trip? Did you get the job?"

Jake thought about how to answer. *I may as well rip this band-aid off right now.* He sat beside her on the bed and said, "I've decided to take the job."

"You did? Tell me about it."

"There's no need. We can't go on like this anymore. We both know the love we shared died somewhere along the way. It's gone, and it's time we acknowledge it. We need to put this marriage out of its misery amicably."

Christy went crazy. She stood, started screaming, crying, throwing things, threatening to kill herself and him. Her face was bright red, eyes bulging, fists clenched—out of control. In forty-five minutes, she played every card there was to play. Jake was sure she needed professional help.

When he stepped into the bathroom to shower, Christy picked up his cell phone. She found the text that read, *Hurry back*. Not recognizing the number, Christy called it. A woman answered, "Hi, Jake. What's up? Did you make it back to Georgia safely?"

Christy ended the call without speaking. It being a woman's voice was all she needed.

With Jake's cell phone in hand, she immediately left to visit the most aggressive divorce attorney in town. She accused her soon-to-be ex-husband of adultery and desertion since she knew he was about to leave.

The following morning, Christy presented him with an ultimatum. "You've got until five o'clock to get yourself and your belongings out of *my house*!"

She pointed out the window and said, "That's *your* pick-up truck, and your utility trailer is behind the barn. Whatever you can load in or on them by five is yours. The rest is mine. Get out. I don't ever want to see your face again."

"Christy. It doesn't have to be this way. I want to help you sell *our* stuff. We own a quarter-million dollars worth of horses together. We've got two houses. It doesn't have to be like this."

"GET OUT. I'VE MADE UP MY MIND!"

Angry and fearing he might do something stupid, like choke her to death, Jake looked at Christy and finally said, "Suit yourself."

When he set about hooking his truck to the trailer, Christy jumped into her vehicle and left the property. As soon as she pulled out of the driveway, Jake called his father.

"I need your help, Dad." He tried to explain the situation as briefly as he could, expressing the urgency of the matter. "I've only got till five this afternoon. I'll explain in more detail later."

G reg came running from the barn, hollering to his wife, "Drop what you're doing, Honey. Jake needs our help. Let's go."

"What are you talking about? Did he call you?"

Greg didn't even look up, which was typical when faced with such opportunities, a regular occurrence during their many years of wedded bliss, before saying, "No. I'm *telepathic.*"

Her nostrils flared, but before she could speak, Greg chuckled and continued, "How do you think I could know it if he didn't call? Get in the truck. I'll explain on the way."

Linda sneered, "I hate you. What the hell's going on?"

"I know, but that's for another time. Come on, we need to hurry."

On the ride over, Greg relayed what little he knew, "All he told me was that he and Christy had a fight, and he was leaving. He needs our help, so that's what we're gonna do."

T he three of them worked hard packing Jake's belongings onto his truck and trailer, intermingled with Linda trying to pull information about what was happening. Jake did his best to be as pleasant as possible without going into much detail, "Mother, please. I'll tell you everything when we have more time. Right now, I'm up against a deadline."

As Jake's vehicles were becoming overloaded, they started packing Greg's. It was beginning to sink in. Jake was facing some gut-wrenching decisions about what to leave behind—his bass boat, horses, ATVs, to name a few.

When Jake was satisfied he had everything he cared most about, they prepared to leave the property for the last time.

Greg looked at his son and said, "Where are we headed?"

"Can we go to the farm? I'd like to go to your house and explain. Over a beer, maybe? Would that be okay with you?"

Greg smiled, "Absolutely. I'll follow *you* to make sure nothing falls off that trailer on the way. I'm not sure how well that load is secured."

They tried to fake a laugh to lighten the mood and headed toward friendlier pastures.

Jake didn't realize that Christy had spent the day closing their joint bank accounts, credit cards, and every access to money he had. He never maintained any personal sources of funds in his name only.

Although he wouldn't discover it until the next day, he was effectively penniless—except for the cash he had on him, which wasn't much.

Greg thought it was fortunate for Jake that the house on the farm had recently become vacant with the dismissal of an employee.

On the trip home, he told Linda, "At least he'll have a place to stay until they get all this worked out."

"Oh, Greg. This is awful. I can't say I'd be sorry if they were to divorce. She's been terrible for a long time. I don't see how he's put up with her for this long, but I've got a feeling about what's coming, and it ain't pretty."

When they arrived at the farm, they followed Jake as he pulled up in front of Greg and Linda's house. They went inside.

Greg began to explain to his son the availability of the house he used to live in. Jake stopped him in mid-sentence. "I won't be needing that, Dad. I'd really like to sleep here tonight, in one of the guest bedrooms, if that's okay. I'll be heading out in the morning. I'm moving to Montana."

Greg and Linda, in unison, said, almost yelling, *"Montana?"*

"I know that must come as quite a shock."

With that, he began his explanation, laying out the entire backstory.

He told them about his affair with Matti that began just months after she came to work at the farm all those years ago. "I'm the reason she left."

Linda asked, "How do you know that?"

"She told me so last week when I saw her."

"You saw her? When?"

"Last week. I just said that."

Linda angrily, "You know what I meant. Where, how, when—did you see her? Explain, please."

Jake went on with further explanation—in detail. He told it all. Jake never was one to lie. He figured his memory wasn't good enough to remember lies, so he always tried to tell the truth, no matter the consequences.

All too often, especially in his adolescent years, his parents sometimes wished they hadn't heard *all* the truth, but that's what they received.

When her son finished, Linda said, "Jake, you must go to her."

He responded, "Thank you."

Greg looked at his son with a lump in his throat and said, "It kills me to see you go, but I agree."

By the time their conversation was over, it was nearly midnight. They had talked through the dinner that Linda had managed to throw together in the midst of it all, but by now, everyone seemed exhausted. It had been a hard day, so they decided to retire for the night.

Before heading to one of the spare bedrooms, Jake asked his mother if he could use her cell phone. "Mom, Christy stole mine, and I'd like to call Matti. May I use yours?"

"Sure, Honey. Here you go. I hope there's enough battery left. It's kinda late, though, don't ya' think?"

"It is here, but it's two hours earlier there, Mom," Jake replied with a forced smile as he took the phone from her. With a quick look at the battery icon, he continued, "Uh, this might be a long conversation. Could I borrow your charger, too, please?"

J ake went to Walmart the following day to purchase a new cell phone and disable his old one. After making his selection, he handed the clerk his debit card. After a moment, she looked at him and said, "I'm sorry, sir. It says your card is declined."

Jake replied, "No. That can't be. I know there's plenty of money in that account. Try it again, please."

Sheepishly, the clerk responded, "I've already tried it three times." She returned his card.

Jake handed her a credit card instead. "Here, try this one."

When "Declined" appeared on the screen, the clerk looked up at Jake empathetically and said, "I'm sorry. You might want to call your bank."

"Duh. If I had a phone, I wouldn't be in here trying to buy a new one. Mine's been stolen." Jake's voice reflected his frustration.

"Oh. I'm sorry." Pointing to the phone on the counter beside her, she said, "We're not allowed to use these phones to call outside, and I don't think there's a pay phone anywhere near here. If you promise not to make a scene and embarrass me or get me in trouble, you can use mine. Okay?"

"I promise. I'll be good and as quiet as I can," Jake replied with gratitude. "I just need to make one call. That's all. Thanks."

He called his bank and discovered what Christy had done regarding their checking account to which the debit card was attached. It was easy for him to conclude she had done the same with the credit card company. He was furious.

Not wanting to go into further detail with the cashier, he returned the phone and said, "It seems I've been hacked, and my identity had been stolen, too. How do I disable my old service contract, and how much is a pre-paid phone?"

"That's not good," the clerk replied. "You'll have to call your carrier. Who provides the service? Is it Verizon, AT&T, T-Mobile? Do you know?"

"Hell. I'm not sure. My wife took care of that." Jake knew. He didn't want to go into it with the cashier. "How much is a pre-paid burner phone?"

They discussed the various options, and he made a purchase using the cash he had on him before returning to his parents' house.

He entered their back door and hollered, "Mom, can I borrow your phone again, please?"

"Jake. You're back already? I thought you had lots of things to do. I didn't expect you this quickly. Is everything okay?"

"Actually, no. Christy's stolen the money from our checking account, and my credit cards don't work. I wonder what else she's done. I gotta make some calls. Can I use your phone again?"

Clearly upset for her son, Linda replied, "Oh, dear. That's a problem. Of course. Here." She handed it to him.

Jake thanked her and began making a series of calls to the credit card companies. All the news he got was terrible. Christy had left him in a mess.

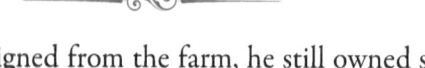

When Jake resigned from the farm, he still owned some tools and equipment he'd left behind for his dad's continued use. He and Greg agreed on their value, and a purchase price of $5,000 was struck.

Linda got involved in the conversation and said, "Honey, how long have you used Jake's equipment on this farm, including the time he worked for us?"

"I don't know, ten years, fifteen maybe. Why?"

"And now you're going to buy it for $5,000? It seems to me you owe him that much again for the lease of the equipment for all those years before any of this happened." Suddenly, the number became $10,000. Greg was not amused but went along with it. After all, Jake was his son, too.

Without any credit cards that worked, cash was the only form of currency Jake had at his disposal. However, the idea of crossing the country carrying all the money he had to his name made him uncomfortable.

"I know you guys always keep some cash in the safe. If you could give me about $2,500 of it, that should be plenty to get me to Montana. Once I get there, I'll open a checking account, and we can arrange for the rest to be wired later. Would that be okay with you?"

It made perfect sense. Linda went to the safe to retrieve the funds. Greg asked his son, "When do you plan to leave?"

"Well, since I no longer had a credit card that worked, I picked up a pre-paid burner phone at Walmart. It's charging as we speak. I was thinking I'd like to work on securing the load on my trailer this afternoon and get a fresh start in the morning. Would you mind if I stayed here again tonight and leave first thing tomorrow? If it's alright with you and Mom, that's what I'd like to do."

Greg assured him, "Staying the night here is fine with me, and you know it'll be fine with your mother, too. You're welcome here anytime. However, no matter when you go, it's gonna break her heart."

"I know, Dad, but I hafta."

"Yeah, I get it." After a pause, his dad continued, "You *do* know this mess with Christy isn't over. Right? She's probably hired an attorney."

"Yeah. I don't care. She can have everything. I just want out."

"I'm sure. You've been strugglin' with this a long time, and I hate it for ya'. I'm sad to see you leave. You're my best friend, you know." With that persistent lump in his throat, Greg concluded, "I'm gonna miss you terribly."

"The feeling's mutual, Dad, but you're right. I've gotta go to Matti. I've loved her for all these years. I tried making a life with Christy. I tried hard, but she's become unbearable. The trip we took this past fall through the northwest was supposed to be an opportunity for us to fix our relationship—but it failed miserably. That was the last straw. I'm done."

"Yeah. I get it. Now, about your stuff in my truck."

"Oh. About *that*. Any chance we can store it here until I can get back down to pick it up?"

Greg chuckled and said, "Of course."

Linda walked back into the room and handed Jake the money. Greg looked at her and said, "Jake's gonna stay with us again tonight and head out first thing in the morning."

"Okay. I figured as much. I'll go lay something out for supper."

Linda turned and walked out to hide that she was about to break down in tears. She went into her bedroom and sobbed, partly because her son was leaving and partly because of the storm she foresaw.

The next morning, Jake left for Montana.

Chapter 14
Jake's Relocation

The trip to Montana was going surprisingly well. Jake had called Matti the night he left Christy and again the evening before departing Georgia. Then, on the trip, about every time he had cell service.

After several calls during that first day of his drive, Matti finally said, "Babe, you've gotta quit calling while I'm at work. I'm a cop, remember? I can't wait for you to get here either, but you're gonna get me in trouble."

"A cop? I thought you were a deputy sheriff."

"You say tomāto, I say tomăto. The words are interchangeable, but I gotta go."

Jake whined, "Okay. Call me when you can. We'll talk then. I've got nothing to do, so you won't be interruptin' me."

Matti couldn't help but chuckle and said, "I love you," before ending the call.

Throughout the rest of her shift, Matti struggled with how she would share the news about Jake with her daughter. On her way home, she summoned the courage to bare her soul. She held nothing back.

To say her daughter didn't take it well doesn't tell the whole story. At nineteen, Shoshoni had already become quite disrespectful to her mother. On this day, it reached a new height.

"My God, Mother! You were having an affair with this guy, sometimes with me in tow, while you were married to your first husband? What was his name? Bryce?

"And now you've invited this *dude*, a man I have no recollection of ever meeting, to come and *move in* with us? And he's in route *right now*? Likely to arrive when? Tonight? Tomorrow? The next day? How am I supposed to deal with this?

"How many men have you been with, Mother? You didn't marry either of the men who got you pregnant, right? You gave up my sister and didn't marry her father, but lucky me, I'm the chosen one. Except, instead of marrying my biological father, you chose to marry Bryce while you were pregnant. Isn't that what you said? And to top it all off, you had an affair with Jake not long after I was born? What's wrong with you?"

Matti was in tears but let her continue.

"Was he the only one? Did you divorce Bryce? Or did he divorce you?"

Matti sat there in stunned disbelief. Through broken sobs, she responded, "I didn't *give up* your sister. I was sixteen when I got pregnant with her. Your grandmother took my rights as her mother away from me. I had no choice in the matter."

Nonetheless, she couldn't deny the substance of her daughter's words. The truth hurt.

Shoshoni waited a moment before continuing. "Then you hook up with Karson, marry him, only to divorce him a few years later. Did you get bored and cheat on him, too?

"He was the closest thing to a *dad* ..." she motioned with air quotes "... I've ever had, but you got ridda him. Do you even *think* about anyone but yourself? What about what *I* want?

"Don't you *EVER* criticize me for *my* sexual escapades. Don't you dare."

Shoshoni was in a rage, red-faced with anger, but she paused to catch her breath, "Oh, I can't wait to meet this, *Jake*. How do you think this is going to go, *Mother*? Do you think I'm going to welcome him with open arms? Is that what you were hoping for? If so, I hate to disappoint you. I really do."

The irate young lady turned and stormed out of the house.

Matti burst into tears—knowing what her daughter had said was mostly true. How it was delivered was painful.

Never had she been so deeply hurt, and it coming from her own daughter made it even worse. *I haven't slept with <u>that</u> many men. I was young and stupid—and got pregnant by the wrong ones.*

On her sixteenth birthday, the sex she had wasn't consensual. Matti, by statutory standards, was raped, but she was too embarrassed and ashamed to tell anybody at the time.

Shortly after she became pregnant with her second child, the man responsible, Ty, showed his true colors by getting arrested for drug possession, a charge for which he would serve time in prison.

It was clear he wouldn't make a good father for their daughter. So, once again, she would choose not to marry the father of her unborn child, even if he asked.

While pregnant, Bryce entered her life. A good man, Bryce fell in love with her almost immediately, and knowing full well she was already pregnant, he asked her to marry him.

Matti agreed. He was a nice enough guy, but she recognized Bryce as an insurance policy against the possibility of her new baby being taken away from her like the first one a few years before.

She had to admit she'd made some bad decisions, but Matti wasn't the kind of woman Shoshoni had suggested. Sure, she had done all the things her daughter had said—and left the only man that really mattered—Jake.

But he was coming home to her—this time forever.

As if her daughter was still in the house, Matti said aloud, "I'll be damned if you, or your little temper tantrums, are going to mess this up!"

She placed the call. "Jake? Are you where we can talk?"

"Yeah. I just filled up and back on the highway. It looks like I've got a pretty good signal. What's up?"

She started telling about her conversation with her daughter. "It's going to be rough when you get here. I fear she's not gonna be very welcoming. How do you think we should handle her?"

They talked and strategized until Jake ran out of cell coverage. They came up with a plan. Jake said, "We have to be as understanding as possible. We'll need to treat her with love and respect. No matter what comes up, we have to find a way to work it out. We can see it through as long as *we're* a team."

Jake had always been a take-charge kind of guy, but he knew when he arrived in Montana to start a new life, he'd have to temper things a bit with his new *family*. After all, it was their lives he was invading. He couldn't just walk in and become the head of the household.

He realized he had a delicate line to walk, with Matti, her friends, and certainly with his new step-daughter. And then there was Cayuga, the daughter he had never met.

Matti had told Jake about her and that she, too, had moved to Montana but lived several hours away. There was no telling how meeting her would go either. These were going to be trying times.

Since Jake's burner phone wasn't equipped with GPS, he had to rely on Matti's directions and maps—old school. He smiled when he started seeing signs and landmarks Matti had mentioned during their conversations. He knew he was close and decided to stop at a service station to use the facilities and brush his teeth. He didn't want to offend his lady when he arrived.

Matti was impatiently staring out the front window when Jake pulled into the driveway. She ran to meet him. They embraced and rocked back and forth for what seemed like five minutes or more, tears running down their cheeks. They were sobbing and laughing at the same time.

After they composed themselves and wiped their tears, they started for the house, carrying what they could of the essential bags, leaving the rest for later.

Once inside, Matti asked, "What would you like first?"

"Honestly? A drink, then a shower."

"Perfect. What would you prefer? I've got water, tea, or beer, or need I ask?"

Jake exhaled and looked at her with a cocked brow. They both broke into uncontrollable laughter. "I'm just so happy to be here. I don't care what you bring me, but a beer sure would be nice."

Closing the fridge door with her elbow, Matti gestured with a bottle in each hand, saying, "Come, let's sit." She led the way to the sofa in the living room, where Jake barely got a word in edgewise. Not turning loose of his free hand, Matti giggled and rambled, often repeating, "I can't believe this has finally happened."

Jake couldn't wipe the grin off his face as he listened. When his beer was nearly gone, he asked, "Is it alright if I shower?"

"Of course. There's only one. It's a small house, but what's mine is yours. C'mon, I'll show you where it is."

Jake downed his last swallow and said, "Good. I'm nasty. It's been a long trip, and I'm eager to get everything that's behind me, off me. Everything. Make sense?"

Matti smiled. "I understand completely."

As she led her guest to the bathroom, she stopped abruptly in the hall. Opening the door, she said. "Linen closet ..." she pulled out a towel and washcloth "... where I keep such items whenever you may need them." After another step, she pointed. "And here's the bathroom."

Once inside, Matti pulled back the shower curtain and motioned with her arm. "There's shampoo, body soap, and conditioner ... anything else you need?"

"No. That'll do just fine." Then, seeing the level at which the showerhead came out of the wall, Jake pointed to it. "What's up with this? Did they build this house for midgets? I'm gonna have to do squats to rinse my shoulders."

Unable to hide how amusing she found the situation, Matti responded, "I knew you'd say something like that. I've imagined you trying to get down far enough to rinse the shampoo out of your hair. I have trouble with that, too, but I'm not sure you'll be able to get there. Should I bring in a stool so you can sit down?"

They cackled together over the mental picture, but when Matti suggested, "Maybe I should set up a video camera and put it on the internet," their hysteria became even more intense.

She turned, shaking her head, still chucking, and exited the bathroom. As she closed the door behind her, Matti looked out the window and decided to carry another bag or two in from the truck.

Walking back inside, it occurred to her what she needed to do. Since Jake had been out of her life for so long, she felt it only appropriate to welcome him home properly.

Matti went into the bedroom and removed her clothes, down to her bra and panties. She slipped into the bathroom and waited for Jake to finish his shower. She lifted his towel from the hook and patiently held it in front of her.

It didn't take long. Jake shut the water off and pulled the curtain back. Seeing Matti, he smiled and raised his hands to squeeze the water from his long hair.

Wearing a sultry look, Matti said, "I thought it might be nice if I helped dry you off. It's been a while since I've been in the presence of a man absent his clothes." She slowed her words, "And a real long time since I've seen *this* ... man ... all clean and shiny ... in the buff. You are a sight for sore eyes, Jake. I wonder how long it might take you to get *me* naked."

As she raised the towel to begin drying her soon-to-be lover's head and face, his manhood began to rise. She couldn't help but notice. Glancing down, she said, "Hmmm, I see it didn't take much to get *him* excited. That makes me *very* happy."

"Making you happy is all he and I *ever* wanted."

Jake brushed his lips against Matti's. Her eagerness was apparent. Her mouth opened, and their kisses grew hot and passionate.

Still dotted with water droplets, he lifted his scantily-clad lady, carried her to the bedroom, and laid her gently on the queen-sized bed. As he stood there looking down at her, his cock fully erect, Matti reached behind her back, unhooked her bra, and tossed it to the side.

He reached for the waistband of her panties. She lifted her backside, and her lover slowly slid them down, revealing the last of her secrets.

He lay beside her, pushed an errant tuft of hair behind her ear, and kissed her. He ventured from her lips and mouth to elsewhere on her face, then her neck—his hunger was insatiable. With wet kisses, he made his way to her collarbone, then down her chest until he found Matti's left breast—he lingered there. Massaging its fullness with his hand, Jake spent time teasing the nipple with his tongue and, gently, his teeth.

Deftly, he moved to her right and focused his attention there. Duplicating his tactics, Jake didn't stop until this nipple, too, was stiff and erect. His lover ran her fingers through his long hair as she squirmed beneath him.

Kissing inch by inch, Jake slowly traced a path down her belly while keeping his hands busy gently caressing her naked body. The warmth of his breath heightened Matti's excitement.

As his mouth teasingly crept closer to the area of Matti's passion, her breathing intensified. Jake used his tongue to explore her deliciousness. Matti moaned and lifted her pelvis to welcome him inside.

She gasped for breath. Jake's playful nibbles drove her crazy, and she squeezed with her thighs at the onset of the first of what would be several orgasms of the session, breathlessly saying, "Oh, how I've missed you."

When the waves subsided, and her body relaxed, Jake returned to Matti's face, kissed her softly, and whispered, "That's one. Let's see how many we can chalk up for you today. Shall we?"

Matti panted. "I hope I lose count."

Lifting her right leg slightly, Jake inserted his stiff and throbbing member slowly inside her wetness. He leaned over to kiss her again, more passionately this time.

Matti groaned with pleasure, feeling her inner muscles squeeze tightly around the length of his shaft. She came again in mere seconds.

After what seemed like a marathon of lovemaking, they both shuddered in another mutual release and were about to pass out. Jake groaned as he collapsed beside her on the bed, "Gawd, I've missed you, too."

Lying on his back with his eyes closed, Matti, with her head upon his chest, gazed at the phallus, flaccid against his belly, glistening in the light from the window, still wet from their lovemaking. The image made her ache.

After catching her breath, she eased her way down with gentle kisses, the last of which landed on the tip of what was, moments ago, the massive and pounding source of her pleasure. After another lick or two of her tongue, Matti's plaything began to respond. It was like new life was being breathed into this favorite part of her lover's anatomy. She enhanced her efforts.

Jake looked down to see his organ rising to the occasion, then disappearing from view inside his lover's delectable mouth. He groaned in ecstasy. After a moment or two of sheer delight, he said, "What do you think you're doing?"

Matti looked up without removing herself from her current activity. Her dazzling blue eyes penetrating his, spoke volumes without words. A little while later, during which neither looked away, the lady lifted herself and said, "I'm still hungry. What should we do about that?"

Jake pulled his lover up to his face, kissed her, and rolled her over, saying, "It would be my pleasure to help with that, my dear."

"We've got a lot of time to make up for, Babe. I've missed you so much. I want you in me all the time. I desire all of you. Nothing makes me happier than when I feel you climax—hot, flowing into my body. I want all you've got. Is that wrong?"

"I'll do my best to make your wish come true," Jake said as he thrust his once-again throbbing member into her. Their lovemaking resumed and continued until they were both completely spent.

Exhausted, they fell asleep, entirely uncovered and wrapped in each other's arms.

Having seen the unfamiliar truck in the driveway, Shoshoni quietly entered as she always did in the late afternoon. Her mother worked a swing shift as a cop, so sleeping during the day wasn't unusual.

Tip-toeing down the hall, Shoshoni walked by her mother's open bedroom door and saw a buck-naked man lying there, cuddled up to her mom. She couldn't resist the opportunity. "Well, you must be Jake."

Matti unsuccessfully reached for the sheet and screamed, "Shoshoni! Get out! Close the damned door!"

Looking first at her mother, then at the *friend* lying next to her, Shoshoni replied, "Not on your life."

Jake responded calmly and without trying to cover himself, "Matti, it's okay."

He got up, completely exposed, walked over, offered his hand, and said, "Hi, you must be Shoshoni. I'm Jake. I've heard a lot about you."

His gesture rejected, he continued, "This isn't quite how I envisioned our meeting, but it's nice to see you again. I knew you when you were *much* younger. You've certainly grown up to be quite beautiful. But, then, with a mother like yours, how could you not?"

Then, using both hands to demonstrate how small she was in height, purposely making no effort to hide his genitals, he continued, "You were only about this tall when I saw you last.

"Now, I think it's only fair, if this conversation is to continue, either your mother and I should put some clothes on, or you should remove yours. Which would you prefer?"

Shoshoni shrieked in feigned outrage, slammed the door, and left for another room. Her performance didn't have quite the impact she had hoped.

While she was determined to make no contact, she couldn't avoid looking down at his manhood. She couldn't escape the fact this guy was better looking than her mother's previous husbands, clearly the fittest—and this one she'd seen entirely naked, so to that she could attest. Mom had done well.

When Shoshoni slammed the door, Matti buried her head in the pillow to stifle the sound of her laughter. Jake tried his best to be quiet, too, knowing she was still in the house and they would be heard.

After she could contain her emotions, Matti whispered, "Well, that didn't go quite how we'd planned. It was *far* better."

Jake agreed, "I know. Right?"

Matti asked, "What would you have done if she had started removing her clothes?"

"Well, I guess I would have enjoyed the show. After all, she's grown up to be a beautiful young lady."

"You bastard! You'd let my daughter strip off naked—with me sitting right beside you?"

"Would you rather I did it in your absence?"

"No, asshole. You know what I meant."

"Yes. I also know it was a *gotcha* question. It worked out exactly the way I figured it would. Shoshoni thought she had the power, but it was taken from her when we didn't try to deny what we'd been doing, and I made no attempt to cover myself. Her position was effectively neutered when I walked over to meet her without shame or embarrassment. Then I offered her a choice."

Matti understood the brilliance of the move, saying, "Just another reason why I love you so much. Did you notice as you walked up to her? She tried to keep her eyes locked on yours but couldn't. She had to sneak a peek. Did you see that?"

"Yeah, I saw it. I hope you're not upset over it. I knew she'd look down even though she was trying so hard not to. I thought it was pretty funny."

"Be careful, Jake."

"No worries on that score, Baby."

The rest of the evening was less awkward than Matti expected. They got through it well, and everybody kept their clothes on.

———— ⚜ ————

A few days later, Jake went to the grocery to pick up some things for the week. He was a great cook and demonstrated his culinary skills whenever he could for Matti and Shoshoni. However, the pantry lacked a few *essential* staples. He thought he'd rectify the situation, noticing how much both ladies seemed to enjoy his abilities in the kitchen.

While he was away, Shoshoni seized the opportunity to quasi-apologize to her mother for how she introduced herself to her new man. "I guess I'm starting to see why you've loved Jake all these years."

Still a little miffed with her daughter, Matti replied, "Is that because you saw him naked?"

Quickly, Shoshoni fired back, "That's not what I meant, *Mother*." Then, after a pause and in a completely different tone, "But he's not bad."

The comment broke the tension, and they chuckled, so she continued, "I can see how much he cares for you, how he dotes on you—and he can cook. We should keep him around just for that."

"Actually, I didn't remember how well he could cook. That's a special bonus. I was drawn to him the first time I met him. It's like I've always loved him. I don't know what it was. There's always been this special connection."

After a moment or two of silence, Shoshoni couldn't help herself. "So, it *was* his cock then?"

They burst into laughter and were still giggling when Jake walked into the house with the groceries.

"Hi, ladies. What's going on? Looks like you're having a good time. What's so funny?"

Matti, composing herself, "Oh, Shoshoni was just telling me about one of her friends and some stupid thing she did with her boyfriend. She's such an idiot. Did you find everything you went after, Honey?"

Shoshoni chimed in, "Yeah, she's so stupid."

Over the next few weeks, Jake settled in the best he could. Whenever Matti was not working, most of her waking hours were spent making love to her man. They couldn't get enough of each other.

When not being intimate with his lover, Jake's attention was focused on fixing things around the house, deciding what he wanted to do regarding gainful employment, and whatever was necessary to make Matti's life as easy and happy as possible.

Especially on the weeks she worked the evening shift, when her *lunch* break didn't happen until around 9 PM, Jake enjoyed serving his favorite officer of the law something tasty but quick in case she had to eat in a hurry.

One night, anticipating her arrival, he had prepared the sides but waited until he received her call to say she was on her way before pan-frying the brown trout filets. Shoshoni was out with her friends.

The timing worked out perfectly. He was removing the filets from the pan when his lover entered the house. When they finished eating, Matti, sitting there in her uniform, looked over the rim of her tea glass at the man she'd longed for all these years and, in her most sultry voice, said, "That was delicious. You look delicious."

Matti stood and reached for his hand, saying, "Come. Over here to the easy chair." She led him the short distance to the living room.

As he turned to sit, she began to unbuckle his belt and unzip his jeans. Jake said, "Matti, you don't have time for us to have sex."

"I know, but I have time for this. Sit down. Lie back and relax."

Matti pushed him down into the chair, grabbed his penis, and engulfed it in her mouth. He immediately became engorged.

After barely a few minutes of immense pleasure, Jake said, "Oh my God, Matti, you've gotta stop. You're gonna make me..." his voice trailed off as every muscle contracted.

Without removing him from her mouth, she looked up and hummed, "Mmm-mmm," nodded slightly, and intensified her efforts.

She continued while keeping her eyes fixed on his until he couldn't hold back any longer. His eyes rolled back in his head, and his body convulsed in ecstasy.

After her lover had finally finished, Matti carefully removed her lips from the end of his manhood. She straightened up, waited for his eyes to reopen, swallowed, licked her lips, smiled, and used her little finger to wipe the edges of her mouth. She stood and leaned down to kiss him deeply before walking the two or three steps around the corner to gaze into the mirror above where her gunbelt was stored.

As she assessed the reflection, peering back at her, Jake said, "That was amazing, but I feel like you got cheated."

"Oh, don't. My panties are soaked. It was good for me, too, Baby. I didn't get cheated. And look, not a hair out of place."

Jake sat there like a zombie in a trance. He was incapable of turning to acknowledge the love of his life's remark.

Matti smiled as she straightened her shirt and strapped on her gun belt to head out to her squad car to finish her shift. As she was about to close the door behind her, she hollered, "I love you."

When Matti finished for the night and arrived home, Jake had been asleep for nearly three hours. She slipped into bed beside him, snuggling to warm her naked body, waking him.

"Hi, Baby. How was work?"

"It was fine. Jake, Honey, can we talk?"

"Uh-Oh. What's wrong, Baby?"

"It's about what I did to you after dinner."

"You didn't like it. I'm sorry. I shouldn't have—"

"No, no, Honey, stop. You are the only man I've ever done that to ... I mean all the way like that. I don't know what possessed me to do it tonight. It was raw, vulgar—and ... I ... LOVED IT! I've thought about little else since. I've been dripping wet all night. Jake, will you make love to me? Please?

"No! Let me rephrase. I want you to fuck my brains out—NOW! PLEASE!"

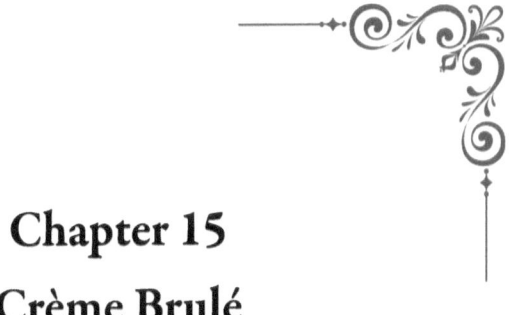

Chapter 15
Crème Brulé

T he following day, they slept in until after ten-thirty. Jake finally got up, pushed the button on the coffee maker, and headed to the bathroom to address his morning routine. With that accomplished, he started breakfast.

Amid the sounds of pans clanking and the smell of bacon frying, the object of his carnage a few hours earlier came dragging out of the bedroom. She staggered down the hall, walked up behind the man she loved, wrapped her arms around him, laid her head against his bare back, and said, "I love you so much, and you look cute wearing my apron ... over your boxers."

With a spatula in hand, her man, facing the stove, looked back at her and said, "Ha. I love you, too, sweetheart, but it's not wise to fry bacon naked. You'd better hurry. Your pancakes are almost ready. The bacon's done, and I'll soon drop your eggs in the skillet."

Matti purred, "The reasons just keep piling up."

With that, she turned and trotted off to the bathroom to brush her teeth, run a comb through her hair, and wash the sleep off her face.

En route, she heard the nearly naked chef holler, "Would you prefer I got rid of the boxers?"

"Eeww! Not while I'm eating. And I don't want my chair soiled, you fool." She laughed heartily.

After a couple of moments, Jake yelled, "Hurry up, Babe. Your eggs are done, and I've poured your coffee."

"I'm hurryin'." She giggled as she ran to the table. Sitting down, she looked at the man across from her and said, "I haven't been this happy in my whole life."

"Wow. I don't think I have either, now that you mention it." Jake smiled at the love of his life.

Matti started eating her breakfast. After a few bites, she said, "This is scrumptious. Where did you learn to cook like this?"

"Babe, this is pretty simple stuff. Bacon, eggs, pancakes. There's nothing special about it. Anybody can do it."

"Maybe so, but it can be easily screwed up. I know because I've done it. This is all delicious—perfect. I am so lucky, so glad you came back to me."

Smiling back at her, he replied, "Wild horses couldn't have kept me away."

Finished with her food, Matti leaned back in her chair, sipped from her coffee cup, looked over the rim into her man's eyes, and said, slowly, dragging each word so they would have more effect, "You really liked what I did to you after dinner last night, didn't you?"

There was a pause during which she smiled and stared at him with those lovely eyes of hers.

Jake gulped, unable to hide his emotions, then finally said, "You have no idea."

"Oh, I think I do. It's written all over you," and she giggled that little, sexy laugh he loved so much.

It's not that he'd never had a blowjob before—but this was different. This was the woman he loved, making love to him in a way he hadn't expected. She didn't do it because she was paid or because it came as a surprise. No. It was intentional—and *her* idea.

"I did, but no more than making love to you the way we normally do," trying to dampen how amazing he found the experience.

"Is that so?"

"Yeah, but I won't ever ask you to do that to me again."

Then, very slowly, with a sexy, wry smile, she replied, "Oh, you won't need to, Baby. Asking won't be necessary."

His heart leapt. He couldn't believe what he was hearing.

This new version of Matti went on to say, "I've never let a man do that before. I've seen girls do it in porn films and thought it was disgusting. I never thought I would."

Jake interrupted, trying to hide his discomfort with the conversation, "When have you ever watched porn films?"

"I'm a cop. I've seen a few. In training, child-porn cases, prostitution—that sort of thing."

This was only partly true. Matti had seen several when she was younger. She wasn't a saint, but she was telling the truth about her feelings on the matter, and she continued. "The other day, after we made love the first time, when I looked down at you, your beautiful cock lying there, still wet from our sex, this overwhelming desire came over me to taste ... us.

"As soon as I took you in, I was overcome with a feeling I can't explain. All my inhibitions vanished. I don't know what it was, but something in me just said, 'I want all of him.' I just had to have you.

"I suspect every man dreams of cumin' down his lover's throat, but I've never had a man I would even consider doing that for. But at that moment, I decided I wanted to do it for you, and last night was the perfect opportunity.

"Then, when you were on the verge, I realized I was in complete control of you. Suddenly, I had *power*. It was exhilarating. It was scary at first, but it was *so* sexy. When you couldn't hold back any longer, and finally released, that's when my own orgasm set in, and oooh, was it a dandy.

"And remember last night at dinner when I said you looked delicious? I was right. When you let go and flooded my mouth, you tasted sweet. It was not nasty at all. Just talking about it makes me hungry all over again."

"Jesus, Baby. You've got *Elvis* awake again."

"Good. I love knowing I arouse you with just conversation. Come on. We can clean up the dishes later."

She reached for Jake's hand and led him to the bedroom. In a flash, they were shed of what few garments they'd donned for breakfast and had begun exploring each other's flesh. This newly found *power* Matti had discovered created a new sense of arousal in her—a heightened sensitivity. There was excitement in the air.

This *vixen* was charged. When she was finally penetrated, she came in an instant—heart pounding, jerking, convulsing. As the waves of her first of what would be multiple orgasms of this session subsided, she returned to the rhythm of her lover.

They continued until both were near exhaustion, at which time Matti removed herself from Jake's manhood. Knowing he had already climaxed at least once, she wanted to test her *power*.

His eyes opened when her tongue touched the tip of his penis. Their eyes remained locked while she worked her magic.

He could feel another orgasm quickly building. Unlike the night before, he made no effort to hold back this time. Instead, he discarded his inhibitions and let go, much to his partner's delight.

As his orgasm washed over him, muscles all over his body stiffened. He began twisting, writhing in ecstasy. It was all Matti could do to hold on, but she managed, never losing control of him, even though she was experiencing another as well.

As her spent partner was recovering, he said, "Are you okay, Baby?"

"I'm better than 'okay.' I've never been this good. I've never cum like that before. You made my entire being shiver. You know, like when a lizard runs across your grave? How does that happen?"

"I don't know, but it was amazing. You are *fucking* amazing!"

Finally, after lying there, wrapped in each other's bodies, nearly falling asleep, Jake rolled over and said, "You don't have to work until the night shift, but I have an interview this afternoon." He headed off to the shower.

Matti stayed behind, relishing the pleasures she'd experienced. After a few minutes, she could hear the shower water still running. She headed naked into the bathroom, slid open the curtain, and stepped in.

"Oh, don't get any ideas. I've got an appointment, Woman."

"What? Me? Get ideas? What are you talking about? Kiss me, Baby," she said in a particularly sexy voice.

Backing away, Jake said, "No. Leave me alone."

Already, his manhood was starting to rise yet again. Quickly, he pulled the opposite end of the shower curtain back and stepped out. Water sprayed all over the bathroom, but neither cared. They were both laughing too hard.

"I've got to go, Baby. I love you, but you're killing me. I've got this job interview with the veterinarian. Besides," looking down at his penis, "poor little 'Elvis' here is just about worn out."

The vixen, still in the shower, pulled the curtain back and, once again, with that sexy, wry smile, looking down at his groin, said, "Well, 'Elvis' looks neither 'little' nor 'worn out' to me. You're gonna have to do better than that, Mister."

Looking into his lady's eyes, he said slowly, "God ... you ... are ... sexy!"

Her baby blues penetrated her lover's like lasers as she spoke. "I hope your interview doesn't take long, Handsome." Then, quickly, she closed the shower curtain.

With great reluctance, he shut the door and headed to the bedroom to dress for his appointment.

The interview went well. He impressed the vet with his presence and experience. Jake landed the job.

He figured Matti would have laid down to nap, so she'd be rested for her night's work. Since he wanted to make something special to show off more of his cooking talents, he decided it was an excellent opportunity to stop for some groceries before heading home.

When he walked in, it woke the lady of the house. In a sleepy voice, she said, "Babe, is that you?"

"I'm sorry, Babe. I didn't think. So stupid of me."

He sat the groceries on the counter and went in to see his sleeping beauty. "I'm sorry. If I'd thought, I'd been quieter and let you sleep. I love seeing you sleep."

"It's okay. It's time for me to get up anyway. I need to start getting ready for work.

He leaned down and kissed her, saying, "By the way, I got the job. Looks like I'm gonna stick around for a while."

Matti squealed and reached around Jake's neck to pull him down on top of her, kissing him deeply. When she finally released him to take a breath, she followed it up with, "I knew you would. I love you so much!"

As she was starting toward the bathroom to get ready for work, the new vet assistant mentioned he had something special planned for dinner and wanted to know when she thought she might be home.

"Never know for sure, but it's pretty slow during the night shift in the middle of the week when school is in session. Hopefully, about nine," she hollered as she closed the bathroom door. "Whatcha plannin' on fixin'?"

Loudly through the closed door, Jake responded, "You'll see. It's a surprise."

"I hate surprises," she yelled back, along with her giggle, indicating it was not at all true.

Jake learned that Matti and her daughter loved chicken fettuccine Alfredo, so he decided that it, along with a Caesar salad and some garlic bread, would be an excellent choice. He made sure Shoshoni knew it was on the menu and dinner would be served around nine. He told her she was invited, should she want to join them.

The rebellious young lady he was trying to win over showed up just in time to set the table and plate the Caesar salad. When her mother walked in, the aroma of garlic bread from the oven filled the kitchen. The fettuccini was being heaped onto the plates, ready to be smothered by the chicken in alfredo sauce—the last touch, fresh, grated Parmesan.

"Oh, my gosh, Babe. This looks and smells *fantastic*! How did you know? This is one of my favorites ... and Shoshoni's, too! Honey, you ... are ... amazing. Thank you."

Looking at her daughter, Matti said, "Jake invited you to have dinner with us? And you came? What a nice surprise."

"Yeah. He called to ask your fav, and I told him we both loved—this ..." and she motioned toward the table. "That's when he asked me to join you guys."

A *family dinner* was something mother and daughter hadn't enjoyed together for quite a while until Jake arrived on the scene. The only thing missing was a nice glass of white wine, but since the deputy was on duty, alcohol was out of the question.

As things were winding down, and it was about time for Matti to go back to work, she once again got that devilish look in her eye. She tipped her tea glass up to her lips, looked at Jake, and asked, "What's for dessert *tonight*, Babe?"

Jake had just taken a sip of his and nearly choked on it. When he recovered, in between coughs, he replied, "Sorry, Hun... no dessert tonight. No time."

Shoshoni, still sitting at the table, innocently said, "Oh, you made dessert for Mom last night? What did you make?"

Astonished he'd been put in this situation, Jake looked at the culprit for help. Not knowing what to say, he looked back at Shoshoni and started, "Uh ...."

That's when her mother spoke up, "Crème Brulé."

"Oh. I don't think I've ever had that. I've heard of it but never tasted it. Is it good?"

Jake was beside himself. His face was turning red.

After letting him suffer a moment, Matti responded, glancing over, smiling, and giving him that devilish look, turned toward Shoshoni, and said, "My dear, it is the most incredible stuff you'll ever have in your mouth. Once you've tasted it, your life will be changed forever."

Jake swallowed hard and looked down at the table to avoid eye contact with anyone because he knew he was about to burst out laughing.

Shoshoni's innocent eyes got big, and she said to Jake, "Wow. Mom makes it sound delicious. I can't wait to try it. Will you make some so I can taste it?"

Matti looked at her lover and said, "Yeah. Will you, Babe? How are you at making Crème Brulé in bigger batches?"

After a moment, he said, "Sure, I'll see what I can do about that. When it's ready, I'll let you know. I'll prepare another dinner it'll go with, something very Italian, maybe. How's that?"

Shoshoni eagerly replied, "Sounds great. I can't wait."

With that, Matti smiled, got up, and kissed her daughter on the cheek. Then she walked over to strap on her gun belt and headed out the door. Jake followed her to the cruiser parked outside.

Once they got to the vehicle, Jake said, "You are evil, and you must die!"

"Yeah, but that was fun. Watching you squirm was hilarious. I loved it. I can't wait to see your Crème Brulé."

Matti climbed into the patrol car. As Jake leaned down to kiss her, a call came in over the radio. She looked up at him, "Duty calls, Hun. Gotta go." She blew her lover a kiss, waved, and headed off.

Jake shook his head laughing, waved back, and went inside, where he found Shoshoni cleaning up the kitchen. Jake helped, and they finished in no time. When they wrapped, she asked, "Is there anything else I can do before I go?"

"No. Thanks for the help, though. I hope you enjoyed dinner."

"I did. It was delicious. I can't wait to try your Crème Brulé."

Jake smiled awkwardly. After he closed the door behind her, he quickly Googled recipes for the dessert.

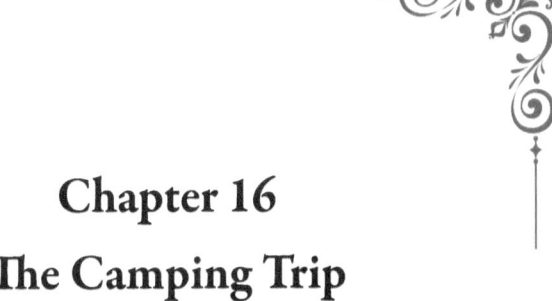

Chapter 16
The Camping Trip

Jake's inherent likability, diverse talents, rugged appearance, and gregarious personality helped him fit right in with the Montana residents. Matti's abundant love for him didn't hurt. Though her social life was limited, everybody who knew Matti loved her, and they eagerly welcomed her new beau.

Jake made it a point to become quite active in the community. His involvement and Matti's position in law enforcement made it easy for people of all stripes to gravitate to them. Their circle of friends grew rapidly.

A few months after Jake moved there, Matti noticed a home for sale a short distance from the house she was renting. She made an appointment to see the property.

Matti asked the realtor if they could have a few minutes of privacy and motioned Jake to follow her to the backyard. "Honey, look at this place. It's newer, bigger, and situated on two lots. Even though it's within the city limits, we'll have *more land* to work with. I love this place. It would be so nice. Do you think there's any way we can afford it?"

Jake nodded and replied, "We'll have to crunch some numbers when we get back to the house, but I think we can."

When they got home, they worked through the numbers, called the bank, and, together, they jumped on it, bought the property, and moved.

Even though the place had more room, Shoshoni decided it was time to move out. They were getting along reasonably well, but she was nearly twenty. She resented having *rules* and found herself being the *third person* in "three's a crowd." She chose to move in with a friend who had an extra bedroom.

Matti was against it, primarily because she felt Shoshoni wasn't mature enough to be out on her own, but secondarily, she disapproved of the roommate's lifestyle.

In a conversation with her lover, Matti said, "This is a terrible idea. Her *friend* is at least a couple of years older and has a young daughter of her own. Who knows who the father is? They'll be living together in a run-down mobile home. I wonder how they'll manage to stay warm during the winter without setting the place on fire."

Her roommate, Natalia, was known to consort with young men who'd been arrested for drug possession and other related offenses. Matti did her best to persuade Shoshoni to reconsider but knew she couldn't forbid it since she was, after all, of legal age.

"If you insist on making this move, remember we have a guest room upstairs. You're welcome to it. But, of course, by then, you'll be accustomed to paying your share of the rent at Natalia's, and you'll have learned how difficult it is living on your own. Then you'll understand what we've been carrying all this time, and I'm sure you won't mind helping out. This new house payment is difficult enough. You can understand that. Right?"

"Thanks, Mom—I think. I can move back home, but I'll have to pay rent if I do. Did I get that right?"

Matti replied, "Living isn't free, my dear. I hate to break it to you, but it's true. You'd better get used to it."

S hoshoni followed through with her plans, and Matti helped her with the move. It didn't take long. They did it while Jake was at work. It took one load since Natalia only had a bedroom available, and Shoshoni didn't have that much stuff anyway.

When Jake got home, he found Matti in a particularly foul mood. "What's the matter, Baby?"

"Oh, my God! You know I helped Shoshoni move her things. Right?"

"Yeah. What did she do to piss you off this time?"

"She's breathing, isn't she?" Their laughter broke the tension. "No, that trailer she's moved into is a dump—it stinks in there. You know what a lazy bum she is anyway. Can you imagine what she's going to be like in a month? Who's gonna clean it up, wash the dishes, vacuum the floors? Who's gonna take care of Natalia's little girl? I am so angry."

Trying to lighten the mood, Jake quipped, "Can I make you a drink? Oh, I see you already have a beer. My bad."

With a cocked brow, Matti stared at him before taking a sip. Tilting the bottle, she said, "No, thanks, I've already got one—asshole." After which, she blew him a kiss and winked.

Jake smiled, walked to the fridge, grabbed two beers, and returned to sit beside his lover. He sat one on the table between them, took a big swig of the other, looked at Matti, and said, "Looks like I'd better catch up."

"Matti quickly drank the last of hers, sat the empty on the table, and said, "Not with this one, you won't." She laughed as she grabbed the unopened bottle, unscrewed the cap, and downed another gulp.

Jake had a way of bringing Matti out of any bad mood. It wasn't long before they sat their bottles down, embraced, kissed, showered, and made love before she had to go to work.

Afterward, as they were lying together, looking up at the ceiling, Jake said, "You know, with Shoshoni gone, we can have sex without the worry of her walking in on us. We can do it anywhere in the house."

"Yep. We should christen every room, don't you think?"

"We should, but do you think we have time? Don't you have to go to work pretty soon?"

Matti shot back, "Not right now, dumbass!" She smacked his chest and buried her head in his neck, laughing again.

It was clear, with the combination of sex and laughter, their relationship was thriving.

The new house needed some work to make it *their home*. So, they set about planning some changes. Several *fixer-upper* and some minor remodeling projects were begun, all of which they could do together. They took them on with the knowledge they would have to live with the mess during the process, and it would take a while. They were okay with that.

Through it all, Matti wanted to keep Shoshoni close, as did Jake. They thought it an excellent way to guide her, ensure she was okay and not in need.

Matti would invite her over for dinner, often at house gatherings. Occasionally, she would include Natalia and her daughter as well. Matti was a cop, and what better way to obtain information?

Jake, being a great cook, loved grilling when the weather permitted. Since their new place came with some land, they constructed an area behind the house where they could enjoy the outdoors during all but the absolute coldest months.

They built a large fire pit, big enough to keep several couples warm even after the temperatures started to fall in autumn and early winter. The area around it was naturally protected by trees and shrubs, shielding it from prying eyes and the wind. Matti added her touches to give it a Native American flair.

Many evenings were spent around the fire. Sometimes, they would start with just Matti and Jake, but it was not unusual for one or several friends to drop by to join them. They were always welcome. "We saw the fire and thought we'd stop to say hello," was the typical greeting.

Their new home became a gathering place for all sorts of activities. As the weather began to warm, there were corn-hole tournaments. They would practice archery in the fall, and Ski Patrol team meetings were occasionally held there leading up to and during the winter.

But during the summer, the big thing was co-ed softball. The community had a park where they had built four ball diamonds that served dual purpose: Little League for young kids and co-ed softball for adults. After his first year there, Jake, Matti, and even Shoshoni played on the team together. By the end of the season, Jake was named team captain and *manager*—by appointment of the other team members.

Perhaps it was because he was the newcomer, and they all ganged up on him, but they tried to make him believe it was because he was their best player and possessed the most knowledge of the game. Truth is, the current manager was all too eager to dump the responsibility onto anyone. Jake happened to be the patsy.

Nonetheless, Jake accepted the burden with pride. He soon understood that trying to organize this *team* and scheduling practices, not to mention games, was like herding cats. Made up of local professionals of all persuasions—doctors, nurses, physical therapists, EMTs, law enforcement officers, firefighters, attorneys—all with different and demanding schedules that are often unpredictable, it's complicated.

Of course, their work demands would trump game and practice schedules, but this would never stop Jake from chastising any *no-shows* for having their priorities *misplaced*.

To combat this problem, Jake maintained several more players on his roster than one would typically think *necessary* in the hope he would have enough players to field a team come game day. Shoshoni even recruited a couple of her friends to play on the team.

Her relationship with Jake seemed to be warming considerably, and she was getting along better with her mother, too.

A local tavern sponsored the team. Shirts and hats, embellished with the tavern's logo, were provided for the players, and if they won, they were rewarded with a complimentary drink and a free appetizer after each game back at the tavern. They could still get a free drink if they lost, but NO FREE APPETIZERS!

The tavern owner, Dave, explained it this way, "That's your incentive. If you win, you eat for free. If you lose, you gotta pay for the food. So, go out there and WIN! Make me and the tavern proud."

The team called themselves the 'Beavers' since the Beaverhead River was nearby. Being a lover of the double entendre, fairly early in the season, as they exited the dugout to take the field, Jake decided to inspire his co-ed team members by reminding them, "Remember, let's go out there and WIN! So we can EAT ... Beavers!"

It took a while before it sunk in for some of the ladies in the group. Most of the guys got it immediately and headed onto the field, laughing and shaking their heads.

Then, as she was running to her position in the infield, one of the female players said, "I can't believe he said that!"

Another yelled, "Oh ... my ... God!" between guffaws.

Another one, playing right field, hollered, "I hope no one hits the ball my way. I won't be able to see it through my tears of laughter."

One young lady screamed, "Come on, guys, play your asses off! We Beavers are ready!"

The whole team cracked up.

After that first time, if Jake didn't say it, somebody would—at least once every game.

E veryone gravitated toward Jake. He was the glue. Even after the season ended, and he and Matti went out to a pub, a crowd would gather around them. They lived in a small town, and word would somehow get out where they were. Their friends would show up. It was strange, almost as if someone attached a homing device to one of them or they had lookouts placed all over town. If they stayed home, it wasn't unusual for their friends to drop by.

Between his time in the military and having worked for so many years on the farm with his father, Jake developed many skills, dealing with animals, working on the equipment, and building things. Consequently, there wasn't much he couldn't do.

Of course, this was good when working around the house, on their personal vehicles, or taking care of Matti's horses, the calves she owned, and the pig they purchased. But when it became known how handy he was, and what an easy mark he was about helping his friends, Jake found himself in high demand.

While they enjoyed time with their friends, they longed for opportunities to get away by themselves.

J ake loved to fly fish, and he was good at it. There may be no better place to practice the sport than Montana. It has some of the finest trout streams and rivers in the United States. Having experience as an outfitter, Matti knew where many prime fishing spots were located, some of which were seldom visited by other humans—a match made in Heaven.

On one of Matti's *weekends* off, which wasn't exactly a weekend, but a 3-day stretch that began on a Sunday, they decided to go on a camping trip. Just the two of them, up to one of her favorite places where Jake could teach her how to use a fly rod.

Jake arranged with the vet to take Monday and Tuesday off. It was late spring, and the weather was supposed to be beautiful, a chance for Matti to get some sun and Jake to put his skills to use.

Matti arrived home around 5 AM Sunday. Jake was packed and ready to leave. She quickly changed clothes, took care of necessities, scarfed down a protein bar, and they were on the road well before six.

It would be a little after eleven, with the sun high in the sky, before they arrived at their destination. Matti slept until nearly ten when Jake turned off the main highway and stopped alongside the road. From there, he needed Matti's help. The directions she provided beyond that point had faded from his memory.

"Matti, where do I go from here?"

"Oh, Honey, I can tell you where to go. I don't need to open my eyes to tell you that." And she gave it her open-mouthed laugh.

Jake couldn't help but crack up, too. "I guess I left myself wide open for that one, didn't I?"

As Matti sat up in the seat, continuing to chuckle, she said, "Yeah, you sure did, but you always do, Baby. You always do. Maybe that's why I love you so much. You're so easy.

"Let's see, where are we? Oh, I see. Yeah, this is where you were supposed to turn." She pointed straight through the windshield and continued, "Head on down this road for a few miles."

"How many is *a few*?"

"I don't know, forty or so, I suppose."

"Forty miles? Matti, this ain't much of a road."

"Jake, I told you, this place is one hardly anybody knows about. Once we get to where we turn off this road, we'll have another twenty miles of a cowpath to navigate. It's a good thing this truck has 4-wheel drive, darlin'. We're goin' back into the wilderness."

Jake was starting to get excited now, "Hot damned, Baby! This could be better than I expected. There may be fish back there that ain't ever seen a human."

Matti came back with, "May be, Honey. May be."

After finding the turnoff and navigating the cowpath, they drove to a point where Matti said, "Jake, this is where we'll have to leave the truck. From here, we have to hike. If I remember right, it can't be much more than about a mile to the spot."

"Much more than a mile? We'll be carrying a lotta gear, you know?"

"I know, Honey, but it'll be worth it. You'll see. Come on. And besides, it's all downhill from here," followed by her trademark giggle.

"Am I about to understand why humans so seldomly visit this place of yours?"

After struggling to position her rucksack, Matti smiled before replying, "If it were easy, everybody would visit. You ready?"

Once they reached their destination, the topography had flattened a bit, and Matti said, "This is where I thought we should make camp."

They set the cooler they carried between them onto the sandy ground and dropped their backpacks. Sparse new shafts of grass were growing, adding new color and a feeling of softness to the area. Matti walked Jake toward the river's edge. The closer they got, the sand gave way to small pebbles. They stopped about three feet from the shore and took in the sight. The river, perhaps a hundred feet across, flowed swiftly from their left to right.

Jake realized they were standing on the inside of a gentle bend, and the campsite Matti had picked was on a natural beach surrounded by the edge of a small mountain range of sorts, the base of it lined with fir trees.

The opposite bank rose sharply to roughly seven feet or more, held in place by numerous willow trees hanging over the water, then extending to an open meadow.

Upstream to their left, the river gradually became more treacherous. The rocks that formed the bottom started getting progressively larger until they became massive boulders. The rise in elevation created a rapid that would test the skill of any Olympic kayaker. The visual was worthy of framing. Jake stared at it momentarily before saying, "Do you see that pool just below the rough water? I'll bet there's trout in there as big as my leg."

"I hope you catch one like that."

"Are you kidding? I wouldn't even be able to turn one that size on the tackle I brought. I'm only using a three-pound tippet, but it'd be fun for a while, though." They laughed together.

To their right, as the river bent around them, the swiftness of the water slowed. A sense of calm seemed to settle in. Jake stood there with his arm around Matti's shoulder, hers around his waist; they were mesmerized.

As if breaking himself from a trance, Jake said, "Thank you for bringing me here. It may be the most beautiful place I've ever seen."

"I knew you'd like it."

Eager to ply his craft, he turned and said, "Come on, let's set up camp so we can catch our *linner*."

"Linner?" Matti replied with that cocked brow of hers.

"Yeah, by the time we catch, clean, and cook 'em, it'll be too late for lunch and too early for dinner, so—*linner*. Doesn't that make sense?"

"If you say so."

Since the area they picked had trees, the self-sheltered hammocks Jake brought worked out well. Jake preferred these over a tent for numerous reasons, except one. They would have to sleep alone. They finished the set-up in no time and headed for the water.

Since Matti had yet to learn the art of fly fishing, Jake brought along a spinning rod with which she was familiar. Once she found a spot and got comfortable, he headed upriver a short distance with his fly rod. In short order, he managed to land three nice trout for their late lunch.

He turned back toward camp, a short walk of about fifty yards, only to see Matti standing on the bank in her hiking shorts and a bikini top. The temperature was nearly seventy degrees. The sun was shining brightly. A big smile formed on Jake's face as his *fishing partner* looked beautiful standing there.

He raised his stringer and hollered to his lover, "I caught us some linner. Then, when I saw you standing there, I thought, what a great marketing ad that picture would be for tourism in Montana. Now I'm thinking it could only be better if maybe you lost the top."

Holding the rod as still as she could, Matti reached behind with one arm. Carefully shifting the fishing rod from one hand to the other to avoid disturbing the bait in the water, she managed to accomplish the task and tossed the bikini top to the ground. Then, without ever shifting her gaze from the stream, standing perfectly erect, the fishing rod properly positioned, and the sun in her face, she said, "Something like this?"

"Uh ... Yeah! Yeah, exactly like that!" Jake could hardly catch his breath—frozen at the sight. She was magnificent. Jake quickly pulled out his phone and snapped Matti's picture. "I'll treasure that one forever!" he yelled to his lover.

"Naw. You'll drop your phone in the river before we leave. We've met." Matti laughed out loud.

Without a cloud in sight, their respective hammocks would be left unoccupied. The anticipation of sleeping together under the starlit sky was too inviting.

Jake had packed a tarp he planned to use to cover the cooking area in case of rain. Instead, he spread it out on the ground, over a soft, flat spot near the fire, where they would zip their two sleeping bags together to form a single one they could share.

They managed to get *some* sleep, but the thought of making love under the stars of the *Big Sky,* next to a campfire in the wilderness, was too much. Most of the night was devoted to pleasures other than slumber.

With the sun peeking through the treetops, Jake was the first to emerge from their cocoon. He quickly slipped on his jeans, boots, and jacket before rekindling the embers. He found the bag of whole coffee beans, poured enough into the pot to cover the bottom, and added the appropriate amount of water. After attaching the lid, Jake placed the pot onto the rack above the burgeoning flames and headed to the river with his toothbrush as his lover watched and smiled.

While Jake was gone, Matti unzipped the sleeping bags, wrapped one around her naked body, slipped her feet into her boots, and shuffled over to the fire. She stoked the flame and added another chunk of wood. She held her hands close to warm them before pulling the log seat, a piece of a large fallen tree branch they had found, close so she could absorb the radiant heat.

She could see from the glass bulb in the lid of the coffee pot that the *magic elixir* had not yet begun to boil, so she reluctantly left it alone above the heat source, impatiently waiting for her man to return and the pot to boil. *It shouldn't be long now.*

Bundled in her sleeping bag, she stared at the flames, lost in her thoughts. Only the movement from her right, picked up in her peripheral vision, brought her out of her trance. "Hi, Honey. Did you *finally* finish?" Then, pretending to be annoyed, "May I *please* have the toothpaste?"

Jake smiled sheepishly as he handed her the tube. "Sorry. Is the coffee not ready? It's chilly out there," nodding toward the water.

"Not quite, but I think it's pretty close. It's probably my fault. You know what they say about a *watched pot*." As she headed toward the river, she joked, "That's all I did while waiting on you!" She quickened her pace as if afraid he would chase after her in retaliation.

Jake laughed and said, *"Thaaat's right!"* emphasizing the sarcasm before quickly donning more clothes and checking to see how the brew was coming along.

He looked up in time to notice Matti drop her sleeping bag wrap and saw that she wasn't wearing anything underneath except her boots. He let out a loud wolf whistle.

Matti immediately reacted by trying to cover her most critical parts with her arms and hands. Obviously embarrassed, she looked around to see if someone else had shown up.

Jake burst out laughing. When she realized no one else was there, Matti yelled, "You're in *so* much trouble. When you least expect it, mister."

"What? I was acknowledging your beauty. What's wrong with that?"

"Uh, huh," Matti replied, shaking her head as she resumed her *necessities*.

When she returned to the campsite, Jake asked, "May I pour you a cup, my love? Or would you prefer to dress first?"

"Who said I intend to get dressed at all today?"

"One coffee coming right up," Jake replied with a big smile as he began to pour.

Wrapped in her sleeping bag, Matti snuggled beside her suiter on the log and eagerly took the steaming cup he offered. After a sip, she sighed, "Ah, that's good."

The fire was now giving off plenty of heat, and as Matti's hands began to warm from the coffee cup, she said, "It just doesn't get much better than this, does it, Jake?"

"I can only think of one thing that might improve it."

Raising her eyebrow once again, Matti looked at him and said, "And what, pray tell, would that be?"

"How about some bacon, hash browns, and a couple eggs? I need to make sure you keep up your nourishment. You never know what might unfold today, and you need to be ready for anything."

"Is that so?" she replied with a suspicious smile.

Jake grinned as he stood before heading toward the cooler, saying, "Learning the finer points of fly fishing can be exhausting. And who knows? You might hook into a trophy."

"Uh-huh. I'm *sure* that'll happen. More likely, I'll bury a hook in you."

"What? You don't consider me a trophy?"

"Ha! Only you would come up with that." Then, musing, "I wonder what the taxidermist would charge. At least then I could hang you on the wall and not have to listen to your BS any longer."

"Oh! That was *cold*."

"Wanna share my sleeping bag?" Matti offered with an onery grin.

"No. I'm mad now," Jake responded, behaving like a petulant child. "And besides, I'm hungry. I'm a man on a mission. The fish are callin' my name. Can you hear 'em?"

Matti giggled and sipped her coffee as Jake set the cast iron skillet on the rack over the fire.

By the time they finished breakfast and a second cup of coffee, the temperature had warmed considerably. Matti said, "That was perfect. I'll take care of cleaning up. You get your stuff together and get out there on the water. I think I *can* hear those fish calling your name, Honey."

Matti threw on a pair of jeans and a flannel shirt while she tidied up around the campsite. She washed the dishes and utensils in the river and put everything away. She shook the debris off the sleeping bags and placed them in the hammocks, ready for the next night's use. Looking around, she brushed her hands together and nodded approvingly. *Good enough.*

It didn't take long for the sun to warm the air to the mid-60s. Jake had headed upstream to the pool below the rapids. Matti was once again down to her hiking shorts and bikini top. She decided to forego fishing and went in search of her man. She walked along the bank to keep him in view, looking for relics or artifacts—stone tools ancient Indians may have left behind.

Then she heard Jake holler, "Fish on."

Matti yelled back, startling Jake, "Way to go, Babe!"

"Oh, hi. I didn't know you were this close. Wow, don't you look cute?"

Matti was about thirty yards downstream from Jake and said, "Well, thank you. I wanted to get some sun. I'm so lily-white."

"Workin' on your tan for summer, huh?"

"Yeah."

Jake laughed, "Don't you know? People in Montana don't tan, Matti."

Matti giggled, "That's why I have to get a head start. I also wasn't sure about the river and didn't want to let you get out of my sight. Wanted to make sure you were okay. I love you so much, remember."

Jake shook his head, "Yeah, I'm okay, Baby. I kinda like you stayin' close and keepin' an eye on me. Dressed like that, you improve the scenery." He blew her a kiss.

"I am about to start working my way downstream, fishing as I go, toward the campsite. Hopefully, I'll catch another fish or two by the time I get there, so we'll have plenty for lunch."

Matti replied, "Oh, that's perfect. I'll head back that way and be waitin' for ya'. Take your time. Good luck."

Jake had reached a point where he could see the beach when he hooked the second trout of the morning, another nice brown. "Fish on!" again rang out. Of course, he couldn't look up when he heard Matti yell, "Yaayyy! Way to go, Honey!"

After taking the hook out of the fish's mouth, he held it up for his lover's approval. He could see her on the riverbank, facing him and waving, wearing nothing but a huge smile. Jake placed the fish in his creel and hollered, "Are you trying to avoid tan lines?"

In a particularly sexy voice, Matti replied, "That's just a side benefit. I'm hungry."

"I've only caught two fish so far."

"I'm not that kinda hungry."

Jake started running toward his lover, "I'm coming, Baby!"

"Oh, you will. Repeatedly, I suspect."

When Jake got to his waiting lover, she immediately began helping him remove his clothes while smothering him with kisses. She had already remade the sleeping bags and spread them neatly, readying them for what was about to happen.

After a marathon lovemaking session that ended with Jake flat on his back, during which Matti's prediction proved correct, Matti, at long last, made her way back up to her lover's face, wet from their encounter, and kissed him all over. "Looks like I made a bit of a mess here. I'm sorry, but you were delicious. Are you okay?"

"Okay? Are you kidding? You were like dessert after a magnificent meal."

"Really? You know how I *love* dessert. Thank you, Honey. This was especially nice. Crème Brulé for two." She giggled before kissing him again.

After the kiss, Jake chuckled. "I love you." They drifted off to sleep.

After the brief nap, Jake decided it was time for Matti's first lesson on the use of the fly rod. He chose to demonstrate, focusing on the forearm and wrist motion, the required patience, and each action's goal while concentrating on technique.

"Here, let me stand behind you. I'll hold your arms to help instill muscle memory."

Matti looked up at him, giggled, and said, "Uh, huh. You just wanna cop a feel."

"What kind of guy do you take me for?" Jake replied, feigning disbelief.

Neither could hold in the laughter, knowing the absence of clothing was bound to turn the activity into another lovemaking session. Little about the art of angling would be learned in their first session.

The lessons were repeated, however, each with a bit more success than the one before, until she was finally able to cast the fly onto the water. Still, they never once did a session end without some form of sexual activity occurring during or at its conclusion.

Matti tried, but it was clear she had more confidence with her spinning rod despite having little success regarding the number of fish caught.

They couldn't swim or lounge in the water. It was way too cold. They could wash, brush their teeth, and clean their utensils, but they had to do it quickly. It was late May, and the water was frigid—and swift.

That was okay with Matti. She would instead wander about looking for *treasures*—artifacts lying around she might find interesting—or watch Jake ply his trade *catching*. She heard Jake say he liked that term better than *fishing*. "Fishing is what people who can't catch them do. I prefer catching."

Matti loved watching Jake standing in or near the water's edge with his fly rod. There was hardly any breeze, the sun was shining brightly, and he made it look like she'd seen it in movies. There was something melodic and beautiful about it—sexy.

As they were packing to head home, Jake said, "I wish we never had to leave this place."

"You know, we can't behave like this just anywhere. Even in Montana, right? Here, and only with you, have I ever been so brazenly naked."

"Oh, then we have to designate this as 'Our spot.'"

Matti responded, "Like our G-spot?"

Jake burst out laughing, and Matti joined in immediately. As soon as he could speak, Jake replied, "Exactly," still chuckling.

They packed the gear neatly onto their rucksack frames for the long hike back to the truck. Before leaving the campsite, they made sure the fire was safely out, and no trash or debris was left behind. They did their best to remove any evidence of them ever having been there and left nothing behind but footprints.

As though she was scanning the area for the last time, Matti said, "I loved this camping trip. Nobody around, so peaceful, so much lovin'—it was perfect. With all the company we seem to have, we can't just do it anytime we want anymore, Jake. I mean, I enjoy the company, but I love having you all to myself, too. I love you so much. I want to eat you up."

"Well, you did a pretty good job of that on this trip. Thank you very much," Jake laughed. "But I know what you mean. This was sooo good. I got to fish, and we got to fuck. What could be better than that?"

They broke into laughter again until Matti said, "I know, right? On both counts and it's nice to have a partner who's so eager to reciprocate."

"Is that an invitation?"

With a sexy yet coy look in her eye, Matti asked, "Do we have time?"

"We're all packed up. There's no place to lie down. We've got at least a four-hour drive ahead of us, and we have to unpack when we get home. So, probably not."

"You're right. I get it. I can tell when I'm not wanted. Let's go."

"Oh! Y're killin' me." He started unbuttoning his shirt. "Here, we can make a bed out of our clothes. Let's lay them here on the grass. We've got time for one more if we hurry."

Matti smiled and said, "That's the man I know and love."

Jake helped his lover get her rucksack loaded onto her back. It was a bit lighter than when they arrived, but hardly enough to notice. He hoisted his, and Matti helped get it adjusted, making it a bit more comfortable for him. They grabbed the cooler and headed off up the trail.

After a few steps, Jake stopped, turned, and looked back for a long moment, "We should come back here often."

Matti agreed, and they vowed never to reveal its location.

Chapter 17

The Proposal

By the time fall rolled around, Jake had an epiphany. He and Matti shared a love that every man hopes for, women dream of, and poets write about. *I can't believe how lucky I am.*

While they were separated, Matti gained a great deal of experience in the mountains as an outfitter and firefighter. She took him to places few humans had ever seen, where big game was plentiful, and the scenery was breathtaking. To Jake, it made her even more attractive.

During his first hunting season in Montana, he and Matti managed to take an elk cow each. Jake also took a big 8-point buck mule deer, while Matti killed an 8-point whitetail. They had plenty of meat for their freezers and a couple of nice trophies for their new home as well—although Matti wasn't quite sure where *two* mounts should be displayed.

When the taxidermist called, saying their head and shoulder mounts were ready, Jake was eager to hit the road.

Matti loved to tease Jake and his obvious excitement provided an excellent opportunity. "What's your hurry? They're not going anywhere. They're dead, remember?"

Jake shook his head and laughed. "What are you talking about? We've been waiting over six months for these. Hell! It's been longer than that. Git y're butt in that truck right now, Woman. We're goin' to see the taxidermist,"

They jumped in the truck and headed off.

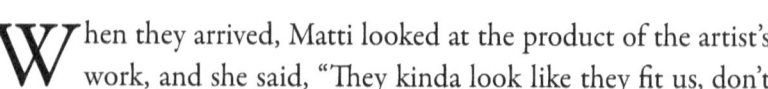

When they arrived, Matti looked at the product of the artist's work, and she said, "They kinda look like they fit us, don't they, Jake?"

"Huh? What do you mean?"

"Well, you know. You killed the mule deer. The bigger, kinda scruffy one—mean lookin'. I killed the whitetail. A bit smaller but more refined. Cleaner lines, just prettier. Kinda like us?" She giggled.

Jake replied with feigned sarcasm in his bold voice, "Oh! *Thaaat's* right!"

All three enjoyed the guffaw that only worsened when the taxidermist looked at Matti and said, "I took great care not to lose a single eyelash on your whitetail, Matti. Like you, he's got great eyes, don't you think?"

"Oh! *Puh-leeze*!" Jake said as he reached down to pick up his mount. "Come on, Brutus. We don't need to put up with this crap from these pansies." As he reached the door, pretending to be insulted, he said, "We're outta here!"

The laughter continued, but Matti stayed behind long enough to pay the craftsman and thank him for his services before turning toward the exit with her whitetail in hand.

Jake helped her load and secure the mounts in the back of the truck, knowing that what went on inside the shop was foreplay. They were eager to get home.

Their banter continued during the ride, only to end in disappointment upon their arrival when they found Shoshoni, Natalia, and Sean, a young man who was quickly becoming one of Jake's best friends, waiting for them to celebrate their trophies.

When Jake turned the corner and saw the cars out front, his heart sank. "Fuck!"

Matti giggled and replied, "Pretty sure that's out of the question, at least for a while, Honey."

"What are *they* doing here?"

"I may have mentioned to Shoshoni where we were going. She must have told Natalia. I don't know about Sean. Come on. Grab a head and put your smile on."

Jake chuckled. "Grab some head? That would surely put a smile on my face."

"That's *not* what I said," Matti replied with a raised eyebrow and a cute smile as she went to the back of the truck. She grabbed her whitetail to carry it into the house, chuckling as she walked, shaking her head. Then, with her back to him, in a low voice he could barely hear, she mumbled, "Maybe later."

Still at the truck, Jake hollered, "I heard that!" He followed with an extra bounce in his step.

As she entered the house, Matti yelled, "Hi, everybody! Look what we've got."

The uninvited guests gathered around to congratulate the hunters and help decide where each trophy should be displayed.

Soon, a consensus was reached and out came the ladder. Jake obediently did the honors and secured each mount in its designated location, and a toast was offered.

Their guests stayed for another couple of hours hearing about the hunt in all its gory detail, and, of course, Matti couldn't help but share her comment with the taxidermist, a point with which everyone agreed.

After a while, the conversation got boring, the *party* broke up, and the guests disbursed. Perhaps it was the time-lapse or the beers they consumed, but the excitement created by the foreplay earlier had dissipated. Instead, Jake fixed a little something to eat, and Matti fell asleep on the sofa. When he brought her food to the living room, he didn't have the heart to wake her, knowing she'd have to get up for work in less than three hours. Jake returned the tray to the kitchen to reheat later when she woke. Sitting in his recliner with a book, he watched his lover sleep peacefully under the coverlet he placed over her body.

There's always much to do in Montana. That's especially true after the snow falls, and Matti knew how to plan.

Matti had encouraged Jake to complete the training program to join the ski patrol that summer. They always needed new members to make up for the natural attrition that occurs in every organization. She was a member, loved it, and thought he would as well.

"As much as you love to ski, I'd think you'd jump at the chance, Honey. Since I'm already a member, it'd mean we'd both get free passes and lift tickets for the season. I'm sure we'd be able to get on the same team, so we'd have to work one weekend and then get the next two off. And, besides, you'd be doing something good for the community. Whaddya say?"

"Oh, for cryin' out loud. Do you nag like this all the time? It's convenient for you that the ski hill doesn't open until after huntin' season closes. Otherwise, there's *no way* I'd agree to it. But anything to shut you up." He grinned. "What do I have to do?"

Matti's past EMT experience was an invaluable asset to the patrol. Jake's skiing ability—honed on the Austrian Alps while serving with the Army in Germany—and his years of experience caring for injured horses would make him an excellent fit, too.

Once the hill opened, Matti and Jake became fixtures on the slopes.

Matti's familiarity with Montana's winters made Jake's acclimatization relatively easy. She knew what to recommend, what to buy, and how to dress him for the cold—temperatures can be brutal there. She made sure to protect him from the potentially life-threatening conditions. *After waiting eighteen years for his return, I don't wanna lose him because I didn't dress him properly.*

On Jake's winter weekends, if they weren't skiing, they were snowmobiling or cutting firewood unless the weather was too brutal. On those days, which they relished, barring unforeseen calamities, they would spend the day wrapped up and *resting*, which usually resulted in making love multiple times. Matti had a way of *teasing* Jake that drove him crazy.

The wood-burning stove was the focal point of the living room. In front of it was a bear skin, tanned and made into a rug. The hair on the hide was long and luxurious. Jake had attached thick carpet padding underneath, making it soft and comfortable to lie on. The room was large enough that walking on it was considered *sinful*. Of course, acts of procreation were perfectly acceptable. With the heat of the fire keeping them warm, the sight of Matti's blonde hair and fair skin, naked against the dark fur of the bear skin rug, was irresistible to Jake. It became one of their favorite spots for such endeavors. Their relationship was thriving.

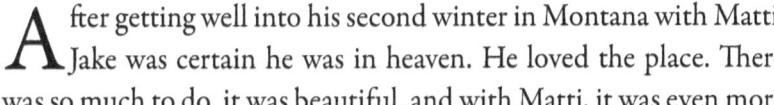

After getting well into his second winter in Montana with Matti, Jake was certain he was in heaven. He loved the place. There was so much to do, it was beautiful, and with Matti, it was even more special. He had proven to himself he could endure the winters.

Having decided he could *not* have been happier, Jake decided to ask Matti to marry him. Then it occurred to him. *Wait a minute, dumbass. What are you thinking? What if she says 'No'? Why would I want to screw up something so perfect? Maybe she'll be uncomfortable about getting married again. Maybe I should re-think this.*

He almost backed out.

After a day or two of careful deliberation, Jake broached the question a little differently. "Matti, would you think it a good idea that we got married—or a stupid one? I mean, I'd really love for you to be my wife, and I'd truly love to be your husband, but do you think it might screw things up somehow?"

Matti looked up and smiled, "Jake, *Honey*, that's way too complicated a question for me to answer. Simplify it for me, please."

Jake sheepishly smiled and replied, "Okay. Will you marry me? I love you *so much*. Whaddya say?"

Wrapping her arms around his neck, Matti said, "I thought you'd *never* ask."

Before long, they were wrapped in a blanket on the floor in the living room, on the bear skin rug—naked and exhausted. They discussed when they should hold the ceremony and officially tie the knot.

They decided a summer wedding might be best. That's when Jake mentioned, "The 22nd of July is Mom and Dad's anniversary."

Matti immediately responded, "Oh! Do you think they'll mind us appropriating their wedding date? We'll need to call them to get their permission and invite them to the wedding. Maybe they won't like sharing that date. You never know. It might be personal to them."

"Oh, *hell* no! Knowing my folks, they'll be thrilled! Trust me. But you're right. We need to ask them. It's the right thing to do. We'll give them a call tomorrow."

Matti snuggled into Jake's shoulder, tears welling in her eyes, and said, "I've dreamt of this moment even before I left the farm so many years ago. I kept telling myself it would never happen but I never gave up hope. There were times I nearly did, but I held on. Now, look at us. Nothing can stop us now. Right, Honey?"

"Right, baby. We'll call my folks tomorrow evening and start making arrangements."

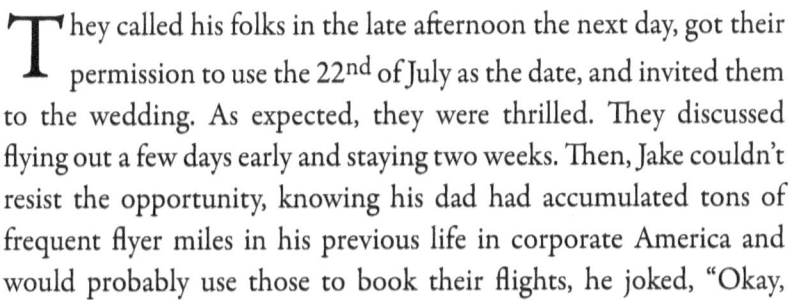

They called his folks in the late afternoon the next day, got their permission to use the 22nd of July as the date, and invited them to the wedding. As expected, they were thrilled. They discussed flying out a few days early and staying two weeks. Then, Jake couldn't resist the opportunity, knowing his dad had accumulated tons of frequent flyer miles in his previous life in corporate America and would probably use those to book their flights, he joked, "Okay, Mom. I'm sure I don't need to tell you this, but it's cheaper if you buy your tickets soon."

Linda snickered. "I'm not even going to respond to that. I'll let you know the details of our flight schedule when we get them worked out. Bye, and congratulations."

Jake and Matti were excited. After they hung up, Matti's grandmother was next to be invited. A call that would take an hour. Granny was ecstatic. She was eighty-seven years young and said, "You're finally marrying Jake? Absolutely, I'll be attending the wedding. I love him. This time, you've got it right, my dear."

Granny didn't like to fly, so she figured she'd recruit someone to accompany her to help drive. "It's a long trip from East Tennessee, you know."

Jake and Matti spent the next few days inviting other family members, most of whom they knew couldn't make the trip, but they wanted them all to know the fantastic news. It seemed everyone in Matti's family knew of her love for Jake all these years and was happy for her.

Jake heard from Linda that Greg had secured airline tickets for them to arrive on Wednesday, the 17th of July.

All Jake and Matti had left to do was select someone to officiate the ceremony, pick out the facility, invite the local guests, and all the other things that go into planning a wedding.

About a week later, Shoshoni walked in the side door from the driveway. Nothing unusual about that, but she looked like she didn't feel well.

Matti asked, "What's the matter, sweety? Are you okay?"

Shoshoni paced the floor, struggling to find the words. Finally, she blurted out, "I'm pregnant."

A flood of emotion washed over Matti, but she was able to catch herself before letting it show. Shoshoni was, after all, four years older than Matti when she became pregnant for the first time.

"Are you sure?"

"Yeah. I'm late, so I did one of those home pregnancy tests. It showed up positive, so I went to the clinic to see a doctor to make sure."

"What do you intend to do?"

"Oh, I intend to have the baby if that's what you mean, *Mother*."

"I figured that. I was just wondering if you even know who the father is and if you intend to marry him." Bracing herself for an angry response, Matti knew Shoshoni was in no position to raise a baby.

Shoshoni's face turned red. She looked like she was about to explode, "*Yes, I know who the father is!* But I'm not going to marry him. I'm seeing someone else now. Me and the baby's father just don't get along. We're like oil and water."

"Does your new boyfriend know?"

"He knows the home test was positive, and it was from before he and I hooked up, but that's about all he knows so far. I came straight here from the doctor's office, and he gave me a due date. That's kinda why I stopped by."

Matti, puzzled, responded, "Oh, what did he tell you?"

"Doctor says I'm due on July 23rd."

"Of course you are!" Matti said incredulously. "You can't make this up."

Matti could see Shoshoni did feel awful about the timing. She had only learned about the wedding plans a few days earlier. The irony was inescapable.

Though Shoshoni felt terrible, she was struggling to avoid breaking out in laughter. "I knew you'd be upset. You probably think I did this on purpose."

"No, I'm sure you didn't plan it." Tears were welling in Matti's eyes as she continued, "It just seems like your actions, whether planned or not, always seem to take a huge dump on my dreams."

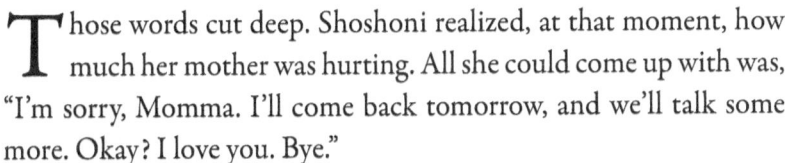

Those words cut deep. Shoshoni realized, at that moment, how much her mother was hurting. All she could come up with was, "I'm sorry, Momma. I'll come back tomorrow, and we'll talk some more. Okay? I love you. Bye."

With that, Shoshoni headed out the door.

Matti sat down in a chair to have a hard cry before getting ready for work. On that particular day, she was scheduled for the early night shift, meaning she had to report by 4:30 PM to start at 5.

Since she had to leave before Jake was expected home, Matti left him a note that read:

"Got some news today we'll need to discuss tonight over dinner. Should be home around 9. See ya then.

Love,
Me"

J ake's day was challenging, and he didn't get home until about 7:30. He saw the note and immediately called Matti. She happened to be on a call when her phone rang. She saw it was her fiancé but couldn't answer. She let it fall into voicemail.

Suddenly, Jake worried. He called the station to check and see if something might have happened to his bride-to-be. His relationship with the folks at headquarters made it easy to find out she was busy working a traffic accident. He felt better.

He decided to get out of his soiled clothes, shower, and get dinner started.

While he was in the shower, Matti returned his call. Of course, Jake didn't hear the phone ringing and never thought to look at it until after Matti arrived home.

When she walked in the door, the first thing Jake said to her was, "Why didn't you call me back?"

"I did. You didn't answer, so I left a voicemail."

Embarrassed, Jake said, "Oh. I musta been in the shower. I'm sorry."

Matti smiled, kissed him on the cheek, and said, "I love you."

Over dinner, she shared the news about Shoshoni's pregnancy.

To say Jake was not happy would be an understatement. "*Oh! That's just fucking great!* That's just what she needs! How does she intend to take care of a child? She can't even take care of herself, for Christ's sake!"

"I know. But you haven't heard the best part. You wanna guess her due date?"

"No! Not July 22nd! It can't be. You've got to be kidding. Right?" Jake was beside himself.

Matti, almost laughing, tried to calm him, "No, no. It's not July 22nd." Then, after a long pause, "It's the 23rd."

"YOU'VE GOT TO BE SHITTING ME!!!! THAT MAY BE EVEN WORSE. OH MY GOD. THAT LITTLE BITCH DID THIS ON PURPOSE! I'M GOING TO KILL HER."

With that bit of tirade, they both broke into uncontrollable laughter. After they calmed down a little, Matti said, "I'm sure she didn't do it on purpose. She's just not that good at planning anything. But it is the most ironic thing that has ever happened to me, or us in this case. It's so awful, it's hilarious. You couldn't make this up if you tried."

Jake followed, saying, "I know. What are we going to do? We can't have our wedding on the 22nd and the baby arrive on or near the same day. No matter what, one overshadows the other. It's not fair to either."

"I know, but your folks and my folks have already made plans—bought airline tickets and everything," Matti said.

After some discussion, Jake and Matti decided to marry in a simple ceremony right away, in April, and hold a reception on July 22nd instead.

Matti suggested, "Honey, the reception could be billed as a party with a threefold purpose: to celebrate our wedding, without holding one; the 52nd anniversary of your mom and dad; and to welcome the arrival of Shoshoni's new baby. That way, all the relatives would have multiple reasons to still come without having to change their original plans. Wouldn't that work?"

Jake replied, "Brilliant!"

Now, all they had to do was tell their relatives back East and let Shoshoni know they weren't going to kill her. She would be relieved.

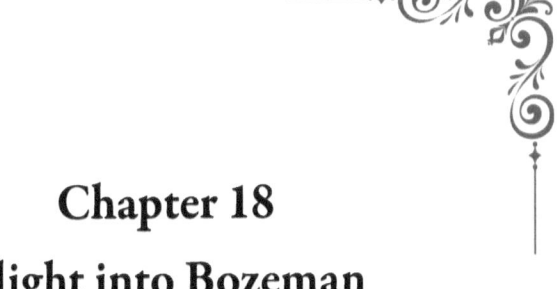

Chapter 18
Flight into Bozeman

Jake and Matti officially were married the weekend after the ski hill closed to the public in early April. There was still adequate snow on the ground, but it was beginning to melt, and the conditions were icy. The owner of Garnet Mountain agreed to open that Saturday expressly for their wedding.

With the veil attached to her ski helmet, Matti accompanied the preacher, best man, maid of honor, and Jake as they rode the designated lift to its culmination, where the ceremony would take place.

At an elevation of 7,000 feet, the wind was whipping. In anticipation, the bride and groom wore their brightly-colored, insulated ski coveralls. The maid of honor exhibited a massive, white, ornate gown, large enough to fit over her winter apparel. The preacher braced himself against the cold in the robe he would wear on any given Sunday, draped over his down-filled jumpsuit and boots.

It was a *short* ceremony. They exchanged vows. The preacher said, "I now pronounce you man and wife. You may kiss the bride." The kiss was, perhaps, the quickest of their time together, and they led the foursome down the slope on their skis to the cheering crowd waiting below.

The wedding was a success, and the party carried on for several hours in the warmth of the lodge before the owner hollered, "Okay, my friends. You don't have to go home, but you can't stay here. We've got to close up for the season. See you next year. Love you all, and congratulations to Matti and Jake."

A few months later, Greg and Linda were on their way, scheduled to arrive in Bozeman at 9:40 PM. It was the 17th of July, five days before the wedding reception and six days before the expected arrival of the new baby.

Unfortunately, Jake was scheduled to participate in a county government meeting that evening. He was heavily involved with Montana Fish, Wildlife & Parks and feared what was on the docket would likely go long, so he asked Matti if she'd provide the necessary delivery services for her new *in-laws*.

"Oh, sure. I'll do your *dirty work*, Honey. Don't you worry about a thing. It'll give me a chance to do some shopping in Bozeman anyway."

Jake objected. "Hey, wait a minute. Who said anything about *shopping*?"

Matti smiled. "You didn't think running your errands was gonna be done for free, did you?"

Pretending to be exasperated, Jake replied, "I suppose not ... but I hoped we could take it out in trade."

"Ha!" Matti chuckled. "You've got that backwards, I'm afraid. All *I* have to do to get that from you is show up. I'm gonna need some *shoppin'* to make this errand right, big fella."

She laughed as she grabbed a piece of scrap paper and a pen. "This list is gonna be a long one."

Matti had worked the previous day and had to the next, as well. She figured if things went as planned, she'd have the arriving parties and their bags in the vehicle and on the road before eleven. The two-hour drive would put them back at home by 1 AM. Conceivably, she could get three hours of sleep—if she was lucky—figuring she'd end up visiting for a while before turning in.

It would be worse. A freak storm blew through and tied up air traffic over the entire northwest for several hours. All Fights were grounded, and it happened *after* Matti had already arrived in Bozeman to do her shopping. She had little choice but to stay and wait it out. She called Linda.

"Yeah. We heard there's a bad storm up there. There's been no indication about when we can expect to leave, so Greg and I are just sittin' here in Minneapolis drinkin' ourselves stupid. There's nothin' else to do. We don't dare leave the gate area. It'd be our luck the plane would take off without us." She and Matti laughed together.

"I know. I've checked the radar. The good news is it appears to be moving fast. It's a big one, but it's heading quickly into Canada, so you shouldn't have to wait much longer. If I weren't facing a two-hour drive home in the dark with precious cargo aboard, I'd start drinkin', too."

"What 'precious cargo'?" Linda asked.

"You guys."

"Oh. Silly girl." Linda burst into laughter.

Despite the Bozeman airport's efficiency, the baggage handling speed, and how close Matti parked to the front door, she would get less than two hours of sleep before returning to work the next day. Greg and Linda's plane didn't land in Bozeman until well past midnight.

It was summer, and the adult co-ed softball season was nearing its
finale. It's a big thing in those parts, and Jake, Matti, and Shoshoni
all played on the same team, along with several of their closest
friends.

Fearing this may not be what his folks wanted to do while in
Montana, Jake broached the subject anyway. "Mom, Dad, this
afternoon is the season's next-to-last game before the year-end
tournament. Now, it's not like we're in the hunt for the league
championship or anything like that, but would you like to come and
watch?"

His mother responded, "After all the years I spent sitting on
bleachers watching you play sports, I never thought I'd drive clear
across the country to do it again."

Everyone chuckled, along with Jake, who bellowed, "I know.
Right? But you didn't drive. You took a plane."

Linda, still grinning, ignored her son's comment and said, "If
it weren't for Matti and this new great-grandbaby on the way, I
wouldn't go, but because of them, you can't keep us away."

"Excellent. Dad, why don't you ride with me? Mom, you can ride
with the girls. Okay?"

"That'll be perfect. I've already spent *way* too much time in those
planes and stuck in airports with your father. Take him off my hands,
will ya'?"

Feigning outrage, Greg responded. "Hey! I'm right here."

"Oh, I'm sorry, Honey. Did you hear that?" Linda replied as she
quickly headed to Matti's side.

Matti wrapped her arm around her and said, "Come on, Mom.
Let's git outta here b'fore you stir up any more trouble."

"I think that's a good idea," Linda giggled as they ran toward her
daughter-in-law's truck.

Chuckling, Greg yelled in their direction. "Yeah, a 'good idea,'
indeed. There's safety in numbers."

When Jake stopped at a convenience store on the way to the ballpark, his father asked "Why are we stopping here?"

Jake waited until the truck came to a stop before responding. Without looking in his dad's direction, he put the shifter in *Park*, shut off the engine, and took a deep breath. Then, as if astonished at the stupidity of the question, he turned and said, "Beer. We can't play the game without beer, Dad. Do you think we're heathens?"

Greg burst out laughing as they jumped out of the truck from either side. "Oh! My bad. What was I thinking? Of course not. I guess it's just been so long since I've played ball, I didn't remember *beer* as part of the standard equipment."

Greg was reveling in having this *time* with his son. It had been nearly two years since they'd seen each other. Oh, they spoke regularly on the phone, at least once a week, but Greg missed his son terribly.

They entered the store, and the clerk behind the cash register, in a loud voice, hollered, *"S'up, Jake."*

"Hey, Joseph. How ya' doin'?"

As they walked on, his father asked, "Do you know everyone in this town?"

"It pays to know everybody, Pop."

They carried two cases of beer to the cashier, where Jake was about to pay when Joseph said, "I didn't know you had a brother."

"He's not my brother! He's my dad, Joseph. His name is Greg. He's here visiting." Shaking his head, Jake continued, *"Brother.* Do you know how tired I am of hearing that?"

"I bet you are," Joseph responded. "You two look so much alike, but with your beard turning grey like it is, pretty soon your dad's gonna look like the *younger* brother." No one could hold back the laughter.

"You're *killing* me, Joseph. This is the last time I'm *ever* coming in here. The only place I get more abuse than this is at home! Oh. By the way, add two big bags of ice, too, please."

"*Okay*. Since you're *never* coming back, I want to get all the money out of you I can on *this* trip."

Jake laughed. "I'm sure you do."

After settling up, Jake looked at his dad, patted the cases of beer, and said, "If you carry these, I'll get the ice and meet you at the truck. Then we'll dump them together in that big cooler."

"Perfect. I'll meet you at the truck."

As they walked out the door together, Jake yelled, "See you tomorrow, Joseph."

"I look forward to it, my friend."

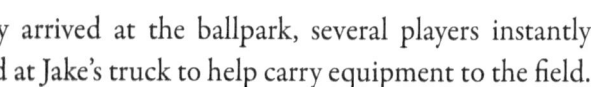

When they arrived at the ballpark, several players instantly appeared at Jake's truck to help carry equipment to the field. Jake seized the opportunity to introduce his dad, and they headed off together across the parking lot.

That oversized beer cooler, eagerly carried by a player on each end, solidified in Greg's mind the team was in it for fun. It became glaringly apparent when his son, in the second inning, went to the mound to pitch with his beer can in hand. Winning *wasn't* their primary objective.

On this night, though, they had a cheering section—Greg and Linda—and they were vocal.

Shoshoni, four or five days shy of her due date, decided she *was* going to play. Linda, of course, was aghast. Dressed in all black, something resembling maternity yoga pants and a shirt that stretched tightly over her belly, Shoshoni's outfit clung to the contours of her body. Linda remarked, "Honey, looking from behind, no one could tell you're pregnant, but when you turn sideways—WOW!"

Shoshoni just smiled and cocked her head.

Linda admonished, "Are you sure you should be playing?"

"I'm gonna get this baby outta me one way or another." She would play first base.

When she stepped into the batter's box for the first time, Shoshoni's belly stuck clear out over home plate. Linda yelled to the pitcher, "Don't hit the baby!"

Everybody on both teams laughed hysterically and then loudly echoed the chant, "Don't hit the baby! Don't hit the baby!" It seemed to come from everywhere.

Linda didn't say it to be funny. She worried about Shoshoni playing at all, but after that first shout-out, the chant erupted organically every time she came to bat. It was a beautiful thing.

When she hit the ball, Shoshoni tried hard to run and support her belly on the journey to first base. When the umpire called her "out," everyone in the cheering section considered it a blessing. When she made it successfully the first time, Jake called a timeout.

He hollered at the umpire and asked, "Could I substitute a runner for my first baseman? Unless someone might be up for maybe delivering a baby right here on the playing field. Whaddya say, ump?"

"I thought you'd never ask," he replied, looking to the opposing team captain to see if *he* had any objections. Seeing none, the ump motioned his approval. A substitute ran in to take Shoshoni's place.

Linda was relieved. *At least she won't have to run the bases, poor thing.*

She had learned Shoshoni had been in and out of the hospital suffering from kidney stones in the days leading up to the game. This being her first child, the mother-to-be thought she was having contractions. Linda worried about her.

The cheering section must have inspired the players, or the ball bounced their way. Their team came away with a victory in a game filled with much laughter, good sportsmanship, no injuries, and lots of fun. From all accounts, both teams had a great time, and, from all appearances, only one beer was spilled.

Since the team's sponsor was on the hook for a free drink plus an appetizer, everybody headed to the tavern where Shoshoni was voted *most valuable player!*

Throughout his life, Jake was a guy people liked to hang around. He was always a gregarious fellow, and so it was in Montana. When he and Matti got together, and with everyone knowing her and their engagement in so many activities, they had many friends. They led exciting lives. People gravitated to them. And so, when the team dispersed from the tavern that evening, some of the players followed Jake, Matti, Greg, and Linda back to the house.

After an hour or two, Matti excused herself and retired to shower and head off to bed. She had been going on very little sleep and had to work the next day, too. *One more wake-up before my vacation starts. When I clock out tomorrow, I'm done for nine whole days.*

The remaining partiers took the hint, but it still took nearly an hour for the last of them to get out of the house and the lights to go out.

Shortly before Jake got home from work the following evening, Matti's eighty-seven-year-old grandmother, Emma Lu, and a friend arrived by car from Tennessee. Before the ladies could drag themselves from the vehicle, the welcoming committee swarmed the SUV.

"Granny!" Matti exclaimed, leaning in to hug her. "I'm so glad you could make it. Who's this you brought with ya'?" she said as she pulled away and headed toward the driver's side.

Emma Lu couldn't respond since Shoshoni, bent over the bulging baby in her tummy, was squeezing her great-grandmother so hard she could not speak as she helped her out of the car.

Stepping from the vehicle, the driver, looking to be in her mid-seventies, said, "Hi. I'm Rose." "You must be Matti. Your grandmother and I have been friends for years. She wasn't comfortable making this drive alone, so she asked me to join her." Smiling from ear to ear, she continued, "We've had a ball. Kinda like Thelma and Louise."

"Well, it's good to know you, Rose. Welcome. I hope this trip doesn't end like the movie," Matti replied with a huge laugh. "Please make sure you both get back home in one piece."

Emma Lu announced to the group, which had grown to include Greg and Linda, "Now that I can speak, thank you, Shoshoni, I'd like to say how grateful I am that Rose came along on this journey. I don't think I could have made it without her help. Thank you, dear friend," and she smiled in her direction.

Matti replied, "Well, you're both welcome here. Let's help y'all get inside. Rose, we've got an inflatable mattress prepared for you upstairs. There's not much privacy, I'm afraid, but I hope it'll work out okay.

"Granny, I don't expect you'll wanna climb those stairs, so we've got another air mattress we can put up in the livin' room. Would that be alright with you?"

"Let's get in there and see whatcha got." Once inside, Emma Lu looked around and said, "If it's all the same to you, I'd just as soon sleep on the sofa. I'm little, and it'll suit me just fine. B'side's I don't wanna be no trouble."

"Trouble? Granny, you can sleep in my bed if you want. You ain't no trouble a'tall."

"Ha! That ain't happenin', child. If it's alright with you, this sofa'll do me fine."

Chapter 19
The Ailing Mare

As Greg enjoyed the first sips of his morning coffee, Jake appeared from around the corner and said, "Mornin', Pop. Would you like to ride with me to check on Shoshoni's mare?"

"And a beautiful mornin' it is, son. I'd be happy to, but I didn't know she had a horse."

"She does, but it seems it's been injured. I'll share all the gory details on the way. You ready?"

"Can I take my coffee?"

"Sure. But let's pour it into this cup." He reached into the cupboard and pulled down one of those expensive, stainless steel, insulated cups with a lid. "The road out there ain't the smoothest and I wanna get this over with."

As they climbed into his truck, Jake explained, "We need to go out to the boarding facility where she keeps her. She, Matti, and Karson owned horses together when they were a family."

On the way, as they watched the fenceposts blur past the windows, Jake explained, "Despite the divorce, Karson's still very much a part of their lives, and somehow, they still get along well—prob'ly better than they ever have." He laughed. "Karson let Shoshoni keep her horse, and he pays the board bill for her. Matti still has her mare—and a gelding—but she keeps them at her other daughter's place about four hours from here."

Jake looked at his dad and continued, laughing, "I guess it was too much to ask the ex-husband to pay board for the ex-wife's horses, too."

Chuckling and laying on the sarcasm, Greg replied, "No! Who could expect an ex-husband to do that?" Jake couldn't help but appreciate the humor and joined in.

"But, given Shoshoni's condition, she hasn't been out to see her mare in the last couple of months. She got a call from the gal that runs the barn telling her about a puncture wound. Said she must have gotten it while in the pasture. She didn't think it was a problem at the time but wanted Shoshoni to be aware.

"Well, now it seems to be a problem, and we're going out to see how bad it is."

"I see. So, this guy, Karson, is Matti's most recent ex-husband?"

Jake nodded, "Correct."

Greg responded, "But when Matti worked for us, I thought she was married to... wasn't his name Bruce? No, Bryce. That was it, Bryce. Wasn't that it? Bryce?"

"Yeah. That's right. But she divorced him a long time ago. Then, after a few years, she married Karson. He's a good guy. I like him a lot. So does Shoshoni. In fact, she calls *him* 'dad.' Still to this day."

Confused, Greg replied, "Well, how long has Karson been out of the picture?"

"I can't say he is 'out of the picture' at all. He's gonna be here for the reception. He'll be stayin' in our camper, in the driveway while he's here—eating and partying with us—and showering in our house, I suspect. We get along fine. You'll like him, too. You'll see.

"He and Matti divorced about a year before she and I got back together, so he knows I had nothing to do with their break up—other than she never quit loving me in the first place."

"Holy crap, Jake. This is freaking amazing. Shoshoni calls Karson 'dad,' but he's not her biological father. That would have been Bryce, right?"

"Actually ... no. That's a long story. Matti was pregnant when she married Bryce, but not by him. He knew about the pregnancy and wanted to marry her anyway."

"Wow! I'm confused. I'm eager to hear the 'long story', but for now, I can't wait to meet Karson. He must be quite a guy," Greg said as they arrived at their destination.

When they walked toward the barn, the facility manager was nowhere to be seen, but Natalia was there with a man who looked strangely familiar to Greg, but he couldn't quite place him. They nodded to each other and exchanged a polite "Hey."

Jake did the same and looked at Natalia, saying, "How's the mare? Have you seen her?"

"Yeah. She looks real sore to me."

Jake walked on toward the stall. She had positioned herself with her butt toward the door and her head facing the opposite corner. She was standing on three legs with the sore one lifted, resting the toe of her hoof on the ground to avoid bearing any weight on her left front.

When Jake slid the stall door open, Greg couldn't help himself, saying, "*That's* not good."

The barn was fitted with wooden shutters to shield the windows against harsh weather—wind, rain, and snow—but they also kept out light. It was summer, and her's was closed. The stall was dark. Nonetheless, Jake could see evidence of drainage coming from a wound high on her leg, very near her shoulder. It looked as though she might have run into a protrusion in a tree or the fence.

Jake asked his dad, "Do you see a halter and lead rope hanging anywhere out there? We need to get her out into the sunlight."

Greg handed his son the necessary equipment. Jake gently slipped the halter past the mare's muzzle and tied it behind her ears while talking calmly, reassuring her that everything would be alright.

He led her out of the stall to an area a few feet in front of the barn. She was reluctant but hobbled the best she could on three legs into the daylight—probably for the first time in several days.

"Hold her for a minute, Pop? We need to irrigate her shoulder. I'll go get the water hose and turn on the spigot."

Greg took hold of the lead, "Couldn't agree more, son."

It became immediately apparent the mare appreciated the cool water. She also enjoyed the bits of carrots Jake brought along.

After several minutes, the water softened the dried drainage that had collected on the mare's leg, and Jake could easily wash it off with a slight rubbing.

Greg occupied the mare's mind with calm whispers, petting her muzzle and a bite of carrot now and then while his son focused on her leg. The mare began to trust Jake's gentleness and let him continue without resistance.

Jake examined the wound. "The problem is, there's no way to tell how deep this puncture is or if there's any debris left inside."

"I *know*. But, *my* concern is its proximity to the shoulder and whether or not the joint's compromised. There's no doubt infection's set in."

Jake's ire was palpable. "Yeah. The vet needs to see this. I 'spect he'll shoot some X-rays."

Even though he was a newcomer to the situation, Greg was fuming.

After a few more minutes of hydrotherapy, Jake administered an oral antibiotic and pain medication he brought along. Since they had done all they could, and the carrot bits were gone, it was time to put the mare back in her stall.

Jake and his dad returned to the truck without another word spoken or any introductions given or received.

Once they got inside and the doors closed, Greg couldn't hold back his emotions. "That mare's poundin' on death's door! She's *sufferin'*. *If* she can be saved from the injury, she'll likely founder during recovery and have to be put down in the end anyway. If she were to recover from the founder, it's not likely she'll be rideable after that, at least not reliably. The bill to save her will end up being ten times her value at least."

Jake replied, "At least! What *really* pisses me off is the barn manager. How long has she been like this? I mean, I know Shoshoni should have been out here more often, even though she is pregnant, but the manager of this place should be shot for letting it go this long."

"I agree. Especially with the trouble Shoshoni's having right now, in and out of the hospital and all. What are you gonna do?"

Before he could answer, Jake raised his finger to interrupt his dad and began leaving a voice message for the veterinarian. After he ended the call, he said, "Now, I'm gonna try and get in touch with the manager of this place."

Over the next several minutes, he engaged in a heated discussion about the mare. Jake learned the manager had an early doctor's appointment and was on her way to the barn as they spoke.

"Jazzy's condition didn't get this way overnight. You couldn't have missed it yesterday if you'd even *looked* at her." Jake didn't try to hide his fury. He continued with instructions on caring for her going forward, including the antibiotic and pain medication until the vet could get there, figuring it might not be later that day. Of course, prescribing and administering medication *was* a bit beyond his purview, but he did it anyway, given the circumstances.

Once it was clear the call had ended and they were pulling out of the facility, Greg asked, "Jazzy?"

"Yeah. Shoshoni says she liked to dance when she rides her, hence the name."

"Ah. I get it. I don't think she'll be doin' much dancin' anytime soon. When do you expect the vet to call back? And, who were those people who met us at the barn?"

"Who knows about the vet? I didn't expect to get an answer. That's pretty much SOP. We'll see.

"The girl was Natalia. She's the young lady Shoshoni lives with now. The guy was Ty, Shoshoni's biological father. I guess he's come up to see his new grandson, which is odd since he hasn't been much a part of Shoshoni's life all these years. I didn't know he was coming. I'm surprised. He lives in Tennessee. I hope he behaves himself. You never know about him. Come to think of it, you've met him before. He's been to the farm."

"I thought he looked familiar," Greg said. "Must have been a long time ago." Then, after a brief pause, "But that's not the guy Matti was married to when she worked for us, right?"

Jake answered, "That's correct. That would have been Bryce. Ty was the one who impregnated her, but Matti couldn't see herself being married to him. Smart move, too. He later spent time in prison for dealing drugs."

"Oh, smart move indeed," Greg agreed. "So, do you expect Bryce to show up, too? This could end up being a real shit show. How do you expect Karson and Ty to get along?"

"I'm not sure how that might go, but I'm confident in Karson's ability to keep things cool."

Greg forced a smile and asked, "What's next?"

"Well, I've been thinking about this ever since we walked into the mare's stall. The first thing I'll do is talk with Matti, fill her in on the mare's condition, and see what she thinks is best. With Shoshoni being in and out of the hospital like she is, I'll be surprised if she wants to share this news with her right now. We'll see."

"I see wisdom is finally visiting you. I'm happy for you, son." Despite the situation, they laughed together.

Jake and Matti talked. "I think we're obligated to share the news with Karson since he's paying the board bill and other costs associated with the mare."

Matti used her phone to place the call and put it on speaker. Jake explained the situation. Karson responded, saying, "I think Shoshoni should make any decisions about *her* mare."

Matti spoke up, saying, "We agree, except she's in the hospital *again*, and I don't think this is the right time to dump this on her. She's having a *real* tough time of it right now, and something like this might push her over the edge."

"Oh. I had no idea. I get where you're comin' from. We prob'ly should wait, then. Let's see what the vet has to say, look at the X-rays, and evaluate the situation from there. Sound good?"

Later that evening, their softball team played their last game of the regular season. On this night, the cheering section for the home team had doubled. In addition to Greg and Linda, the crowd now included Granny and Rose.

Shoshoni couldn't play because the hospital *refused* to release her, but Matti was catching behind home plate. Jake was on the mound—with his beer.

They played the best team in the league, that had gone undefeated all season. Despite the intense crowd noise, the home team lost—badly—by the ten-run rule in the sixth inning. "If only Shoshoni could have played. Maybe *that* would have turned the tide," Jake hollered in jest as he walked toward the bleachers and the awaiting fans.

Later that evening, the twentieth, Ava, one of Matti's cousins, arrived. Rose and Granny picked her up at the airport and made it back to the house sometime after midnight. Another inflatable mattress had been prepared upstairs, again with little privacy, adding one more to share the small bathroom up there.

While Ava, Matti, and Granny were all very close—related by blood and grew up together—Greg and Linda had never met Ava or Rose, nor had Rose and Ava ever crossed paths. Despite that, somehow, it didn't even seem awkward. Everybody got along great—seamlessly. The chemistry worked.

Jake and Matti had strategized and planned activities to keep their guests busy in the days leading up to the wedding reception ... and the arrival of River. They had *not* prepared for the difficulty Shoshoni would experience and the numerous trips in and out of the hospital.

Karson arrived the next day, the twenty-first, in the middle of the afternoon. He'd been on the road for several days and was thankful when Matti offered him the use of their shower.

When it looked like the house couldn't hold another person, Jake saw a car pull up in front of the house. It was Natalia, and Ty was with her. He quickly headed out to meet them, saying, "Given Shoshoni's current circumstances, we haven't mentioned her mare's condition. We think it's best to wait until the vet assesses the situation before breaking the news."

Reluctantly, they agreed to avoid any discussion about Jazzy's condition.

With that, Jake welcomed them into his home. "Try to squeeze in. Things are kinda tight, but make yourselves as comfortable as possible. You wanna beer?"

Afterward, they all had dinner together. There were ten that evening, eating wherever one could find a spot since the table could only seat six. Everyone staying at the house was there, and Shoshoni had been released from the hospital, too. Sean had dropped by with his dog, a young Golden Retriever named Sax.

Granny started a big pot of potatoes, green beans, and ham earlier in the day. It proved a great move because everybody had plenty to eat, and they loved it.

Linda watched as everyone helped themselves to the food from the seemingly endless kettle and remarked to Granny, "I don't know how that one pot of ham, beans, and potatoes is feeding all these people."

Granny, deeply religious, replied, "It's kinda like the miracle of the 'loaves and fishes,' isn't it, darlin'?"

Linda smiled and nodded in agreement.

Food and beer were plentiful, the mood was happy, and everybody enjoyed getting to know one another or renewing acquaintances, telling tales, and spinning yarns.

After Karson got comfortable, especially with the new *in-laws*, it became apparent why he, Matti, and Jake could still get along. He fit in easily. Greg and Linda embraced him right away.

The party lasted well into the night. Everyone ate too much, drank too much, and laughed a lot—but behaved admirably.

Gradually, things started dying down. Rose quietly slipped off and climbed the stairs to her bed. Granny stretched out on the couch, and people started getting the hint.

Sean gathered up Sax and addressed the crowd before making his way out the door. "Good night, everybody. It was nice to meet all you folks whom I've never met before. See you at the reception,"

Natalia and Ty said their goodbyes and followed behind.

Shoshoni, Jake, and Karson went out to the driveway to check on the camper, familiarize the evening's occupant with its features, and ensure he had everything he needed. Once accomplished, Jake left them so the two could spend a few minutes of dad-and-daughter time together.

Greg moved furniture back into place and helped gather dishes and debris left by the guests. Ava, Matti, and Linda were doing the more challenging clean-up chores.

When Jake returned inside, seeing the work winding down and his dad a bit bewildered, not knowing what to do, he offered, "Hey, Pop. How about a dram of single malt for a nightcap?"

Greg, without hesitation, responded, "*Perfect*," despite the raised eyebrow of Linda, who was still wiping counters.

The next day, Monday the twenty-secondof July was initially intended to be the day of the reception. However, Jake discovered a few weeks prior that another party had already reserved the pavilion. He decided a postponement of one day was better than finding another, less suitable venue.

With Jake's involvement with Montana Forestry and Parks, often attending county council meetings, and Matti a Deputy Sheriff, they expected several city and county officials to attend.

When Greg learned about the people his son had invited, he said, "Holy cow, Jake. How many people do you expect at this party?"

"You never know, Pop. I'm guessin' somewhere between a hundurd—hundurd-fifty. Maybe more. The mayor said he'd be here."

"The mayor? Seriously?"

"Yeah. I'm involved in so many of those county council meetings. I think he prob'ly feels obligated." Jake chuckled. "And he likes me."

"Always an asset, son."

Karson had to leave that morning to head back to his home in Utah since he had another trip run. "I am so sorry for not being able to stick around for the party but so glad I was able to meet everybody. If everything goes as planned, I'll return to see the new baby on the twenty-sixth.

"Jake, please keep me informed about the vet's opinion on what we need to do regarding the mare. Okay?"

"I surely will."

As it turned out, shortly after Karson left town, was when the vet could finally make it out with the necessary equipment to shoot X-rays. Jake and Greg headed to the barn to get there a little before the vet's scheduled appointment. It's never good for the vet to arrive before the horse's owner or a representative. The bill usually reflects the vet's displeasure with being kept waiting.

Half an hour before the vet was expected, the two men pulled up at the barn. When they walked into Jazzy's stall, they found her lying dead on the floor. Neither was all that surprised, given what they had seen two days before. Tragic though it was, it was a blessing.

Jake quickly called the vet to advise him of the situation. "No need to come. The mare you were coming to examine has died."

His next call was to fulfill his promise. Karson responded, "Well, one thing about it. It saves *us* from having to make the decision to put her down."

"You're right about that. I'll let Matti know, but I can't do it just yet. She took Shoshoni back to the hospital in the wee hours this morning. She's with her as we speak."

Karson mused, "I sure don't think this is something Shoshoni needs to deal with right now. Do you, Jake?"

"Couldn't agree more." They said their goodbyes and ended the call.

Jake then got the barn manager on the phone. "Do you know you've got a dead mare in your barn?"

She screeched, "What?"

"Yep. Jazzy's dead. It's 11 AM. You're the barn manager, and you don't even know it. Rigor mortis has already set in, so she's been dead for at least an hour or two. I assume she was alive when you fed this morning. Or did you feed? Have you even *been* to the barn yet today? This is not a good look for you, *barn manager.*"

She defensively replied, "I had another early doctor's appointment this morning and just got back. I haven't been down there yet. I am *sooo* sorry. I'll be there in just a minute."

When she arrived, Jake expressed his displeasure... again. He then worked with her regarding arrangements for the mare to be buried at the facility. "I would like to ask that Jazzy's tail and forelock be brushed, braided, and clipped so they can be given to Shoshoni after her baby arrives. Would you do that for me?

"Shoshoni's been in and out of the hospital with this pregnancy, so we haven't even told her about the severity of her mare's injury. We don't intend to tell her about any of this until we know she and her baby are safe. She doesn't need any more stress in her life right now. I hope you'll respect our wishes about keeping this on the hush-hush." The barn manager understood and agreed.

As they pulled out of the driveway, Greg asked, "How you bettin' on this secret bein' kept?"

"Ha! With all the players involved, I'd say the safe money's against it."

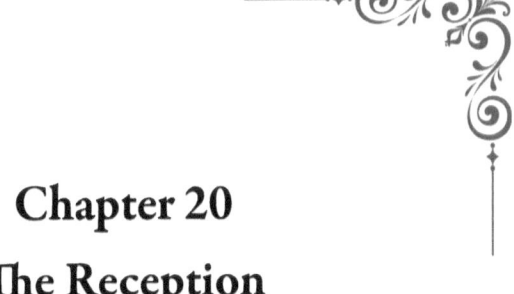

Chapter 20
The Reception

L ate morning on the twenty-third, long before the crowd began to assemble at the pavilion, Jake, with his dad in tow, arrived to prepare for the day's festivities.

Jake was in his element. He had decided to treat his guests to something many in that part of the world had never experienced—a *low-country boil.*

He gathered huge pots, propane burners, and everything else needed to make it happen. What equipment Jake didn't already have, he borrowed from neighbors and friends. He had brought in crawfish and shrimp from Louisiana.

From a local butcher friend of his, he purchased andouille sausage. The day before, he and his father stopped by the local grocery to pick up copious quantities of potatoes, onions, butter, and corn on the cob.

Jake explained to his dad, "The trick to the perfect low-country boil is knowing when to add each ingredient. Some take longer to cook than others, and since everything's cooking in the same pot, timing is critical. But we can't forget the seasonings. I have my own special concoction.

"And, when y're feedin' this many people all at once, the task becomes a bit more challenging."

Jake envisioned the space and noticed the only potable water source, a frost-free hydrant protruding from the ground about fifty feet away from the pavilion. "There's no sense carryin' pots full of water farther than we hafta. The cook station should go here. We'll do that first." Motioning with his hands to an area next to where he was standing, he continued, "We'll drag a picnic table over there for a prep surface."

"I'm on it," Greg replied as he started toward the truck.

Linda and her gaggle of eastern visitors arrived as Jake and his dad assembled the cook station. "What can we do to help?" echoed the question. Neither of the men knew for sure who asked it.

Keenly aware of the challenges of four women trying to get ready with only two bathrooms at their disposal, Jake couldn't resist the opportunity to poke them with a stick. "I'm sure glad y'all could make it. We've about got it now."

Linda playfully smacked her son on the shoulder and said, "Oh, shut up, Jake."

"What? We could have used your help an hour ago. That's all I'm sayin'."

"You two weren't even here an hour ago. Besides, it takes time to get this beautiful in the morning. Doesn't it, girls?" Linda patted her curls as the words left her lips. The ladies gleefully chimed in with their agreement.

Father and son set the picnic table in place for their workstation, and in a complete change of sentiment, Jake asked, "Matti is still at the hospital?"

"Yeah. Shoshoni's due to be released this morning, but you know how that goes. I expect her any time, though. Doc says it was just those darn kidney stones and not contractions. Matti called me on the drive here. She said she tried to call you, but it went directly to voicemail."

"Yeah. I'm not surprised. We're in kind of a canyon here. Cell coverage might be dicey. Hope the girl gets better. Today's supposed to be a party, and it's tough to have a good time when you're feelin' poorly."

Shifting his attention to the group and pointing to the picnic table they had just placed, Jake said, "Okaaaay, we thought we'd use this end as our workstation, but you can use the other end for whatever you guys need. Maybe store the paper plates and stuff like that. Will that be enough room for y'all's stuff?"

Linda looked at the girls. They talked among themselves and finally nodded or shrugged. Linda spoke for the group. "We think so. We'll set it up so people can walk by, pick up what they need, and store bigger boxes underneath. Yeah, we can make this work."

"Excellent. If you'll start bringing everything you need from the truck and arranging it how you want, that'd be great." They got to work, and there was *excitement* in the air.

As the girls headed off, guests started to trickle in, and Jake said to his dad, "If you'll chop onions, I'll fill this here pot with water. Better get this show on the road." He started toward the hydrant several yards away.

As his son walked, Greg asked, "How many you want chopped?"

Jake hollered over his shoulder, "How many we got?"

Greg thought about it for a second, then, as if a light bulb went off, responded, "Forget I asked."

Jake smiled, kept walking, and yelled at a softball team member getting out of his truck. "Luke. How's it hangin'? Do me a favor, would ya'?"

Luke waved, "Sure. Whatcha need?"

"There's a buncha stuff in the back of my truck, games, and equipment to keep everybody occupied while the food's a cookin'. Would ya' start draggin' it out and settin' it up for me?"

"No problem."

When Luke got to the back of Jake's truck, his eyes got big. *Holy shit. I'm gonna need some help to set all this up.*

Jake had brought two pairs of corn-hole boards, a badminton set, a volleyball net, and board games for younger kids to keep them occupied. The facility had a horseshoe pit, shoes for tossing, and a basketball goal. Several guests brought fishing poles. There was much to do while their feast was being prepared.

Having watched the exchange between her son and husband unfold, Linda quietly mentioned to Greg, "Convenient having water so close, but why is that pipe sticking so far out of the ground like that? And what kind of gadget is that?"

Greg smiled, "It is convenient, but we're in Montana. It gets cold here. It's called a frost-free hydrant. The pipe is tall, so large containers can be filled under it, like the pot Jake has now.

"Do you see that blue handle on top? It activates a valve deep in the ground, below the frost line. Do you see the rocks at the base of the pipe?"

"Yes. Held in place by the steel ring?"

"Exactly. When Jake pushes that handle down, it closes the valve below ground. All the water in the pipe drains out into those rocks. That's what keeps everything from bursting in the winter."

"Ohhhh. That makes a lot more sense."

Greg thought about it. *Oh, what the heck.* "Don't tell me. When you heard the word *hydrant*, you started looking around for a red *fire* hydrant. Right? It's true, isn't it."

Linda couldn't hide it. "You don't know me." She giggled.

Greg laughed with her and said, "You're so pretty."

Their levity was interrupted when Jake hollered, "Hey, Pop. You wanna help me carry this over to the burner?"

"That thing get a little heavier?"

"It did! I have no idea how much water this damned thing holds, but it's a good thing there's a handle on each side. You see, it's designed to be carried by two people."

"Uh, huh." Greg chuckled as he walked toward his son, wiping his hands. As he grabbed hold of the handle and began to lift, he said, "Dang, this thing *is* heavy."

Jake summoned up his *tough guy* persona, "Nah. Nothin' a man can't handle. I just didn't want to splash water on m'self. B'sides, looked like you was about to cry—needed a break from those onions."

His dad looked up at him with a raised eyebrow, smiled, and murmured, "Mmm-mm." To the burner they walked, being as careful as they could not to spill a drop, trying their best to hold in their laughter.

Jake lit the propane burner under the pot while Greg resumed his kitchen duties. "There's sausage that needs slicin' too," his son reminded him.

Linda asked, "What can we do next?"

Jake replied, "Would you ladies like to start shucking corn? Or, better yet, how about peeling potatoes? We need a bunch of those and cut into bite-sized chunks."

In no time, the ladies had pulled a trash can close, a new liner installed, and the tasks done.

Jake dumped half the potatoes and a bag of his pre-mixed seasonings into the near-boiling water on the burner. He asked Greg to fill the other pot. "It's time to get the next one goin', Pop."

His dad was quick to respond, "Gotcha," and headed to the spigot.

------ ⟋᠙⟍ ------

After deciding the potatoes had reached the appropriate level of *doneness*, Jake added the onions, then, at the right time, the sausage. When the potatoes were soft enough, in went the corn, each cob cut into manageable lengths. The seafood was last to enter the boiling cauldron.

As the pots were cooking, Jake directed two picnic tables be placed together, end-to-end. He then asked Linda to get some help to spread out layers of butcher paper he had brought. "Mom. Would you please get somebody to help you with that big roll and spread it down the length of the two tables? I'll need multiple layers overlapping, so the top's well-covered with at least four thicknesses of paper. Would you do that for me, please?"

Knowing his mother well, Jake said with a smile and no attempt to hide his tease, "I know how you're always trying to save me money, Mom, but on this occasion, please don't. We want clean-up to be easy. Okay?"

The first batch of food was ready as soon as Linda had finished. Jake summoned a friend for help. They each donned potholder mittens and slowly lifted the inner basket out of the cooking pot to allow the boiling water to drain. As they did so, Jake hollered, "Make way, we're coming with treats, and they're HOT!"

Jake and his friend, a deputy with whom Matti worked, each holding a basket handle with the picnic table between them, began dumping hot food, forming a line of steaming delicacies down the center of the butcher paper Linda had just prepared. Greg followed immediately behind, dusting the fare as it fell from the basket with one last measure of seasoning.

When the basket finally emptied, the line of food reached the middle of the second table. Bystanders frantically blocked corn cob sections from rolling off the table's edge while others couldn't stand the temptation. They'd snatch a crawfish or shrimp and look for a trash can to toss the empty shells after they devoured the meat hidden inside.

Jake returned the basket to the cook station and noticed some people staring at the food, wondering what to do. A few started politely putting bits of food on their paper plates. That's when he decided some instructions were in order.

He went to the table and said, "This is how you do it." He reached down, picked up a crawfish, and broke the shell in half, removing the tail section from the upper body. He sucked the head and laid the empty half on the table neatly in front of him. He showed them how to break the tail shell with their fingers to free the meat. He glanced around the crowd before popping it into his mouth, saying, "*Succulent.*" He kissed his fingertips and threw his hand in the air, simulating an explosion.

After discarding the shells in the nearby trash, he noticed a man he didn't recognize holding a plate. Jake asked, "May I borrow that?"

Without hesitation, the surprised fellow handed it to him. Taking it, Jake demonstrated proper etiquette. "If you choose to use a plate or similar device, at some point, you're gonna realize we have a serious shortage of utensils." He paused to nod and lift his arm. "You're gonna get your these things dirty."

His massive hand raised in the air, fingers spread wide and wiggling, Jake said, "Don't be shy." He plunged it into the pile of steaming food like a grappling hook. "Pick up what you want to eat, and put it onto whatever container you have. It's all good. Make sure you get an ear of corn, and then get the hell outta the way."

The paper plate he borrowed barely held what Jake had in his grip. He handed the heaping dish to the attendee from whom it was borrowed, saying, "I hope you don't mind my hands. If it's a problem, I'll gladly enjoy this pile of deliciousness."

His new friend responded, "No, no. I'm guessing your hands have been in this food all day." Briefly examining its contents, he said, "That's everything I was gonna put on that plate myself. Thanks, Jake." He quickly took it from him and headed for a calmer place away from the fray.

With that, Jake let out his signature laugh and yelled, "Dig in everybody!"

Suddenly, there was a mad dash for the food. Many reached in and followed Jake's instructions to the letter. Most would then retire to nearby seating, only to quickly return for seconds or thirds.

Some, lucky enough to get to the main tables first, sat where the food was within arm's reach. They stayed until they were full.

Many stood behind those sitting at the front. They'd reach over the shoulders of the seated and pick whatever they wanted, like poachers. A crawfish or a shrimp, step back to eat it, and toss the shell into the trash can. They'd repeatedly edge their way back for another helping until a seat opened up. Watching it unfold, Greg said to his son, "Reminds me of *musical chairs*. Remember that game?"

Jake laughed, "I know. Right?"

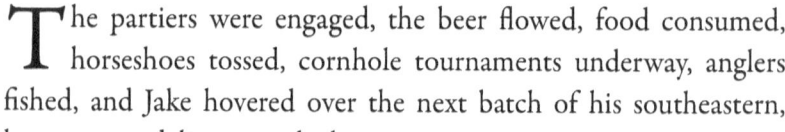

The partiers were engaged, the beer flowed, food consumed, horseshoes tossed, cornhole tournaments underway, anglers fished, and Jake hovered over the next batch of his southeastern, low-country delicacy on the burner.

The feeding frenzy resumed when the second basket was ceremoniously dispensed. In the end, there was virtually nothing left over. The attendees raved about the food. Many had never even heard of a low-country boil, much less eaten that kind of fare.

The mayor indeed did come by, and he stayed about an hour. Shoshoni was there, too, but she wasn't feeling well, seldom wearing a smile. She sat away from the crowd, usually with Matti close at hand.

Shoshoni had worked at a bakery in town until she got too far along in her pregnancy to continue. She couldn't *make* the cake for the party because of her condition, but the creation of its design—that she could handle. Her ex-co-workers took care of the rest.

A beautiful composition depicting all three reasons for the celebration, Shoshoni beamed as she unveiled the cake despite her discomfort. When she opened the enormous box, people close enough to see it couldn't hold back their admiration. "Oh, my." "How beautiful." "Wow!" were only some of the accolades expressed.

Shoshoni summoned as much energy as possible and addressed the crowd. "I'd like to say..." she took a deep breath, "... Congratulations to my mom and Jake on their wedding, to Greg and Linda on their 52nd wedding anniversary, and to my new baby boy, River, who I hope will hurry up and get here so I can get this over with."

The crowd erupted in applause, whistles, and cheers.

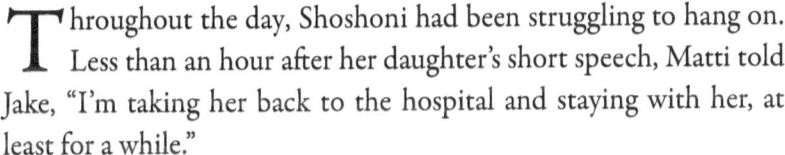

Throughout the day, Shoshoni had been struggling to hang on. Less than an hour after her daughter's short speech, Matti told Jake, "I'm taking her back to the hospital and staying with her, at least for a while."

Seeing the two leave, it didn't take long for the party to start winding down. After the debris was collected and the tables returned to their original locations, Jake and his newfound residents packed the gear and headed back to his house for the evening.

The doctor examined Shoshoni and felt the baby might come during the night. Shoshoni begged her mother, "Momma, please don't leave me. I'm scared."

"I won't leave you, Honey. I'll be right here—by your side."

Matti called Jake and asked him to bring her a change of clothes, her pajamas, a toothbrush, and other grooming supplies. She was staying the night.

Early the following morning, Jake called his wife. "Do we have a new member of the family?"

"Not yet."

After a quick breakfast, Jake and all the temporary residents piled into two vehicles and headed to the hospital.

They arrived and made their way to the appropriate wing. They followed signs to a waiting area. It was a small hospital, and Jake was surprised to see so many people already assembled there, only three of whom he recognized: Natalia, Ty, and Clayton, Shoshoni's current boyfriend. Jake made the introductions as best he could. He politely nodded to the others in the small room with insufficient chairs.

Fortunately, one chair was empty, and Emma Lu, at eighty-seven, made a beeline for it. Ty gave up his so Rose, in her mid-seventies, could sit. But that meant the rest would have to stand leaning against a wall.

Jake had earlier texted Matti that they were on their way to the waiting room, and just as his introductions were wrapping up, she walked in to complete them.

The first she chose to introduce was a handsome fellow sitting on the windowsill who looked to be about Shoshoni's age. Matti pointed in his direction and said, "This young man is Jacob. He's the baby's father. I'm glad you're here, Jacob."

Next was Jacob's mother, an attractive woman, about forty years of age, neatly dressed and looked as though she might be a schoolteacher or a preacher's wife.

"And this lovely lady is Jacob's mother, Nancy. And, Nancy, I can't tell you how happy I am to see you here. Thank you so much."

Jacob's father was next, standing against the wall near the door with his arms folded across his chest. She didn't mention his name in the introduction. Matti would later reveal that she knew him professionally. He and his motorcycle gang were on her radar as a Sheriff's deputy. She was involved in his arrest only once but knew of his numerous altercations with the law. Covered in tattoos and piercings, he proudly wore the typical leather vest with his gang's logo. He also appeared to be a bodybuilder with broad shoulders, the sleeves of his T-shirt stretched tight over his muscular arms. If he was trying to look the part of a motorcycle gangster, he succeeded.

His response was a nod and some *guttural sound* rather than a word—no offer of a handshake toward Jake or Greg.

Across from him was his newest wife. She, too, looked the part. She was wearing shorts and a halter top, and about every bit of exposed skin, of which there was a lot, was either covered in tattoos, pierced, or both.

She had a daughter, eight or nine years old. The daughter clung to her mother like a tick on a dog—never got off her mother's lap or spoke.

Matti pointed in her direction and said, "And this is Jacob's stepmother and her daughter." The mother's response was a timid nod while the child merely looked at the floor, emotionless.

Matti pulled Jake aside and led him out into the hall. Once away from the others, she said, "At my count, there are fifteen people in an area with five chairs. Granted, some are sitting on the wide windowsill, and a couple are on the floor, but too many are left standing.

"There is no way of knowing how long the wait will be. You know how it may take with the first pregnancy. The doctors think the baby may not come for several hours. Honey, I *hafta* stay here, but you've got a game to play. Take your dad and anybody else who'll go, too. It'll relieve the overcrowding here in the waiting room. While you're gone, I'll see if I can find better accommodations for this group."

As if Jake needed a reminder about the game—it weighed on his mind like an anvil. He was the team captain, after all, and they were scheduled to play the first game of the single-elimination, end-of-season tournament later that morning. It wasn't like they expected to come away with a trophy or anything, but forfeiting? That's not how he envisioned the season ending, and he knew the other players didn't want it to go that way, either.

Wearing a tormented expression, Jake asked, "Are you *sure*?"

Matti continued, "Of course, I'm sure. With the team we've drawn, it'll probably be the last game of the season anyway. I'll hold down the fort here. Go on. Gather up the girls and get out of here."

"I can tell you right now, not one of those ladies is gonna leave this place to come to a softball game. That in itself makes me feel *real* awkward about doin' it, too."

"I don't care. You have a responsibility to your team. I can handle things here, and if you stay, you'll be doing nothing but sitting—or *standing*—and wringing your hands, feeling like you let your team down. No good will come from you being here. Now go. I love you."

Jake replied, "Okay. If you say so."

He turned to his dad to tell him of the plan. Together, they tried their best to recruit others to accompany them, but their attempts proved futile. No one else would leave the hospital. Reluctantly, they headed to the ballpark.

Hurrying down the hospital corridor, Greg asked, "Are you *sure* Matti said it was okay for us to leave? Linda didn't look too pleased when we were walkin' out."

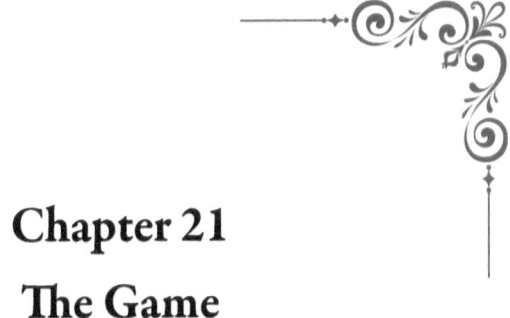

Chapter 21
The Game

Jake had to stop at his favorite mini-market to pick up beer and ice. Once they arrived at the park, several team members gathered to help carry the cooler and equipment to the appointed diamond.

In his attempt to fill out the roster, Jake realized a problem. Matti and Shoshoni would not be there, for obvious reasons, but to add to his troubles, a fire had broken out about a week earlier, some thirty miles to the northwest. Smoke covered the sky in that direction, past the mountains to the horizon. Three of his players were wildland firefighters and had been called up, so they wouldn't be there either.

Greg could see his son's frustration. Without enough players to field a team, Jake looked at his dad and said, "We're gonna have to forfeit after all, Pop."

"Not enough players? Where is everybody?"

"Comedy of errors, I guess. Baby River about to show up, and that damned fire. Everybody has something else they think's more important," he joked. "I've only got eight players. We could play without the roving shortstop, but I can't field a team with only eight. But what the hell? This team's gonna kill us anyway, so it really doesn't matter."

Greg had been a pretty good athlete during his younger days. He played a lot of baseball and softball during those years, so he had experience. Seeing his son torn by the decision, he offered a solution. "Let me catch. See if the other team will go for it. I can't hit or run the bases—I'm wearing flip-flops for crying out loud. I'll just catch behind the plate. Run it past 'em and see if they'll be okay with it."

"Are you kidding me, Dad? You're 70 years old. You don't need to be out there."

"I want to. Come on. See if they'll bite. Hell, you said we're gonna get our asses kicked anyway. Right?"

Jake laughed, "Well, you've got a point there." He walked over to the other dugout to float the idea.

After conferring with his teammates, the opposing captain said, "As long as the ump has no objection, it's fine by us."

Together, the two captains approached the umpire to discuss the situation. There, they talked briefly before Jake motioned for his dad to join them behind home plate, where the ump instructed, "You may substitute as the catcher but not participate in the batting rotation. Understood?"

"Yes, sir." Greg was excited but now suddenly a bit nervous. He realized it may have been twenty-five years since he had thrown a softball or slid his hand into a glove. *Oh well, it's like riding a bicycle. Right?*

Some say Jake got his gregarious personality from his dad. Those in attendance that day might attest to it. Greg's chosen position when he played organized baseball as a youngster was *catcher*. He didn't have command of a curveball, slider, or anything fancy, so he washed out as a pitcher. Other positions didn't offer enough activity for Greg. He wanted to be involved in every play, every pitch, and being the catcher provided that.

Greg was very vocal in that position. He talked to the batter, the umpire, the pitcher, always trying to engage them in conversation. His specialty was antagonizing the batter. He did everything he could to get his mind off the pitch coming in—tell jokes, say things to make the batter mad. Nothing was off-limits.

Greg was in his element. Jake was pitching, tossing a few warm-ups. Mind you, we're talking slow-pitch, co-ed softball, where the pitcher lobs the ball to the plate with an arc of at least six but no more than twelve feet above the ground.

"Okay, he's ready," Greg yelled as he stepped out and threw to third to start the *around-the-horn* routine. As the experience played out, Greg felt thirty years younger, walking down memory lane with his son. He tossed the ball back to Jake to start the game. Wearing a huge grin, he headed behind the plate.

As Greg approached, the lead-off batter was ready to take his place in the box, bat in hand. Greg looked at him and said, "You're all rearing to go, ain't ya'? My name's Greg. What's yours?"

The would-be batter mumbled, "Bobby."

As Greg squatted behind the plate, he replied, "Good to know you, Bobby. What position do you play?"

"Centerfield."

"Ahh. You fancy yourself more like Mickey Mantle or Willie Mays?"

Bobby turned to look at the catcher in disbelief. The two were great ball players, to be sure, but the obvious difference was race, and there was no denying Bobby was Caucasian. With Bobby's attention diverted, Jake seized the opportunity to toss the pitch.

"Ball one," the umpire called out as he raised his right hand and registered the count in his clicker.

Astonished, Jake extended his arms and said, "That was right down the middle."

The umpire replied, "Too high."

Bobby had stepped out of the box and looked first at Jake, then to the ump, and finally to Greg. Nodding, he said, "That was cold."

"I know. I'm sorry. I didn't know Jake was gonna throw that pitch while we were talkin', tryin' to get to know one another. It was pretty cold."

Chuckling as he stepped into the box, Bobby said, "Uh, huh. And if I believe that, you've got a bridge for sale."

Greg never let up, "You from around here? I'm from Georgia. It sure is beautiful here, ain't it?" Then, without waiting for an answer, Greg yelled, loud enough to break the batter's eardrums, "Come on, Jake, throw that wicked fastball in here."

Then back to the soft tone to the batter, "You've got to watch this guy's fastball. It is *wicked*—a lot of movement. You think it's coming in over the plate, and at the last minute, it darts up and in. It'll pop ya' right in the eye if you ain't careful!"

Greg was reeling off crap—one-liner after one-liner. Jake had already let the pitch fly, but the batter was laughing too hard to swing. The umpire yelled, "Stee-rike one."

The batter stepped out of the box, looked at Greg, smiled, and shook his head. Greg grinned and replied, "What? Was it something I said?" They both laughed together.

The batter continued shaking his head as he stepped back into the batter's box, and Greg's chatter began again. "Okay, this time, I'm going to move over here," he stepped to his right, calling for the pitch way outside. "I've signaled for a slider. This one'll start like it's gonna miss the plate, then at the last minute, it breaks hard right and catches the outside corner for strike two. Be ready."

When Jake tossed the pitch, it went straight to Greg's target—never broke. The umpire yelled, "Ball."

Greg hollered at Jake as he stepped toward the mound, pretending to be mad, "Do we need to go over the signs again, or did you just not see when I flashed it? Or maybe you can't throw that slider anymore. Is that it? Have you lost your touch in your old age?"

He threw the ball sharply back to him, turned, and headed toward the plate, saying, "Jeez, you can't get good help anymore."

Jake yelled, "I know, Dad. I guess I'm just not warmed up yet." Smiling, he added, "I'll do better."

Greg hollered, "Alright, son. Bear down now. Let's go." He slammed his fist into his glove and walked to the plate, chuckling. "I thought I trained that boy better'n that."

Greg was having a blast. The batter and the umpire were shaking their heads and laughing, too.

As Greg settled in, the chatter resumed, but it was interrupted when Jake said, "How about the knuckler this time, Pop?" The ball was in the air and on its way.

It wobbled in flight as if crazed—possessed. The batter didn't swing but stepped out of the box. The umpire snickered and boldly called, "Strike two."

Bobby looked at Greg and said, "Holy shit. Did you see that?"

Greg chuckled and replied, "I did. But I'm not sure I believe what I saw. We need to have the ump inspect the ball. That can't be legal."

When Jake heard that, he yelled, "Hey, Dad, whose team are you on?"

Bobby jokingly nodded, saying, "Yeah, we need a close look at that ball. What did you put inside that thing?"

Jake shouted, "Well, you've heard of a *spitter,* right? What you saw was a legal variation. I just rubbed it with beer and got it drunk. That's what an intoxicated softball does in flight."

Laughter came from every direction: the dugout, the infield, even the umpire chimed in.

The ump couldn't find anything wrong with it, so he returned the ball to Greg, and the game resumed. With the count at two balls and two strikes, Jake prepared to deliver the next pitch—which the batter promptly hit over the left-field fence for the game's first home run.

Greg said, as the batter rounded the bases and approached home plate, "Oh, *thaaaat's* right. We were having a good time until you did that. I see how it is now. No more Mister Nice Guy from now on, *Bobby*. No sir." Then he held up his hand for a high-five with a huge smile to congratulate him as he passed. He squeezed in a "nice hit" before he made it to the dugout.

I n co-ed softball, no two male batters can hit in succession, so the next person to bat had to be female. Greg didn't let gender dampen his chatter. Except with the women, he chose a slightly different approach. He'd ask about the perfume they wore, whether they were married or seeing anyone.

He'd ask directions to a town he'd heard about. Greg didn't care where it was. He was simply trying to distract from the task at hand—the ball coming toward the plate. If those weren't effective, Greg would try disparaging remarks about boyfriends, husbands, or girlfriends if he thought they might lean the other way.

Greg noticed a female batter near the bottom of the order approaching the plate in the second inning who appeared unusually psyched. He decided she represented a challenge. "Wow. You look determined. What's your name? Mine's Greg."

When he received no reply, Greg said, "What's the matter, cat got your tongue?"

She ignored Greg again and stood in the batter's box, glaring at the pitcher taking half swings with the bat. After a moment, Greg stood, raised both hands and called, "Time."

He stepped in front of the plate and yelled loud enough for everyone to hear, speaking slowly and enunciating carefully, looking back and forth between the batter and the mound. "Jake, you need to take it easy on this one. It seems she's deaf and unable to speak, so be gentle. Nothing fancy. Okay?"

He turned to the batter and, accentuating his words even more, said,

"C a n ... y o u ... r e a d ... l i p s?"

Trying to hold it together, she stood there, her body rigid. She made a fist with her free hand, her bat in the other—until one side of her upper lip curled into a smile. She held it briefly before breaking into a full-blown come-apart. She probably hated herself for it, but she couldn't hold it in.

Greg laughed along with her and returned to his position behind the plate. He assumed his crouch, glove open between his knees, inviting the pitcher to *fire at will*, and began his conversation. "You know, this pitcher can be very dangerous. You need to watch out for pitches that come inside and high. They can knock your teeth out or worse. One time, I saw this guy get hit in the helmet. He went down like a hammer. A bad concussion, so look out for that. Yeah, it was bad. Watch for backward spin on the ball. When you see that, it means it's gonna bend toward ya.'"

Astonished at the absurdity of his remarks, the young lady turned to Greg and flashed a look that expressed, *you're so full a' shit.*

She shifted her attention to the pitcher at the very second the ball landed in Greg's glove.

In a sympathetic tone, the umpire raised his right hand and said, "Strike one."

Anger flew all over the batter. She glared, first toward the man behind the mask who made the call, then toward Greg. She was fuming.

When the next pitch came in, she was determined. It was too high, but she let her rage get the best of her. She swung anyway, with all her might—tried to take out her frustrations on the ball. Instead, she hit a dribbler to the mound. Jake threw her out at first.

And so it went as the game progressed. Jake would carry his beer to the mound to imbibe between batters. He would carefully set the can on the rubber's end and begin his wind-up.

When the lead-off hitter came to the plate for the second time, he mimicked Babe Ruth when *The Great Bambino* gestured with his bat toward the right field fence, indicating where he would hit his next home run. Except Bobby pointed his bat at the beverage on the mound. Jake looked in horror and yelled, "Don't hit my beer!"

Bobby looked to the umpire and asked, "Wouldn't that be considered an automatic ground-rule double? Interference from an outside object that wasn't supposed to be on the field anyway? Right?"

The final arbiter responded, "Well, he's gotta point, Jake."

"Oh. That's just wrong." Turning his attention to the batter and holding up his left hand, Jake challenged him. "It's a good thing I've got this here glove. I'll snag whatever you hit this way."

Greg egged Bobby on. "I don't think you can hit it. I mean, I saw you hit a nice home run, but c'mon, man. It's only because Jake offered you that sweet layup. Even your grandmother could have hit that one out of the park. It's gonna take *precision* to hit that can, and I don't think ya' got it in ya'. That's all I'm sayin'."

With the target set up outside, Greg yelled, "Throw him that slider, Jake."

"Ball one," was heard by all.

Greg laid it on, "Alright. Your slider isn't breaking like it should. Toss him your curve. Put some spin on it this time." He set up his target way inside.

The pitch would have hit him if the batter hadn't stepped out of the box. Being hit by the pitch would have sent Bobby to first base. He didn't want to be deprived of a chance to hit Jake's beer.

"Ball two," came the call.

Greg hollered to his son, "Huh. Looks like we're in trouble. *None* of your stuff's workin'. Maybe it's time for your fastball. Fire it in here. He won't be expecting that."

Both teams erupted hysterically. From the dugout, a voice shouted, "Yeah, that should do it."

Jake responded, "I know, Pop. Maybe this'll do the trick." Another knuckler was on its way. It wobbled and danced toward the plate.

The batter couldn't resist. He took a mighty swing. The ball headed toward the defenseless can at blistering speed.

Jake quickly reached with his glove to intercept it, but he was too late. The trajectory carried the ball barely an inch above the stranded container.

Fortunately for the home team, having realized the batter's aiming point, Jake had repositioned the shortstop. He fielded the ball on one hop and threw the runner out at first. No harm done.

The opposing team consisted of young, talented male and female players who were good sports. They seemed to enjoy the banter Greg dished out and heaped it right back, which made it all the more fun.

Jake's *Beavers* lost to this first-placed team in the standings via the ten-run rule after five innings when they played them earlier in the spring. No one had beaten them all season, so everyone knew the odds were stacked against Jake's team.

On this day, the home team was down eight runs in the top of the 7th and final inning. The bases were loaded with Jake on the mound, a female runner on third, and one out.

If one run scored, it's okay. The *Beavers* would have one more chance at the plate. If two runs scored, the game would be over—the ten-run rule.

The man at bat hit a line drive to left field. The runners froze, ready to take off if the ball was caught on the fly. The left fielder came up a few feet, caught the ball, and fired it to Greg at home to get the female runner attempting to score.

The throw was on target but a little short. Greg moved a step or two in front of the plate to catch the incoming throw and then had to dive back toward the runner to make the tag. She had already touched home.

The umpire yelled and motioned with his arms out wide. "Safe!"

Greg, fully aware the call was correct, adopted his best *Yogi Bera* imitation, got up, mocked at kicking the dirt as much as he could in his flip-flops, and screamed in disgust—all the while trying to hide his smile. "Safe? Have you lost your mind? Are you blind? Anybody could see the runner was out! This game is rigged—"

"You'd better watch it, mister. You're not too old for me to throw you outta here. It's not too late, you know," trying his best to look serious.

With a salute, Greg replied, "Yes, sir." He turned to Jake and said, "I'm sorry, son. I gave it my best shot."

"Holy shit, Pop. You're bleeding! I'd say you did. Are you okay?

"I'm fine. It's like you always say, 'Nothin' a man can't handle.' Let's play ball."

Jake replied, "Okay, then. We've got two outs. All we need is one more. Let's do this."

J ake tossed the next batter, a female, his famous knuckler. As she started to swing, the wobbling ball darted down. Her bat caught just the top, making it more like a bunt.

There were two outs with runners on second and third. First base was open, so they should have held because Jake could never make the play at first.

But, the guy on third broke for home. Realizing the ball would only make it about halfway to the mound, Jake screamed to the catcher, "Stay there."

Greg stood blocking the plate. Jake's only play would be to field the ball with his bare hand and, in one motion, toss it to his dad.

Greg positioned himself, stretched out and ready. The throw and the timing were perfect. Dad made the tag.

The Umpire screamed, "Out!" The first half of the inning was over. The Beavers had one more chance.

When they assembled in the dugout, a beautiful young woman, Sharon, a Physician's Assistant in her mid-thirties, a friend of Jake and Matti, who played second base, rushed over to Greg to check on his injuries. He was bleeding from abrasions to several appendages—both knees and his left elbow.

As she cleaned the catcher's wounds using materials from the team's first aid kit, Greg looked up at his son and said, "Keanu Reeves was right. 'Pain heals, chicks dig scars, and glory lasts forever.'"

While Jake and everybody else in the dugout enjoyed the quip, Sharon seized the opportunity to remind Greg who was in charge. She pressed a little harder on his knee at just that moment and said, "Now that I have your attention, *Superstar*, you'll want to ensure these don't get infected. Keep them clean—especially this one.

"You may want to put some anti-biotic salve on these and cover them with non-stick bandages. I don't have any big enough, I'm sad to say. You *have* done a number on yourself, but you'll be fine." She pressed hard again on his knee, just for good measure. "Okay?"

Greg flinched, "Ouch. Yes, ma'am." Looking over at his son, he continued, "Dang, these Montana women are tough, Jake."

"I know, Pop. You gotta be careful around them, especially Sharon. She's as tough as they come. She's not just another pretty face—no, she's mean, too."

Greg replied saying, "And to think, I only sacrificed myself because I figured she'd be the one who'd be taking care of my injuries. Pretty as she was, I figured it'd be worth the sufferin'. Boy, was I wrong. She...is...heartless, I tell you."

With that, even Sharon had to laugh, along with the entire dugout.

T he team had one remaining chance to at least tie the game in the last half of the 7th inning. The Beavers only led once when they went ahead in the bottom of the first, three to two. Since then, they'd been consistently outscored, standing at fifteen to six. If Jake's team could put up nine runs, they'd go into extra innings. If they score ten, they win the game outright.

It was a daunting task, but the Beavers were giving it their best shot. The rally began. Maybe the spilling of Greg's blood had something to do with it, but the ball started bouncing their way. Five runs had already crossed the plate, but there were two outs. The bases were loaded, an excellent female hitter up to bat, and Jake, one of their best home run hitters, on deck.

She got her pitch, swung, and connected with a sharply hit ground ball up the middle, scoring the runner on third. Safe all around. The Beavers were three runs behind, bases loaded, and Jake at-bat with a chance to hit a grand slam to win the game.

As he stepped into the batter's box, Jake eyed the pitcher, took a couple half swings, and drew a deep breath of determination. He watched the ball drift too far outside. He let it pass.

The umpire called, "Ball one."

Jake never took his eyes off the man on the mound. He watched as the second pitch sailed toward him, this one too high. Jake stepped back and waited.

The ump called, "Ball two."

Feeling in control, Jake stepped into the box and breathed deeply. This pitch looked good but too far outside for him to pull toward left field, the shortest distance to the fence. He chose not to swing.

"Strike one," was the call.

C'mon. A little more inside.

The next pitch mirrored the last.

Jake took that one, too. *Damn it. He's in a groove.*

"Strike two."

Jake knew he had to guard the plate. He watched the ball coming toward him. It wasn't the pitch he was hoping for, but he couldn't take the chance he might be called out on strikes.

He took a deep breath and coiled his body like a spring. Everyone heard the mighty grunt when Jake unleashed before their eyes. They watched the blur of his arms and bat until the ball jumped skyward as if shot from a cannon. It flew high toward left-center field.

Bobby ran to the fence and waited for the ball to come down—it seemed like an eternity. He leaped at just the right instant, possibly higher than he ever had, leaning over the fence. The momentum of the ball's trajectory pulled his body headfirst over the barrier, where the centerfielder landed on his back. He managed to jump to his feet, the white of the ball shining through the gaps in his glove, robbing Jake of the home run and saving the win for his team.

Halfway between first and second, Jake shook his head before whining, "Of course, it's you, *Bobby*."

Bobby's grin seemed wider than his face. He jumped the fence and rejoined his teammates, who were whooping and hollering in celebration, running to greet him in the outfield.

As the players from both teams lined up and congratulated each other, with Greg in the mix, the opposition's captain leaned into him and said, "One thing about it, we all agreed your banter sure added some welcomed spice to the game and made it more fun."

Greg's joy was impossible to contain, "I had a blast. Thanks for allowing me to play. You guys were great sports."

Jake overhead the conversation, and when he and his dad walked away together, he said, "How cool was that?"

With tears welling, Greg replied, "Awesome, actually. Freaking awesome. I'm seventy years old and in Montana. Do you know the odds against me doing this today? Who'd a thunk it?"

Jake smiled and threw his arm around his dad's shoulder.

As they walked toward their dugout, Greg said, "You know, if you'd a pulled that just a little bit further left, there's no way he coulda caught that. Right?"

Jake looked at his dad, pulled his arm abruptly off him, and said. "I'm not speaking to you anymore all day. I'm done. In fact, I'm not sure how you're gettin' home." He picked up the pace and stomped off, feigning anger.

Greg replied with a chuckle, "I was just sayin'."

As the team members collected equipment and gathered their gear for departure, Jake's phone rang, "Shoshoni's in delivery."

"We'll be right there. Yeah, we just finished the game. We're loading up. Should we go home and shower?" He paused, waiting for an answer. "Okay. See you in a few minutes. Bye."

Hearing only his son's parting statement, Greg asked, "Where are we going to be in a few minutes?"

Jake explained the situation and informed his dad why they were *not* going to the tavern for free beer. "We're heading directly to the hospital, Pop."

"Son, don't you think we're a bit dirty, sweaty, nasty, and stinky to be going to a hospital? I'm certainly *not* needing medical attention, so I assume River is on his way, or has he arrived?"

"Hey, I'm just doing what I was told. Remember, I'm married now."

"Good talk, son. I forgot."

Their laughter didn't fade until they pulled into the hospital parking lot, a short drive from the ball field.

Chapter 22
River's Debut

G reg felt self-conscious as they walked through the hospital's
main entrance, especially since he was still bleeding from the
wounds suffered on the softball diamond. They were getting strange
looks from nurses and other personnel, but Jake was undaunted, so
the injured catcher did his best to keep up.

Jake, at 6' 4", had legs a bit longer than his dad's, and his fast walk
was more like a steady trot for Greg.

Hurriedly, they made their way through the corridors to the
new, larger waiting room where everyone had transitioned. The same
gaggle of visitors was still there, smiling and eagerly awaiting their
first look at River. They had heard mom and baby were doing fine, so
the mood was cheerful.

When the ball players walked in, a hush fell over the room.
A couple of the women softly gasped. One put her hand over her
mouth. Seeing her husband's bloody appendages, Linda broke the
silence by asking Jake, "What have you done to your father?"

Greg was about to defend his son when Jake spoke up, "Well,
Ma, it's a long and difficult story, but it's all my fault."

Then, looking at his father, he said, "Think of me as your
attorney, Pop. Don't say anything without looking at me first. Trust
me, anything *you* say *will* be held against you."

Everybody broke into robust laughter. So much so that Granny admonished the group to quiet down, reminding everyone where they were. It helped a little, but not much.

Jake continued, almost whispering, "You see, Ma, it's actually Matti and Shoshoni's fault—maybe River's too. Since both women were *here* and not at the game, we didn't have enough players. And, in case you didn't know, the mountains just to the north are on fire, so we lost a couple more players who were up there fighting those. I had to recruit Dad or forfeit the game. So, I added him to the roster. He filled in as our catcher. He played a hell of a game today."

Linda shifted her gaze slightly toward Greg, smiled sarcastically, and said, "Of course you did. You two are a pair."

Turning to her son, she continued, "Look, Jake," pointing to his father, "apparently, you tried to kill him. He's bleeding from virtually every joint."

Jake, doing his best to hide his amusement, said, "Mom, I promise you. We came straight here. We didn't stop off at any *joints*. He got those on the ball diamond."

Trying to hold on to her *mean* face, Linda said, "Don't you pull that crap with me."

"Well, I know, but the game was on the line. And *dear old Dad* felt like he *had* to make the play. The team depended on him. Don't you get it?"

Jake's play-acting was admirable, but his sincerity may have been lacking. He could barely hide how much fun he had with the exchange, and the audience enjoyed the show.

When Jake finished, Linda asked, "So, you won?"

Jake dropped his head and replied in a low, despondent voice, "No. We lost."

With that, the room fell apart. Nobody could hold back their laughter.

J ake and his dad had done their best to clean themselves up before entering the hospital, brushing the dust off one another. Greg had rinsed his wounds. The bleeding had stopped, but one especially was still oozing and running down his shin.

Linda handed her husband a tissue and said, "Here, use this to keep them from leaking all over everything."

Both men felt awkward being there—but they *were* following orders.

A s Greg sat, he studied the people's interactions.

Jacob, River's father, was a strikingly handsome young man, barely twenty years old. He seemed polite and respectful but didn't interact much. He kept to himself and spoke only when asked a direct question. Shoshoni had made it clear to Jake and Matti that she couldn't see herself in a relationship with him but provided no reason why.

Nancy, Jacob's mother, had just become River's paternal grandmother. She was an attractive woman with a delightful personality. She interacted with everyone in the waiting room, getting to know all her new *relatives*.

Jacob's father, his new wife, and their daughter never participated in any conversation. If they spoke, they did so in whispers among themselves but did nothing to cause any trouble or disruption.

Clayton, Shoshoni's current boyfriend, was a slimy-looking person—not at all handsome. Greg could not imagine what she saw in him, especially when Jacob was in the room. The contrast was stark.

Clayton never took his face away from his phone and didn't interact with anyone.

K G WAUTHIER

Ty, Shoshoni's biological father, about whom everyone was most worried, epitomized the classic Tennessee redneck. He was uneducated, crude, and unpolished, but on this occasion, he was a perfect gentleman. He was polite and engaged in conversation when appropriate.

Natalia was there in support of her best friend.

Linda, Ava, Rose, Granny, and Jake rounded out the menagerie, anxiously awaiting the first look at River and his new mother.

Matti, of course, had never left her daughter's side. Shoshoni wanted her mother there. She gave birth in the same room she had spent the night before. A far different experience than Greg witnessed when Linda gave birth to their two children so many years ago. Back then they wheeled the expectant *mom* into a separate room for delivery. Not so anymore.

Greg and Jake sat in the waiting room with the others for well over an hour. He looked at his son and whispered, "We woulda had time. Coulda stopped off at the house and showered."

As Jake was chuckling and nodding in agreement, the door to the room finally opened, and Matti stepped out. She walked calmly toward her husband with a big smile on her face. She motioned for him to follow and led him away from the group.

She spoke with him only for a few seconds. Jake nodded in agreement and started back toward his seat. Matti then turned and said, "Jacob, would you like to meet your son?"

Jacob looked up, astonished. "Me?"

"You're the father, aren't you?"

Jacob asked, "Can Mom come in, too?"

"I don't know. The doctor asked me to come and invite you. She didn't say anything about your mom. I guess we'll have to ask her when we get there," Matti said as she winked at Nancy and motioned for her to follow.

Matti whispered as they walked. "We've got to be really quiet when we go in, Jacob. The doctor will tell us what we can and can't do. Okay?"

When they got to the room, the doctor was there waiting for them. She helped Jacob with a protective gown. As she was doing so, Matti said, "Jacob has requested River's other grandmother accompany him. Do you think that would be okay, doctor?"

With an inviting smile, the doctor said, "I suppose we could make that exception. This *is* such an auspicious occasion, after all."

Nancy's face revealed the relief that washed over her. She was delighted to be among the first to see the new baby boy with her son, the new father.

The doctor admonished, "Enjoy yourselves. Just try to avoid loud noises and be brief. Remember, many want to see him, and he's brand new."

They walked in to see Shoshoni holding River, wrapped in a tiny blanket. It was a beautiful picture. Even though Shoshoni had been through a lot, it may have been her most perfect moment.

Nancy looked at her and said, "Oh, my Lord! You look so beautiful sitting there holding him, my dear. May we see?"

Shoshoni adjusted the blanket and shifted the baby's position to improve everyone's view.

Nancy was in awe. "I think he's the most beautiful baby I've ever seen—and I'm not saying that just because he's my grandson."

Jacob's head snapped toward his mother standing next to him.

"Yeah, I hate to admit it, but he's even prettier than *you* when you were born, and that's saying something."

Acting crushed, with his hand over his heart, Jacob said, "Mom. I didn't think I'd ever hear you say such a thing." After a pause, he finished, "He *is* a handsome little guy, isn't he?"

Through teary eyes, Nancy smiled.

Shoshoni spoke up, "And he's perfect too. The doctor said so. She checked him out already. I knew it right off, though. He's got ten fingers and ten toes. I counted them. I'm so lucky."

Nancy chuckled, looked at Shoshoni, and said, "I'm so happy for you, dear, but how are *you* feeling?"

"Oh, much better now. I'm *so* glad it's over. I've been hurtin' really bad. We'll see how the next few days go."

Overcome with emotion, the tears in Nancy's eyes said everything. Bursting with happiness, she realized that River was beautiful, healthy... and she was a grandmother. "If there's anything I can do to help, please let me know. Okay? I want to play as large a role as you'll let me."

Shoshoni smiled, mouthed, "Thank you," looked up at Jacob, and asked, "Would you like to hold your son?"

Jacob stood speechless. Then, after a moment, his mouth formed the words, "Do you think it's safe? I mean, he's just been born."

Shoshoni giggled and replied, "You don't plan on dropping him, do you? I haven't held one this young, either. But then, neither of us have ever been parents before, have we?"

Jacob stepped closer, reached down, and awkwardly took River from his mother.

Trembling with excitement, Nancy tried to hold her cell phone steady as she took pictures. The image of her son holding her grandson was almost too much to bear.

After a few awkward moments, several facial contortions reflecting something between terror and excitement, and dozens of photos, Jacob asked, "Can Mom hold him?"

Wearing a broad smile, Shoshoni replied, "Of course."

Nancy laid the phone on the bed, taking the baby from her son's arms. Overcome with joy, she pulled River close to kiss his tiny face, saying, "What a beautiful baby boy you two have created. Do you know when they'll let you go home, my dear?"

Shoshoni replied, "I haven't heard anything about that yet."

Another few minutes passed, and Matti, standing away from the group, noticed the doctor flashing a signal. It was time for a shift change. Others wanted to see the new arrival, too. Matti suggested that Jacob should stay in the room. Nancy would be replaced by her ex-husband and company.

Matti escorted Nancy out of the room and walked the new paternal grandfather, his new wife, and Jacob's half-sister in to see the baby. They did as instructed, stayed less than five minutes, and exited with Jacob.

When they returned to the waiting room, the new grandfather agreed the baby was beautiful, explained how it had been nice to have met everyone, "...but it's been a big day, and we've got a long drive back home, so we need to be on our way."

Their rapid departure came as no surprise to anyone. Clearly, they would have preferred to have been anywhere other than there. They did their obligatory duty for *his* son but couldn't wait for it to end.

Jacob had ridden with his dad, so he left the hospital, leaving behind his mother, who lived in a different town. Nancy chose to stay for a while. She couldn't stop talking about her new grandson.

Matti stood in the waiting room looking around until she finally said, "Where's Clayton?"

Linda responded, "I saw him slip out a short time ago. I thought he might be heading to the restroom, but he hasn't come back. He left right after Jacob went in to see the baby."

Granny, Ava, and Linda were next to go in for a visit. Rose was invited but felt awkward about going in, saying, "I'm not a *relative*. I'll wait until mom and baby come home. You guys go ahead. He's going to get too much company anyway."

Ty and Natalia went in next. When he looked at his new grandson, Ty couldn't find the words. After staring at him for a long moment, a few finally came, "Wow, Shoshoni. You done real good."

"I did, didn't I?"

Natalia asked her friend, "How you feelin', sweetie?"

"Pretty good. Gettin' tired, though."

After a couple more minutes of small talk, Ty and Natalia left the room. Matti walked up to Rose and invited her one more time. She declined again, saying, "Thank you, Matti. I'd rather wait until they both come home if you don't mind. I'll be fine with that."

"Okay, Rose. Whatever you want, Honey."

Taking one last unsuccessful look around for Clayton, Matti turned to Jake and his dad, "I guess you two losers are the only ones left. You guys want to come in and see River?"

Greg looked at his son and said, "Did you hear what your wife called us?"

Jake shrugged, "Well, we *didn't* win, Pop."

His dad responded, "True. But that was *cold*."

Chuckles came from nearly everyone remaining in the waiting area. Greg questioned the wisdom of the two men entering, dirty as they were. Matti assured them they wouldn't be allowed to touch the baby, but they would at least be able to see him, and Shoshoni too.

As they headed toward the room, Matti motioned to Linda, "Wanna join them?"

"I don't wanna be seen with *either* of them, actually, but I will if you insist."

The room erupted. The men felt as out of place as...two men in a maternity ward, filthy and bleeding after playing softball. Yeah, that's how they felt. Linda's presence, the room's laughter, and the gowns they had to wear helped a bit.

Shoshoni was tired, so they didn't stay long. When they left, Matti announced that Shoshoni and the baby would try to get some rest, "Y'all may as well go home and relax. I'll keep you posted with any further news. Right now, it's unclear when they'll be released, but I doubt coming home tonight is in the cards. We'll see."

Everybody followed orders, and Matti arrived home a couple of hours later. Her prediction proved correct. The doctor decided it best for Shoshoni and the baby to stay overnight for observation.

A happy mood filled the house. Beer flowed, conversation ensued, and food was enjoyed, but Matti seemed worried.

Granny spoke up first and asked, "What's the matter, sweetheart?"

"I don't know, Granny. I'm not sure how ready Shoshoni is to be a mom. She's so immature. River hasn't latched on to her breast yet. I wouldn't be surprised if I don't get a call in the middle of the night."

"From the hospital?"

"No, from Shoshoni. She'll start freaking out, not knowing what to do. When that happens, she'll do what she always does. She hates me most of the time, but when she can't figure things out, who does she call?"

In unison, almost yelling, everybody chimed in, "Ghostbusters!"

Even Matti couldn't hold it back. She shook her head. "Who didn't know that was coming? Right?"

A great tension breaker, to be sure, but everybody knew Matti was troubled.

A little before midnight, Matti's phone rang. "Sure. I'll be there in a few minutes. It'll be okay. Stop. Dry your tears. If you're crying, River *certainly* won't stop. He probably thinks there's a reason to cry. Toughen up, girl. I'll be there in a few. Hold on."

Jake whispered, "Do you want me to go with you?"

"Oh, hell no. You and your dad are *going* on that float trip in the morning, and you have to get up early. You need your sleep. You two have been looking forward to this all week. I'm not gonna let *this* screw it up for you guys. Close your eyes, Baby. I'll be fine. I'll get *some* rest at the hospital."

Matti quietly dressed and slipped out without anyone else knowing she had left.

Chapter 23
The Homecoming

Greg's alarm went off at 5 AM. He rose quickly to silence it in a futile attempt to prevent disturbing Ava and Rose in the adjoining room. A light sleeper, waking Linda was inevitable. Besides, she wouldn't let her men leave without having coffee, fixing a sandwich or two for them to take on their trip, and seeing them off properly.

Greg found the coffee already made, hot, and ready when he descended the stairs. Hearing Linda's footsteps, he poured her a cup.

As his dad placed the pot back on the burner, Jake joined them in the kitchen and whispered, "Mornin'."

Linda asked, "Matti still in bed?"

"No. Tryin' not to wake Granny."

A voice from the living room answered. "Too late. The perkin' of the coffee pot did it. But, y'all sound like a herd a turtles, too." She giggled. "Don't mind me. I'm a light sleeper. Go on about yer business. I'll be fine."

"Sorry, Granny," they replied in unison.

Jake quietly informed Linda that Shoshoni had called around midnight. "Matti spent the night back at the hospital. I'm sure she'll call a little later to let everybody know what's goin' on. Since Dad and I'll be on the water, my guess is she'll prob'ly call you, Mom. Okay?"

"Oh, sure. No problem. Let me make something for you guys to take with you for lunch. What about the guide? He'll need to eat, too, won't he?"

"No, he'll have his own lunch. There's some cold cuts in the fridge, Mom. Dad and I'll be outside getting things ready in the truck." He motioned to his dad, and they headed out the side door together.

As they were assembling their gear, Matti called. Sounding all bright and chipper, Jake answered, "Good morning. How's the new mom and baby?"

Never to miss an opportunity to poke her husband with a stick, Matti, with more than a *hint* of feigned irritation in her voice, asked, "*Oh?* You don't care how *I'm* doing?"

Seeing right through her petulance, Jake responded, "Of course, I care about *you*, *darling*. But knowing how empathetic you are and that you'd never think of yourself first, I had a feeling the two of them would be top of mind for *you* this morning. Your well-being would be *way down* on the list of *your* priorities. Are you doing okay, Precious?"

"Oh, my God! I think I'm gonna gag."

As soon as her words were spoken, Jake said, "Holy crap! That message came through in stereo. Matti, while you were saying that through my phone, Dad said the same thing, standing beside me. You two must have planned it."

Matti responded, "No, Jake, what you were feeding us made us both sick."

Jake pushed the speaker button on his phone, relayed what his wife had said, and asked, "Do you feel sick, Dad?"

They all had a good chuckle. Matti went on to explain that River had been fussy during the night, and Shoshoni just needed some *mamma* support. "They're having a hard time getting Shoshoni's milk to come down as well as it should, and River doesn't seem to be adjusting to what little there is. In short, they aren't quite ready to release them yet. Personally, I think there's more to it than that, but that's all they're sharing."

Matti went on to explain she'd call Linda a bit later to have the other *girls* come up to the hospital for some playtime with the baby. "The doctor said she thought it'd be okay."

"That sounds great." Jake and Greg both agreed as they were finishing the task of stowing their gear at the back of the pickup truck.

Jake kept Matti on the phone chatting while they walked back into the house. As he approached Linda, he said, "Here's Mom. You can fill her in while we freshen our coffees for the road. We're about to head off to meet the guide." He handed the phone to Linda.

Surprised, Linda took the phone and said, "Good morning, new grandma. Everything okay?"

Matti assured her all was fine, but a release date had not yet been set. After a bit of small talk and a brief explanation of the plan, Jake made it clear to Linda that she needed to hurry. He and Greg were ready to get to the river.

"Okay, Honey. We'll be there as soon as I can get the girls moving. See you soon. Seems Jake is ready and wants his phone back. You can call me on mine if you'd like. Bye."

Her voice trailed off because Jake was pulling the phone from his mother's hand and away from her mouth. He said to both into the phone, "I'm sorry ladies, Dad and I've gotta go now. We love you. Bye." He disconnected the call.

Jake said as the two men walked toward the door, "Love you, Mom. Don't worry about *us*. We'll have a good time. Bye-bye."

Greg hurriedly whispered loudly, "Ditto! And thanks for the lunches." He blew Linda a kiss as he closed the door behind him on their way to the truck.

Greg was excited about the trip because he had never fished from a drift boat and knew nothing about the tactics they would employ.

Before they loaded into the vessel, the guide offered some instructions while they stood on the river's edge. "You won't be *casting* like you would if you were fishing from the bank or how you see on TV. No. I'll put you on the water you'll be fishing. Most of the time your bait will be less than ten feet from the end of your rod. You won't need much line out."

The guide asked Greg, "May I use your rod to demonstrate?" Once in his hand, he stripped off some line and flipped it a short distance upriver. "This is how you'll *cast*. Toss your line like this to wherever you think the fish will be.

"Lay it out gently like this on the water, slightly upstream from our position. The nymph will sink, but the strike indicator will float. Watch it closely as it drifts along with us. If you notice any disturbance, if it stops, goes under, or moves in another direction, set the hook.

"Make sure you're always ready. Watch the line and the strike indicator at all times because when a fish takes the bait, it will only take him a second to figure out it's not real food and spit it out. You may have missed the biggest fish of the day. I'll take care of navigating the craft. You focus on the trophy."

As they boarded, Jake insisted his dad be in the bow, giving him the first crack at the wary fish. He would take up position in the stern. The guide would sit in the center, manning the oars.

No sooner than they pushed off, Greg heard a voice from the center seat, "You can't catch a fish if your line isn't wet."

He chuckled and replied, "You're right about that," dropped his line in the water, and just like that, a nice rainbow took the bait and headed upstream on a tear. The fish broke water several times in unsuccessful attempts to free himself from the hook in his jaw.

"Way to go, Pop," Jake said as he scooped the exhausted fish with his landing net and offered it to his dad. "Hold him up so I can get a picture."

Greg removed the hook, lifted the tired fish from the net, and asked, "Okay, but how are we gonna get him home for the fryin' pan?"

The guide piped up, "He's a Rainbow Trout. You can't keep any of those out of this river. They're catch-and-release only. You can keep Browns within size limits, but since you didn't bring a cooler to store fish, I didn't figure you were plannin' on keepin' any. You know you can't hang a stringer off any watercraft in this kind of water, with rapids like these, right?"

Jake looked at his dad and said, "I guess we're fishin' just for the braggin' rights today, Pop. You're off to a good start, though. This guy looks like he's nearly three pounds, wouldn't you say?"

The guide snickered, and Greg replied, "I guess it depends on how far out in front of me I hold him for the picture." All three chuckled as Jake photographed his dad at various degrees of arm extension before releasing the trout into the swift water.

As he watched him swim off, Greg joked, "Do ya' think we'll have to switch colors? He'll prob'ly tell all his buddies not to bite on those black ones after *his* experience."

The guide quickly responded, "Naw. He'll take that message to his friends upstream. We've already drifted down from where he's heading. It's bad news for the guys coming up behind us, but the fish under us right now have no clue."

Before the guide's dialogue concluded, Jake called out, "Fish on."

Mere seconds later, Greg hooked one, "Me, too."

Before either could be landed, the guide said, "You guys had better steady yourselves. We're heading into a bit of a rapid. Careful, you don't fall overboard."

Greg replied, "Perfect. What could possibly go wrong?"

Both fishermen continued to fight their prey as they were maneuvered around big rocks through the rough water and drop-offs, steadying themselves, starting with a knee against the gunnel. Then, when things got rougher, a free hand when it could be spared, or an elbow, or even their butt occasionally when all else failed.

When they finally reached the eddy on the other side, both fishermen were able to land their bounty, along with a tale to tell where not only did the size of the fish swell but so did the enormity of the boulders along with the treacherousness of the rapids.

And so it went throughout the trip, fish after fish, photo after photo, rapid after rapid, release after release.

They stopped on a small beach, where they disembarked and had lunch. They listened to the guide tell tales of trophy fish he and his customers had caught on this stretch of the river.

They were enthralled until Greg finally asked, "Why haven't we seen one of those six-pounders this morning?"

The guide smiled before replying, "You never know. One might be waiting around the next bend."

Jake looked at his dad and said, "Wouldn't that be somethin', Pop?"

"It would indeed. But we can't catch 'em if we're sittin' here."

The guide agreed, and they were on their way.

While he didn't catch the tr*ophy* he'd envisioned, Greg was amazed at how such a small river could produce so many quality fish. Had they brought a cooler, they would have limited out on Brown Trout before they stopped for lunch.

The weather cooperated, and the scenery's magnificence alone was enough to fill a photo album. The guide's ability to maneuver the boat through the rough waters and keep the fishermen in the right place for maximum production was impressive.

The generous tip he received reflected the quality of the experience. Greg was pleased.

Snuggled in her robe, Linda kicked back in the recliner, not far from Granny lying on the sofa, maybe pretending to be asleep under a blanket. She hoped to catch a few z's before the others began to stir.

Ava was the first to find her way down the stairs, searching for a shot of caffeine.

Granny lifted her head from the pillow, opened one eye, and murmured, "What's the meanin' of all these interruptions?"

Linda softly mumbled, "Poor upbringin', I'd reckon."

As Granny laid her head back into the softness of the down, she replied, "Hmph. 'Spect so."

From the kitchen, Ava said, "I heard that."

Linda watched Granny smile before adding boldly, "Mind fixin' your elders a cup since you're there? Mine's the one's already been drunk out of."

"Sure, how ya like it?"

Granny replied, "Cream and sugar, please."

Linda suggested, "There's half and half in the fridge, and honey on the counter if you'd like that instead of sugar. It's up to y'all. A little half and half for me, please."

Perhaps it was the time of day or simply too much for Ava to contemplate without caffeine, but things were about to get confusing. "Granny, you said 'cream and sugar.' Would half and half be okay, or would you rather have milk?"

"Sure, Honey. Either is fine."

"Oh. So you want honey instead of sugar?"

"No. That's not what I meant, but honey sounds okay, too. I like honey. Whatever's easier for ya'... Honey." Granny looked at Linda and winked, trying hard to keep from losing it.

Ava's head was about to explode. She poured herself a cup and hurriedly sipped to calm her nerves. The pot had been sitting on the heating pad for nearly two hours. When the taste set in, her face twisted and formed something resembling a giant prune.

She thought about spitting it into the sink, but that wouldn't be ladylike, and she needed the caffeine. She swallowed and said, "Let me do us *all* a favor. This stuff is nasty. I'll make some fresh, and we can enjoy some *good* coffee even if we have to wait a few minutes. How's that?"

Granny replied, "'At'd make me real happy. Now, if y'all'd be quiet, I could get a few more minutes' sleep."

Linda settled back in the recliner as Ava prepared the brew.

As the hot water dripped through the basket of grounds, Rose descended the stairs, saw Ava sitting at the kitchen counter, and chirped, "Good morning."

Linda turned her head toward Granny and opened one eye with a cocked brow.

Granny must have felt her stare and peeked, lifting a single lid.

What started with a snicker and a giggle quickly turned into snorts and chuckles heard in the kitchen.

Rose, taken aback, asked, "What's so funny?"

Granny regained her composure, "Nothin', dear. We're just delirious, that's all. Is the coffee done yet?"

Ava replied, "Almost, Granny. Almost."

Granny slid from under her blanket, sat up, and said, "Good. I may as well get up. I can tell y'all have decided it's time." She headed toward the bathroom, seemingly in a huff.

Linda joined the others in the kitchen. Seeing the pot nearly full, she said, "I think it's ready enough." She poured three cups and set one each in front of her guests. "Here, ladies." She added a touch of half and half to hers before placing the container within their reach. "You'll have to dress yours to your liking."

When Linda saw her heading back toward the kitchen, she said, "I told these girls they should quit trying to run your life, Granny."

Together, Rose and Ava screeched, "*Linda!*"

Ava continued, "You said no such a thing."

In a performance worthy of an Oscar, Granny, with her nose in the air, replied, "Thank ya' for settin' 'em straight. I'm glad you could see it, too, my dear."

"*Granny!*" Ava blurted.

Struggling to hide her amusement, Linda poured another cup, "Would you like a little half and half in here, darlin', or would you prefer milk? How about a little honey instead of sugar ... honey? It's a natural antibiotic, you know."

Over their coffee, Linda explained the situation, and they were at the hospital by ten.

The four of them, even Rose, spent most of the morning and some of the afternoon in the room with River and his mom. It resembled a hen party with all the fussin' over a baby chick.

River seemed to enjoy the company. Very active for a newborn, he tried hard to hold his head up to take in all the sights, sounds and smells.

When mom and her new son began to fade, and a nap was in order, the visitors left for the cafeteria to have lunch.

Linda would later tell Greg, "Seeing Granny sitting in the hospital room, holding River, her great-great-grandson, and kissing him all over his little face was one of the sweetest things I've ever witnessed. It made tears roll down my cheeks."

Granny, Ava, and Rose especially relished their time since they had announced they were leaving the next day to begin their long drive back to Tennessee.

When Jake and his dad returned home from their fishing trip, the ladies were already back at the house. Linda took over the lead duties of preparing dinner. Matti stayed behind at the hospital.

When the men walked in the door, meal preparations were well underway. As they entered the kitchen, Linda's first words were, "Where's the fish?"

Jake replied, "We didn't bring any home. It was a catch-and-release trip."

"What? You paid all that money and didn't bring any fish home? How stupid is that?"

Jake defended their insanity by saying, "We took lotsa pictures."

Linda sneered, "I wonder how those pictures are gonna taste. How are they best prepared, fried, or baked? Maybe blackened would be good. Whaddya think?" Shaking her head, she said, "You guys are somethin'. Did ya' have a good time? You smell like ya' did."

They responded, "We had a GREAT time!"

Greg added, "The scenery was amazing. To think such a small river can hold so many fish. The water is so cold—and swift—it makes you wonder how a fish can survive there, but they do, in vast numbers."

Jake broke in, "And some big ones, too."

"Yeah, we didn't hook into any *trophies* on this trip, but the guide said the section we fished was notorious for five and six-pounders. The biggest we caught was, what, Jake, three pounds? Two and a half at least, don't you think?"

"Yeah. Prob'ly 'bout right."

Then, as if rehearsed, they said, "It depends on how far out in front you hold it for the pictures." They couldn't hold it back. The two men bent double in hysterics. Of course, inside jokes are only funny to those in on them. No one else even smiled.

Granny couldn't resist, "Yeah, yeah, yeah, always how it goes. 'You shoulda been here *last* week,' or 'You shoulda' seen the one that got away.' You fishermen are all alike. Nothin' but excuses."

Jake shook his head. "I know it, Granny. We're nothing but a couple a no-count losers."

Everybody sighed, "Awwhhh."

Linda came to the rescue, "Yeah, but they're *our* no-count losers, and we love 'em. Don't we, girls?"

The pile-on began. Granny was first. "Yeah, I reckon we do. Heck, we don't have much to choose from, so I guess we'd better love 'em."

Rose followed, "Of course we love 'em. I've only known 'em for a few days, and I love 'em to death. I wouldn't take nothin' for 'em." After a pause, "No. I'd have to get a little somethin' at least." The room erupted.

Ava finally chimed in, "Well, I love 'em. I don't care *what* y'all say. They don't need to bring home fish for *me* to love 'em. No sir. I don't care *a'tall* they can't catch fish."

The girls were having a lot of fun at the guys' expense. The more Greg and Jake tried to defend the fact they caught a lot of fish but released them, the worse it got.

At some point during the ruckus, Matti walked in. She loved every minute, saying, "Are you girls picking on my men?"

Granny responded with, "Lord no, Honey. We were letting them know how much we love 'em despite their ineptitude. That's all." And the laughter erupted again.

Just as Jake was thinking, or maybe hoping Matti might defend them, she waited until the right moment and said, "I know, Granny. That's why they need our love even more."

Jake threw up his hands. "OH, THAAAAT'S RIGHT!"

Greg looked at his son and suggested, "Maybe we should leave. Go someplace, have a beer, and come back later. This might resemble your home again with friendlier people when we come back. What do you think?"

Jake agreed, "Might be a good idea. I hear there's a fish fry at the Moose Lodge."

Linda quickly pointed out the absurdity of the suggestion by saying, "Don't even think about it. You try to head for the door, and I'll shoot you in the pinky-toe. Both of you."

Jake looked at his mother, "In the 'pinky-toe'?"

"Yeah. And I mean it, too."

"Mother, you're not that good a shot."

"Exactly why you should be worried."

Jake's eye caught his dad's. "She has a point there, Pop."

"She does. You never know where the bullet might land."

Heading toward the fridge, Jake replied, "True, and she never was one to bluff."

Greg said, "Sheezz! This is bad. We can't win, and we can't leave. What are we gonna do, Jake? Show 'em the pictures. Show 'em we caught fish."

"It won't do any good, Pop. They're not listenin'. Here, have a beer." He tossed a can to his dad from the refrigerator.

Catching the flying container, Greg replied, "Thanks, Bud. Prob'ly the best course of action."

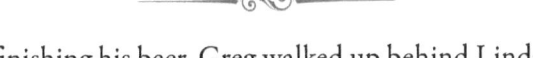

After finishing his beer, Greg walked up behind Linda, stirring a pot at the stove. He leaned over and kissed her neck. "Whatcha cookin', Baby?"

Not turning around or resisting, Linda said, "Oh, that's just like a man. Kiss her on the nape of the neck and talk softly. That'll melt her and fix everything. Right?"

Greg, between kisses, asked, "Is it working?"

Linda slowly reached behind her with her free hand and gently rubbed her husband's thigh, "I don't know. Is it?"

Greg responded, "Mmm, maybe."

At the right moment, Linda squeezed hard, where it hurt the most, and said, "Get away from me, you loser. You smell like a dead fish."

Releasing her grip, she continued, "But after you get a shower and some food in your belly, I could change my mind about you. I'm fickle, you know."

Smiling, Greg headed toward the stairs. "I knew you weren't as tough as you let on."

"You think you're so smooth, don't ya'?"

Bounding up the steps, Greg asked, "What's that, Baby? I didn't hear ya.'"

Linda nodded. "Uh, huh. You heard me."

Matti arrived at the hospital the following morning before 10 AM and discovered the discharge papers were being processed.

Shoshoni, recognizing she wasn't ready to care for her newborn son alone, asked her mother, "Would it be okay if we stayed with you for a while till we work through this learning curve?"

"Of course, Sweetheart. You can stay as long as you need."

When Matti found an opportunity to slip out of the room, she called Jake to share the news about Shoshoni and baby staying with them for some indefinite period.

After hearing the news, Jake began calling people he thought might enjoy hearing about River's pending release. While he had each on the phone, he invited them, one by one, to welcome River to "Grandma and Grandpa's home."

Granny explained to Jake, "We Tennesseeans have decided to delay our departure in anticipation of the new mom and baby's arrival if that's okay."

Jake smiled broadly. "Of course, it's okay, Granny. Wouldn't have it any other way."

Before it was over, quite a crowd had gathered. Jake made sure there was a place left in the driveway for Matti to park since every spot on the block in both directions was lined with automobiles.

At the hospital, Matti helped Shoshoni and River get situated in the truck. After closing the rear door on the passenger side, she called her husband. "Hi, Honey. We're about to leave the hospital."

"Good. Just a heads-up, I've invited a few people over to welcome River and his mom to Grandma and Grandpa's home. I've saved you a spot in the driveway, so don't be surprised with all the cars parked along the street."

At first, Matti wasn't sure it was a good idea, but she didn't want to toss a wet blanket on his plan, especially since it was already well underway. She finished the conversation before opening the driver's door because she didn't want to ruin the surprise for her daughter.

River seemed to enjoy his first ride in the fancy car seat on the trip home. He kept looking around, attuned to the new sounds and bright light of the sun. Shoshoni barely took her eyes off her phone. When Matti turned into the driveway, taking the last remaining parking space, Shoshoni finally became aware of the guests.

It was a beautiful, warm, sunny day, with many outside waiting for them—a homecoming filled with happy tears, hugs, and kisses.

Soon, the procession made it indoors, with Matti leading the way. Inside, Granny was waiting for them beside two surprise visitors. Matti's mother made the trip from Flagstaff for the occasion, and Shoshoni's sister, Cayuga, drove in from Lewiston.

Matti put aside the resentment she'd carried all these years. She knew, deep in her heart, her mother's actions were probably for the best, but it was hard having all parental rights taken away. "Hi, Mom. I'm so glad you could make it. How are you feeling?"

"Pretty good... all things considered. It was a long trip. How about you?"

"I'm good, too ..." They laughed as they repeated together, "All things considered."

Reaching to embrace Cayuga, they hugged. Matti squeezed her tight and said, "I didn't expect you to make the long drive, but I'm glad you did. I've missed you."

"Yeah. Mom called to let me know she was coming, so I figured I'd better get here, or there'd be hell to pay. Right?"

Still holding her close, Matti whispered, "She's your *grandmother*, remember? Last time I checked, I was the one who carried you for nine months and gave you life." Matti stepped back and raised her hands. "But it's okay. I get it. This is too precious an occasion. I'm sorry."

"I'm sorry, too, *Mom*. Old habits die hard. I didn't mean anything by it."

Matti wrapped her arm around her eldest daughter. "I understand. She raised you. It just stung a little. Come on. Check out this baby boy."

Now, there were five generations in the room. Many of them clamoring over the newborn child. They would pass him around from one to the other, if only for a moment or two, before the next pair of eager, loving hands snatched him away.

The *Homecoming Party* lasted only about an hour. Those in attendance were eager to welcome River to his new life outside the confines of the hospital, but they recognized it was a lot for mom and baby to endure. When he got fussy, it was clear mom and baby needed some rest, and privacy too.

As much of the crowd dispersed, Granny seized the opportunity. "I think it's time we head out, sweetheart."

Matti responded, "No. Do you have to leave today?"

"Yeah. I hate to say it, but we do. My cohorts need to be gittin' back, and you just received two more guests to take care of. You're runnin' outta room. We loaded the car this mornin'." Granny kissed her cheek. "I love you."

Matti wrapped her arms around her grandmother and wept. Through her tears, she whispered, "I love you so much."

Sitting together, watching the remaining family members who stayed behind, Greg quietly told his wife, "It's remarkable how River's arrival bonded so many people of such diverse backgrounds together in such a beautiful way."

Linda smiled. "A new baby often has that effect."

"I suppose, but in this case, you have three men who at one time or another, or maybe still, all loved Matti and should not have gotten along—but did, remarkably well. Ty's heading back to the southeast, but Karson and Jake act like close friends."

"That's certainly true. I can't get over how those two clicked. You don't see that very often. What I enjoy most is watching Matti with her mom and both daughters together. She's *beaming*, isn't she?"

"She is, but did you catch that dig about '*mom*'?"

"Oh, with Cayuga? Yeah. Some scars may never heal. But I'm proud Matti dropped it as quickly as she did."

Greg agreed, "Indeed. But it sounded like she wouldn't have come if Matti's mother hadn't called her. Did you catch that?"

"I did. I wonder how Matti feels about that. I doubt she'll share her thoughts with Shoshoni. She won't want to shatter the sister love between them. That's how Matti is, you know."

"I'm sure you're right about that. Prob'ly comes with that book on motherhood. Huh?"

Linda giggled and said, "I suppose it does. And don't you love Jacob's mother, Nancy? Right there in the mix of things."

"I do! She seems awfully proud to be a grandmother. Let's hope that continues."

Linda assured him, "Oh, it will. Just look at her. She's all in. She'll be *actively* involved."

"Yeah. My worry is Jacob. I hope he steps up to the plate as a new father and is engaged in raising River."

Linda chuckled. "I think he'll have to answer to Nancy if he doesn't."

"I wonder if Shoshoni and Jacob will ever become a couple."

"Time will tell. It would be nice, wouldn't it? He seems like he's trying to do the right thing. And he's a handsome young man, isn't he?"

Greg replied, "I can't disagree. One thing is clear, though: River's the glue, the magnet that pulled this unlikely group of people from all across the country together and, at least for a while, mended a few fences and salved wounds."

That evening, after all the guests had gone home, Jake asked, "Hey, Pop, share a single malt with me?"

Greg chuckled. "I'd prefer a glass of my own if you don't mind."

Overhearing the exchange, Linda interjected, "He thinks he's so clever, Jake. Ignore him."

Jake smiled, "I had that one comin', Mom. Want a cigar to go with it, Pop? I'll even splurge and give you one you can have all to yourself."

"Ha! Sounds great, son. I assume you've got the necessary accoutrements that I can use?"

"If you mean the cutter and a lighter, I do, but you may find the rental fee a bit excessive."

Both men laughed heartily before Greg said, "Nothing short of what I'd expect from a carnival barker like yourself. Take advantage of a captive audience."

Linda chimed in once again, "Cigars? You know I hate those nasty things." She stepped closer to her husband, leaned against him, put her hand on his chest, looked into his eyes, and, in her sexiest voice, said, "We have the upstairs all to ourselves again. No longer need to worry about offending the sensitive ears of interlopers in the next room. You wouldn't want to ruin such an opportunity with one of those awful, disgusting, smelly things I despise, would you?"

Jake came up behind his mother, set a glass of the amber liquid on the counter in full view of his dad, and held up two cigars. He winked at him and said, "I'll see you on the porch, Pop."

Greg leaned down to kiss his wife. When their lips parted, he said, "I'll be up in a few."

Seeing the stogies in Jake's hand, a grimace formed on Linda's face. "You're gonna smoke one of those damned things, aren't you?"

Greg smiled.

A frustrated Linda turned and stomped off to join Matti.

It was a gorgeous night outside on the porch. Greg looked up at the cloudless *Big Sky* of Montana. The minimal ambient light provided quite a backdrop for his reflection on events during their stay. He was choking back tears, wondering how many summers he had left to spend with his son, daughter-in-law, and new family. His mother had passed when she was sixty-three, his dad at seventy-seven. Chronologically, Greg was right in the middle. But geographically, he was separated from this part of his family by over 3,000 miles.

Jake said, "Here."

"Huh?"

"A golf tee. I use this instead of a cutter. It keeps the end cleaner. Besides, that way I don't have to charge you that exorbitant fee I mentioned."

Greg welcomed the comic relief. It tore him from those depressing thoughts.

After successfully igniting his own, Jake said, "I suppose you're gonna need this, too." He handed the lighter to his dad.

"Thanks. Your generosity is overwhelming."

As he sat back in his chair, Jake quipped, "Wait 'till you get my bill in the mail."

Greg smiled, lit his cigar, and gazed at the stars through his smoke ring for a long moment before he said, "This has been an incredible couple of weeks. There were some extra-special moments, like when River was fussy earlier. Shoshoni was tired and didn't know what to do. Linda cradled River against her bosom and sat in the recliner while his mom napped on the couch. All three fell asleep. It was the sweetest sight I've seen in a long time.

Jake smiled at his dad. "Mom has a way."

"We packed a lotta pretty amazing stuff into these two weeks despite all the challenges. Thank you, son."

"It was my pleasure, Dad. I'm glad everything worked out the way it did."

Greg continued, "You realize River, my new great-grandson, arrived during what will probably be the last organized team sporting event you and I will ever have a chance to participate in together. Right?"

After a pause, Jake responded, "Yeah... maybe. I guess."

"You know, I shed my blood on that field. Do you think they'll name the park after me?"

"I don't think so, Pop."

"Hang a plaque?"

Jake shook his head, "Doubt it. Sorry."

After a couple moments of silence, Greg held up his glass as a toast and said, "Oh, well. No matter. The way I see it, it ranks up there as *The Greatest Softball Game* ever played. What say you?"

Jake touched his glass to his dad's, nodded in agreement, and replied, "And to think, it wasn't even televised."

They laughed, leaned back in their chairs, sipped their scotch, and puffed on their cigars before Jake added, "It's one *we'll* never forget."

The End

Don't miss out!

Visit the website below and you can sign up to receive emails whenever K G Wauthier publishes a new book. There's no charge and no obligation.

https://books2read.com/r/B-A-AFBS-UTPWB

BOOKS 2 READ

Connecting independent readers to independent writers.

About the Author

K G Wauthier is a decorated combat veteran who served in Vietnam. He was born in the Midwest but spent his development years growing up in California and Florida, where he gained a wealth of experience.

He met and married the woman of his dreams when he was eighteen, and they have built a relationship that endures to this day. Together, they took on life and the world headlong, continuing to add to his experience.

The Greatest Softball Game is his first book. It's a series of events that could happen to real people, sprinkled with the spice of sexual escapades from his own experiences, that will leave you eager to read about their next adventures.

Be on the lookout for his next book, Chase & The Spirit of the Trestle, to be released by Christmas.

Read more at https://books2read.com/ap/RwdkqW/ K-G-Wauthier.

www.ingramcontent.com/pod-product-compliance
Lightning Source LLC
Chambersburg PA
CBHW031052020726
47495CB00007B/1836